Dear Lois...

L.W.KING

DEDICATION

For all of those who are, or have been on a
journey of self-discovery...Remember
that there is always a rainbow that
follows the storm, X

ACKNOWLEDGMENTS

I give thanks to… Divine inspiration

Dear Lois.....

CHAPTER ONE

Usual chaos met Lois as she edged towards the staircase, and again the same as every working day, that familiar feeling of dread filled her as she stepped quietly down into the boxing ring, which was once her kitchen. She inhaled deeply as she walked into the room unnoticed by her family members who were sparring with one another as ever. Amber, her daughter, aged ten was pulling at the cereal box held by her younger brother Jake aged seven, who was clinging on to said cereal box with his life, meanwhile, the sorry excuse for a father, Kevin, was screaming at them both, due to yet another raging hangover.

Lois shook her head solemnly as she walked to the kettle, the need for one last coffee before the school run and then work was imperative if she were to cope with whatever the day would bring. She jumped as the front door slammed shut signalling that Kevin had left the house for work, today being one of the rare occasions that he could be bothered to crawl out of bed and go. Still, then again, it was payday for him, which would mean only one thing, he would fall through the door in the early hours after whiling the hours away in the pub, surrounded by the many who would wait for his imminent arrival and weighty wallet. Lois sighed, was this what she signed herself up for on what was supposed to be the happiest time of her life? She thought as she sipped at the hot coffee, knowing that anytime now the house would erupt into absolute mayhem when she would chase the children around the house on the hunt for school ties, bookbags and other miscellaneous necessities.

As they drove towards the school, Jake began the usual routine of crying, even though he had support in place, due to his diagnosis of autism, still every day, he would break his heart at the thought of six hours in an environment which made him feel so incredibly insecure and uncomfortable,

"Do we have to go to Julie's house after school?" Amber whined as Lois tried her hardest to calm Jake's tears, "Mum! I said do.."

"I heard what you said Amber, and yes, I'm sorry but I have to work," Lois replied as she pulled up in her usual parking space and climbed out of the car.

"Mrs Parker, could I have a word?" Mrs Turnball, school principal and general bitch from hell asked as Jake clung relentlessly to Lois's legs. Lois put on her best fake smile and nodded, "We really need to discuss matters concerning Jake's focus and concentration, it is quite a cause for concern," she stated sternly, Katie, Jake's keyworker joined them and peeled Jake away from Lois, dragging him kicking and screaming into the ancient school building, "Mr Davies informed me that that yesterday, Jake spent the majority of his day staring out of the window, so much so, that he was forced to move him to the inner wall and still he stared into space," she continued, Lois drew her gaze to the harsh looking woman after she had harrowingly watched her son being dragged into school,

"Forgive me if I am mistaken but this is a school is it not?" Lois replied harshly,

"Yes," Mrs Turnball replied in bewilderment, shocked by Lois's unexpected attitude,

"My son has Autism, and he struggles with concentration amongst other things, you receive extra funding to support him, so maybe you should think about tailoring an education that suits him, not the other way round, now if you will excuse me, I am already late for work," Lois fumed as she then turned and jogged back to her car.

The A&E department was busy as usual, and as Lois rushed through the full waiting area, she could see that it was likely to stay that way, she threw her bag and coat in the nurse's room and ran to the station to await instruction,

"Fashionably late as usual," Jackie the ward manager stated and shook her head as Lois approached the desk,

"Sorry, Jake's principal insisted on having a word," Lois replied and winced, she hated being late, before she had children she would pride herself on being early and now that seemed to be a thing of the past,

"Hmm, that's three handovers you have missed this week," Jackie said as she looked through a pile of notes on the desk,

"I am sorry, I will make sure that I am early tomorrow," Lois replied humbly, her work was her lifeline, a place where she felt that she truly made a difference, at home, life was just one great battle, the red phone bleeped and lit up as the words RTA resounded through the department, everyone ran to prepare, it was every nurse's worse nightmare when the red phone bleeped, especially when it was a road traffic accident, and even more so when it involved a motorcycle, and unfortunately, this one did.

Much to Lois's horror she, along with two colleagues had been allocated the motorcycle rider and they waited with bated breath as the paramedics rushed him through on a stretcher, they immediately set to work on removing, what little pieces of material still remained, carefully taking as much from the wounds as was possible. The rider was in his thirties, unconscious, he had severe lacerations to his legs and back, with a possible fracture to the femur, and as they waited for an X-ray, he began to regain consciousness, he tried to sit up and Lois quietly whispered for him to remain still as she explained where he was and why he was there, the realisation of the situation set in and it clearly filled him with terror, so Lois sat with him, providing constant reassurance that everything would be fine.

The X-ray revealed that he did indeed have a significant fracture, one which required immediate surgery, Lois walked beside him as they wheeled him down to the theatre, as they reached the doors, she stooped so as he could hear her,

"This is where we say goodbye, I'm sure that everything will be fine, you are in good hands," Lois said quietly, he grabbed her hand,

"What's your name?" He asked,

"Lois," she replied and smiled,

"Thank you, Lois, I will never forget you," he said as he disappeared through the double doors and into the hands of the surgeons.

A little later once the department quietened, Lois walked to the staff café for lunch, she grabbed a salad and a coffee and sat at her favourite table beside the window,

"Mind if I join you?" Mark, her friend and colleague asked, she smiled and nodded,

"I hear that Jabba was on the warpath this morning," he said and chuckled as he sat down opposite her, Lois chuckled,

"It's my fault, I was twenty minutes late again, you can't blame her," Lois replied,

"What was it this time, did you have to drag that tosser of a husband out of bed again?" Mark asked and raised his eyebrows,

"Nah, it's his payday," Lois replied as Mark gave a knowing nod, there was no love lost between Mark and Kevin, Mark had witnessed first-hand how abusive and vile Kevin could be and he constantly nagged Lois to take the children to stay with him, he was middle-aged, gay, and single, and continuously moaned about how he rambled around his large four bedroomed house alone. "I was bawled out by Jake's Principle," she continued, Mark shook his head,

"Honestly, I have no idea how you cope," he sighed, Lois checked her watch,

"Shit I had better go," she said as she then gulped down the remainder of her coffee and ran back to the department.

After an afternoon filled with youngsters overdosing on what they thought were recreational drugs, but following the toxicology reports, discovered that they could have sourced the ingredients from a local garage, two heart attacks and a stroke, Lois was relieved to be driving to Julie's house to collect the children, where she spent an hour offloading to her poor friend Julie, who despite having three children of her own had kindly offered to collect Lois's two from school every day, and then on their way home they stopped at the chippie and then sat and ate fish and chips in front of the television as a treat.

She tucked Jake into bed with his favourite Sonic the Hedgehog snuggled up safely beside him, and kissed him on the head,

"Mummy, where's Dad?" he asked,

"Oh he's busy with his friends," Lois replied diplomatically, of course what she wanted to say was, he is spending what little money he has earned this month in the pub so that tomorrow he can sit in the house, drink whatever he can lay his hands on and then bark orders at the three of us, but she relented.

"Mummy, I don't like Daddy, he's mean, can we send him away," Jake asked, Lois chuckled,

"Go to sleep, only one day left of school this week," she said as she walked to the door,

"Yippee," Jake replied sleepily.

She sat on the bed as thoughts of the day swam through her mind, she opened her bedside table drawer and took out her journal:

Thursday 22nd October 1995.

Dear Lois,

What a day! We had a pretty horrific RTA today, a really sweet guy called Alex had been hit by a Land Rover on his bike, he was so scared. I accompanied him to the theatre, and he said that he would never forget me, the strange thing is, I got the feeling that I knew him, he had a sense of familiarity about him, and since then I have not been able to get him out of my thoughts, to the point that I almost rang HDU to see how he was doing? Am I losing it?

As per, Kevin has gone to prop up the bar at the Coach and Horses yet again! I expect that there will be a row when he either gets turfed out of the pub or his latest bit on the side has had enough. Why do I stay? Mark asked me today, I am afraid to start again, I would have to move away, I know that he would never let us alone if we stayed nearby, and then the kids would have to start new schools, for Jake that would be a nightmare. Well, I had better sign off for today, Amber is whingeing that she needs a drink but is too afraid to go downstairs on her own. One day life will be simple. xxx.

Just as she expected she heard a loud crash at four thirty am, as Kevin fell through the front doorway and into the door, she turned over, pulling the quilt over her head as she heard the thudding footsteps awkwardly climbing the stairs becoming ever closer, the bedroom door flew open and he staggered to the bed, the stench of alcohol filled the room as he began to attempt to undress, throwing his discarded clothes all over the bedroom floor, he fell into bed and pushed Lois hard as he tried to dominate the area, she clung to the side of the bed, fearing that she might fall out, saying not a word for fear of confrontation, again he slammed into her, this time sending her out of bed and onto the floor with a thud. She knew she had two choices, to stand and fight or disappear down the stairs, like she mostly did, she didn't want the children to witness yet another showdown and she was too tired to fight, so she picked herself up and slipped out of the bedroom, unnoticed.

She looked at the antique clock which had belonged to her Grandmother, sitting idly on the mantlepiece, it was nearly five a.m., thinking that there was no point in trying to sleep on the uncomfortable sofa that had been a wedding gift from Kevin's overbearing mother, she took herself into the kitchen and boiled the kettle. As she stood at the back door taking in the fresh autumnal air, thoughts of her parents filled her mind, she had not spoken to either of them for six years, since that fated day when they arrived unannounced, Kevin was in a drunken stupor and his level of emotional abuse was on top form that day, of course, her Dad told him that his behaviour was unacceptable, which was not accepted gracefully as Kevin physically threw him out of the front door onto the drive, her Mum screaming as he did, and Lois standing with Jake, just a baby in her arms not knowing which way to turn as she tried to calm little Amber who was close to hysterical. Her Mum called later that day and begged her to move back home with the children, how could she? Her parents were in their twilight years, and Kevin being Kevin would never leave them alone, she couldn't put that on her parents, how could she? She gently declined the offer and was then told that until she left him, there would be no contact from her or her dad, and to this day it still sang true.

She often drove up the pretty avenue where they lived, hoping that she would catch a glimpse, how she missed them both terribly, but, she had made a dreadful decision against their advice and now she and only she would deal with the consequences.

Owing to the fact that she had been awake since four thirty am, Lois arrived at work gloriously early, with time to grab a coffee before handover, Jackie looked as though she were in a state of shock when she arrived at the desk to find Lois sorting through the patient's discharge notes as she sipped her coffee,

"Well this is a most pleasant surprise I must say," Jackie said breathlessly as she removed her raincoat, the weather was abominable, as a storm with high winds and a deluge of rain swept across the area.

The morning flew by, and as expected the department was once again teeming, Lois was looking for the transfer notes of a patient when Mark walked through the double doors and joined her at the desk, he was on the afternoon shift, and looked as bright as a button, Lois, on the other hand, did not, as the lack of sleep and the stress of life began to creep up on her and she yawned,

"You look like shite," Mark said, wearing a look of concern,

"Thanks, babe," Lois chuckled,

"Bad night with him again?" Lois nodded and walked to the waiting porter with the patient notes, on her return Mark looked ever more concerned,

"What's wrong?" Lois asked,

"HDU have called down, someone called Alex is asking to see you," he said in bafflement, Lois frowned,

"He wants to see me?" she asked requiring reiteration, Mark nodded,

"Apparently so," he replied,

"Cover for me will you?" Lois asked as she removed the plastic apron and headed towards the doors.

She walked to the nurses station on HDU where Carol, the lead staff nurse was standing, "Quite the celebrity aren't you?" she said as she looked up,

"Am I?" Lois asked,

"He's in room two," she replied, and slowly Lois walked towards the door, she peered through the small glass window of the door and seeing that he was alone, she quietly slipped inside, and as she walked to the bed he opened his eyes,

"Lois, thank you for coming," he said quietly,

"You are welcome, how are you feeling?" she asked as she pulled up a chair,

"I have had better days," he replied and attempted to laugh, but the pain was overwhelming, "I wanted to thank you for yesterday," he continued when he stopped wincing,

"No need to thank me, it's what I'm paid for,"

"No, I disagree, it goes way past that, kindness I mean, it takes a special kind of person to exude kindness like you do," he said weakly, Lois smiled, it was moments like this that made her life a little more bearable,

"I feel that we have met before, since I opened my eyes yesterday and looked into your eyes I feel that I have looked into those eyes before, have you always lived here?" he asked, Lois was taken aback, she had felt the same, to the point that she wrote it in her journal,

"Er, yes, yes I have," she replied awkwardly,

"Hmm, I was afraid that you would say that you see I was only passing through, I was on my way to a friend's house in Brighton, I come from Surrey, have you ever been?" he asked,

"To Brighton or Surrey?"

"Sorry, to Surrey," he asked as he chuckled, which given the pain that he was in was all that he could muster,

"No, I never have," she replied and smiled a gentle smile, his eyes wore such a kindness as she had never seen before,

"Well, maybe, when I get out of here, you might like to come and visit?" he asked, Lois frowned,

"I can't, it's against company policy, we are not allowed to socialise with patients," she replied sadly, as the small smile on his face disappeared and an expression of disappointment washed across his face,

"Yes, of course, sorry, I shouldn't have asked," he replied as he looked down at the bed,

"But all the while that you are here as a patient I can drop by and visit," Lois suggested to ease the bitter disappointment that they were both now feeling,

"Would you, that would be wonderful, " he said as the smile returned. The door opened and Carol peered around the door,

"You are wanted, another RTA," she said sternly wearing a look of disapproval,

"Shit, I had better go, I'll pop up and see you when I finish," she said as she rushed out of the room and back towards A&E.

Chapter two

"Can we play out when we get home?" Amber asked loudly from the back seat of the car, almost deafening Lois as she did.

"Yes, as long as you change out of your uniforms first," Lois said as she pulled up on the drive, the two children ran ahead and were scuffling with one another as to who could get in the house first, "Stop or you won't be going anywhere," Lois stated sternly as she placed the key in the lock and opened the front door, to be met with the reek of alcohol and cigarette smoke. As both children ran up the stairs to change, Lois sighed as she walked slowly to the kitchen, where she placed her bag down and walked through to the lounge. Kevin had invited some of his so-called drinking buddies around to play cards, the living room stank as they all sat around the table drinking and smoking, and not one of them looked as though they had seen a flannel or bathtub for months!

"Oi, go down the offy and grab some beers," Kevin hollered as she turned to leave the room and its vile occupants, she shook her head in dismay as she walked back to the kitchen and grabbed her bag and car keys, "Tell him to get them himself," she heard the voice in her head say,

"He will only kick off if I do," she sighed as she walked to the front door and back out to the car.

Upon her return she could hear that the children were clearly distraught and upset as she walked back through the front door, she marched into the lounge and looked in horror as both children were sitting on the sofa red-faced, red-legged with tear-stained faces,

"What's going on? What's happened?" Lois asked as she rushed to where the children were sitting,

"Dad slapped our legs," Amber sniffed,

"Yeah, and he bloody well will again if you don't shut up," Kevin roared from the table as one of the other men laughed,

"Kids should be seen and not heard," he sneered and looked at Kevin. It was at that very moment Lois saw red, he could do what he liked to her but hit her children, no, this was the point of no return,

"GET OUT OF MY HOUSE," she screamed as she grabbed the empty cans from the table and pointed to the door,

"WHO THE HELL DO YOU THINK YOU ARE TALKING TO, IT'S MY HOUSE!" Kevin stood and roared in her face,

"I pay the mortgage, I pay the bills, so you and your friends can get the fuck out!" Lois screamed as both children sat with their hands over their ears as they rocked back and forth in a plight to self soothe, she ran to the kitchen and grabbed her purse, pulling out a handful of notes which she had saved to treat the children at the weekend, she ran back into the lounge and shoved the money into Kevin's hand, "Now take that and find somewhere else to drink," She shouted, Kevin looked at the handful of notes, counted them, nodded, and gestured for his friends to join him at the pub, which thankfully they did.

Once she had her house back and cleaned up the mess, she

cooked the three of them a lovely meal and they sat together as they ate, Lois trying her hardest to make up for their earlier ordeal. They watched the television for a while and once the children were tucked up in bed, Lois made herself a cup of tea and took it to her bedroom, where she sat on the bed and took out her journal:

Friday 23rd Oct 95

Dear Lois,

What began as a nightmare, then turned into a good day and then I came home to World War Three! I was up again at 4.30, yes you guessed it, he came home pissed and more or less kicked me out of bed, but at least I wasn't late for work and today was the first day since he started school that Jake did not cry when I took him, hooray! I suppose I should be grateful for small mercies eh. Moving on from that, I was pleasantly surprised today when Alex asked to see me in HDU, you know the guy from the motorbike accident, anyway, I went up to see him, and still, the same sense of familiarity was there, but he felt it too, how weird, he asked if we had met before? It turns out that he is from Surrey, he asked if I would visit him when he is discharged, but I said that company policy didn't allow it, despite the fact that I am an unhappily married woman. He has the kindest eyes, eyes that you could easily find yourself lost in, anyway, I digress, I told him that I would pop up and see him every day until he is discharged, which pleased us both.

I then came home to Kevin and his band of scummers in my living room, drinking smoking and smelling bad. Long story short, he smacked both Amber and Jake while stupid me was fetching him more beer. I gave them all their marching orders and then spent the evening trying to make it up to my poor children.

I know that I cannot allow his vile temper and abusive nature to carry over onto the children, I know that I have to get out of here, but I have no idea how to, maybe we should go and stay with Mark?

I should have listened to my Dad on the way to the church all those years ago, he told me then that I shouldn't go through with it, but did I listen, no, and I now am living to regret that.

Anyway, I am going now, I am so tired, and I want to get the children up and out of the house early tomorrow, until then. Xxx

She woke up to what could only be described as the sounds that resound from a pig sty as he lay on his back, his foul breathe filling the room as he snored and groaned loudly, Lois slipped out, grabbing her clothes as she crept across the landing to wake the children, quickly they washed and dressed and were out of the door before eight am, on the promise of a breakfast along the way. Lois had decided to take them out to a wildlife park, which was a thirty-minute drive from the house, and on the route was their favourite café, which sold the best crumpets this side of the Channel! After the breakfast stop, they continued on their journey and Lois smiled as she pulled up into the car park, to the cheers of her children.

After what was a most wonderful day, full of memory-making and feeding wild animals, Lois told them it was time to leave, Jake became distraught at the thought of going home,
"Come on, I'm cooking your favourite tonight, and you can choose the movie, how does that sound," Lois said, trying her hardest to console him, but to no avail, very soon he was wailing like a banshee as the many other visitors to the attraction were climbing into their cars and staring in Lois's direction,
"I am not going home! I hate Dad, he hits me!" Jake shouted Lois's face reddened as the onlookers gasped in horror at Jake's revelation,
"Please Jakey, I promise that we will leave Daddy, you just have to give me time to arrange it," Lois pleaded as her son stood beside the car, his arms folded tight across his body in refusal,
"Jakey, come on get in the car, it's not fair on Mummy, is it? She doesn't hit us, she tries her best," Amber said as she gently moved him towards the car door, at that moment Lois was fighting hard to chase back the tears which were threatening a downpour, as the beautiful words from her ten-year-old daughter rang out.

Thankfully when they arrived home the house was in complete darkness, and Lois breathed a huge sigh of relief upon seeing this as so too did the children. Amber and Jake sat in the lounge watching the television while Lois set about cooking the spaghetti Bolognese, which was Jake's favourite, sensory issues made certain food types unpalatable for Jake and usually if it weren't chicken covered in breadcrumbs, he would not eat it, except for Spaghetti Bolognese, which he would happily eat every day if Lois allowed him to.

They had a wonderful, peaceful evening watching movies and eating treats, and by ten they were all tucked up in bed, Lois was exhausted, so much so that she hadn't even the energy to write in her journal, thinking that she would catch up the following day as the weight of her eyelids became too much and she drifted off to sleep.

She woke the following morning to find two stowaways camped in her bed beside her, she grinned at Amber's big cheesy smile as she sat herself up, "And to what do I owe the pleasure?" Lois asked and chuckled, it had been years since they had snuggled up beside her in bed, she was thinking, "Well, Dad's not here and you looked really snug, so we thought that we would join you," Amber said, and Jake nodded in agreement,
"You mean the big bad wolf didn't come home?" Lois asked as her eyes widened and both children began to howl with laughter as they shook their heads in unison,
"Well, come on then, what are we waiting for, this calls for a celebration, pancakes I think," Lois said as she jumped out of bed, Amber and Jake following her cheering as they did.

Following a stroll through a local forest, foraging for all things Autumn, and a quick, yet harrowing trip to the supermarket, Jake always went into sensory overload in the supermarket, the afternoon for Lois was filled with ironing the freshly washed and dried uniforms, catching up on the household chores, and preparing the evening meal. As she stood chopping vegetables a childhood memory popped into her thoughts, Sundays as a child were always the same, Sunday morning, her Dad would take her out for a couple of hours, dropping her off at the local

25

swimming pool on his way to the pub, she would spend an hour or two, depending on the lifeguard, in the pool with her friends, before the slow walk home, then at two o'clock on the dot, Sunday roast was served, followed by an afternoon of football on the TV, her Dad snoring as he slept in the armchair and Mum lying on her bed so she could rest her eyes. How times had changed, she thought as she placed a tray of chicken dippers in the oven and stirred the simmering curry on the hob.

Sunday 25th Oct 1995
Dear Lois,
Why do weekends fly by so quickly, no sooner than you are climbing out of bed on a Saturday, it is already Sunday night, and the weekend has all but gone. The kids and I have had a lovely weekend, probably because Kevin is on another of his away days. We visited a wildlife park on Saturday and had a lovely forest walk today, where we collected a full bag of pine cones and acorns, ready for crafting in the half term.
I have to be honest here, you are the only person I would say this to, but my mind has been elsewhere for much of the weekend, twice today I had to stop myself from calling HDU to see how Alex is doing. He constantly fills my thoughts, so much so, that I even made him an apple pie to take in tomorrow, Friday we were chatting, and he told me that the worst thing of adulthood is not eating his Mum's cooking and apple pie was his favourite, I just hope that I have done it some justice, if not he may discharge himself and travel back to eat his Mum's apple pie!

What is it about him? Why can't I stop thinking about him? It is driving me insane!

Anyhow, enough of my nonsense, my eyes are heavy, and I CAN NOT be late for work tomorrow, so I'll bid you a good night,

As always Xxx

Another morning of earliness and no tears from Jake when she left him at Julie's, had put a smile on Lois's face as she drove to work, with the radio blaring, the sun shining, the rich autumn colours filling the landscape, Oasis played on the radio and Lois sang along, '*I would like to leave this city*', as she sang, the words resounded in her mind, how true they were, she had spent twenty-eight years of existence in the same seaside town, yet always as a youngster and beyond, she dreamed of living in the middle of nowhere, surrounded by trees and all things natural, and yet here she was, still in the same place, doing the same job, day after day. It was although a bomb of inspiration had dropped at that very moment, and she realised that if she wanted her dream to become a reality, then she and only she could make it happen, and at that very moment she promised herself that she would.

Strangely, A&E was pretty quiet, which allowed the staff to catch up with things that sometimes got left to one side, Lois was sitting behind the desk sorting through paperwork when Jackie approached the desk,

"How's the young man in HDU doing?" She asked and grinned, Lois looked up and blushed,

"He was doing okay on Friday when I popped in to see him, why?" she replied, Jackie looked at the clock and sighed,

"It's quiet, why don't you head on up there now, at least you won't be late collecting the children," she suggested and winked,

"Really?" Lois asked, now completely bewildered by Jabba's sudden change in attitude, Jackie smiled and nodded as Lois wasted no time at all in rushing to grab her coat and bag. She ran through the corridor and then realised that she had left the apple pie in the staff fridge, so she sprinted back and grabbed it, bumping into Mark as she ran out of the door,
"Whoa there! Where's the fire?" he asked and chuckled,
"What? No, I was just about to del... never mind, meet me in the canteen in half an hour," she called out as she ran towards the stairs.
She tapped on the door and walked in, she was taken aback when she saw Alex as he sat in the chair beside the bed, he turned to look at her and smiled,
"Wow! You look heaps better! I er I made you this, it's probably nowhere near as good as your mum's," Lois stammered awkwardly, Alex began to laugh,
"Well, what is it?" he asked as Lois clung to the bag as if her life depended on it.
"Oh, it's apple pie," she said as her face reddened with embarrassment and she passed it to him, he held it to his nose and sniffed,
"Hmm, smells wonderful," he said as his eyes sparkled in the sunlight, how different he looked, hospital gowns were not designed to be attractive, but as he sat in a t-shirt and cargo pants, he looked gorgeous, Lois was thinking, he pressed the buzzer and Lois frowned, "I need a knife," he said on noticing her confused expression.
As he tucked into his third helping of the pie, Lois was again lost in her thoughts,
"I bet you struggled to get dressed didn't you?" she asked, her thoughts jumping out of her mouth, Alex almost choked on his mouthful as he chuckled and watched Lois writhe in mortification,

"It would have been easier and far more pleasant if I had had your assistance," he replied and winked causing Lois to burst out laughing as Josh, Alex's named nurse walked in with a cup of something that loosely resembled tea, Lois checked her watch and realised that she should have met Mark five minutes ago,

"Right, well, I had better get a move on," Lois said as she climbed off of the chair, Alex's expression told a story of its own,

"That's a shame, I haven't seen much of you," he said quietly,

"I know, I'm sorry, but, well I have to be straight with you Alex, I have two children and they are waiting to be collected," she replied sadly, knowing that this would probably be the last time that he would want her to visit,

"I suppose that you are happily married too?" he asked solemnly, she smiled a small smile,

"Married yes, happily, no," she replied as the smile then returned to his face,

"The pie was delicious, will you come and see me tomorrow?" he asked as he smiled his beautiful smile,

"How can I resist," she replied and leaned over to gently kiss his cheek, he turned his head and their lips brushed as her tummy filled with butterflies and her legs turned to jelly,

"I'll see you tomorrow beautiful," he said as she walked to the door, she skipped down the corridor with a spring in her step, her head spinning with emotion.

"What took you, where have you been?" Mark asked as she ran into the canteen,

"Do you like a roast?" she asked, still in a state of bliss, Mark chuckled,

"Yes, I love a good roast, why?" he replied,

"No Mark, I said do you like a roast, nobody said anything about it being good, I love a roast, but the kids won't eat it, do

you fancy popping around tonight and I'll cook us one, I can
fill you in then," she said as she stepped back, edging closer to
the double doors,
"What time?" he called out as she began to disappear,
"Seven, bring wine," she shouted, sprinting along the corridor
towards the main exit.

CHAPTER THREE

She grabbed the children a guilty pleasure, namely a take-out burger and fries on the way home and once inside, cracked on with preparing roast beef, Amber and Jake were playing up in their rooms with some neighbourhood friends, and relievedly, there was still no sign of the big bad wolf.

The doorbell rang out at seven prompt and Lois ran to the door as both children were engrossed in the new series of Goosebumps on the TV, Mark grinned as he waved Lois's favourite bottle of wine in the air, which she gratefully accepted and beckoned him inside. He went straight into the lounge to see the children, he was a natural around children and they both loved him, Jake especially, Lois went back to the confines of the kitchen where she put the finishing touches to the roast, namely gravy, and placed it into the oven to warm as she rounded the children up for bed.

"You were right, that wasn't a good roast," Mark said as he sat back in his chair and Lois scowled, "It was an exquisite roast darling!" he continued and rubbed his full belly,

"Well, thank you," Lois said as she gracefully accepted his compliment,

"So come on, what was with all the cloak and dagger earlier?" he leaned forward and asked, Lois spent a while explaining about Alex, and the trouble that she had been having with Kevin, Mark, took a sip of wine, wiped his mouth on a napkin, sighed and then looked at Lois,

"You need to leave him, you know that don't you," he sighed,

"It's a bit difficult when he is not here to leave," she replied, chuckled, and hiccupped, placing her glass back down on the table,

"You know what I mean," Mark said sternly, Lois nodded, she knew he was right, she knew it was inevitable,

"I'm scared Mark, the last time that I tried to leave him, he stalked us and threatened to kill me," Lois said and downed the remainder of the wine that was in her glass,

"So, you make it a completely fresh start, somewhere he would never dream of looking," Mark suggested,

"But what about the children?"

"What about them, from what you have just told me, both are terrified of him,"

"Yes I know, but they would have to leave everything that they know, their home, friends, school," Lois said,

"Lois, darling, they are children, they will adapt, make new friends, feel excited and not be afraid to go home," he said as he poured them both another glass, Lois nodded, she knew that everything that he was saying was true, she was just so scared of venturing out into the big bad world by herself.

"Where would I begin?" she asked quietly as she drew her finger around the rim of her glass in deep contemplation, Mark stood and walked out to the hallway, soon returning with a brochure, which as he took his seat, he handed to Lois, she took it from him and studied the contents, frowning as she did,

"My brother runs a small estate agent up in the lakes, we were chatting on the phone a few days ago and I took the liberty of asking if there were any suitable properties for you and the children," He said and smiled, Lois looked again, a small cottage nestled deep within a valley jumped out at her,

"But where would I work?" she asked,

"Lois, you are one of the best nurses I have ever worked with, I am pretty sure that even in the arse end of nowhere, they still require medical attention, one way or another," he replied, Lois nodded,

"Let me sleep on it," she said as she folded the brochure and placed it into the back pocket of her jeans.

Monday 26th October

Dear Lois,

Well, what can I tell you about today? In many respects, it has been a little out of the ordinary. The kids are on half-term break and came home full of news about their day at the park with Julie, I am slightly jealous, I would have loved to spend the week with them, but we have to eat, and the bills won't pay themselves!

I took Alex's apple pie in today and he loved it! Phew! I told him about the children, which didn't seem to bother him, and then I kissed his cheek, and he turned his head, our lips brushed and for a moment I thought that I was in heaven! Luckily, we didn't get caught. There has been no return of the big bad wolf, which I am over the moon about, the children always seem so much happier when he isn't around, which leads me to my next revelation.

After a lovely dinner with Mark, we chatted about life, and he advised me to leave Kevin, which I know is inevitable, I explained how afraid I was to go, I just know he will come looking, and as fate would have it, Mark's brother runs an estates agents in the Lakes, which has certainly given me food for thought... but now there is another person to factor into matters, namely Alex, I know it may seem that I am jumping the gun a little, but I truly feel that we are meant to be, but if the children and I move hundreds of miles away, then I guess that any prospect of romantic interest concerning Alex would go well and truly out of the window.

Saying that however, I have decided that during my break tomorrow, I will contact some of the local estate agents with a view to putting the house on the market, wish me luck!

It's that time again, you know, where my eyes are heavy and dreamland is a calling, so I will bid you a goodnight, As ever Xxx

The week toddled along nicely, Lois had been given various price suggestions for the house and still no sign of the big bad wolf, which was somewhat relieving, she had been to visit Alex every day and was shocked at his recovery progress, he was certainly not one to give in to incapacity! Each time she visited, their friendship forged forever deeper as it was clear for all to see that they were wildly attracted to one another, that was until Thursday…..

Which began stressful with Jake's refusal to go to Julie's he stood at the car, arms folded tightly, adamantly shaking his head, "I'M NOT GOING!" he screamed, Lois looked at Amber, who was shaking her head in disapproval of her younger brother's outburst,

"Why Jake, why today?" Lois asked as she began to give up all hope of getting to work at all,

"Mum, I know why," Amber whispered as she stood beside Lois,

"DON'T TELL HER, YOU PROMISED!" Jake bellowed,
Lois turned and looked at Amber gesturing for her to continue,
"He had a fight with Thomas yesterday and Julie told them
both off," Amber said as Jake began to wail,
"Why? Why did you fight with Thomas?" Lois asked,
completely baffled by the revelation, they were usually the best
of friends,
"He said that his Dad is better than mine and that he doesn't
get smacked, so I hit him," Jake sobbed, Lois swept him up
into her arms and held him tightly,
"Why don't we go, and I'll have a word with Julie, it's only two
more days and then I'm off and we can spend the weekend
making the Halloween decorations, how does that sound?"
Lois pleaded, what she really wanted to do was say fuck work,
turn around and go back inside, but if she were to set her plans
in motion, she needed all the money that she could make.
Jake reluctantly nodded his head, Lois wiped his tears away and
when they arrived at Julie's, after she had apologised profusely
for Thomas's behaviour, she made Lois aware that Thomas
had gone to stay with his Grandma for a few days, which
brought the smile back to Jake's sad face.

Work was no better, the department was a constant throng of
emergency admissions, Lois had not taken a break all day and
her shift had overran by half an hour, she had no time to visit
Alex, especially as Jake was in such a delicate mind frame, so
she ran out to her car to collect the children.
Once home, Amber was in the bath, while Jake happily played
video games, and Lois was in the kitchen preparing the evening
meal, when there was a loud knock on the door, which sent
Jake into a frenzy as he ran to Lois and grabbed her legs as he
trembled, she walked to the door and could see through the
glass panel that there were two police officers, she slowly
opened the door,

"Mrs Parker?" One officer asked, Lois nodded,
"Could we step inside a moment?" the female officer asked,
Lois nodded,
"Of course," she said as she now began to tremble,
"There has been an accident, a collision between two vehicles
on the M5," the male officer said,
"Oh God! Is he dead?" she asked, automatically thinking that
any involvement was centred around Kevin,
"Sorry, who?" the officer asked,
"My husband Mr Parker,"
"No madame, you must be mistaken, we are led to believe that
your parents Mr and Mrs Stone, were involved, *your parents, Mr
and Mrs Stone, your parents, Mr and Mrs Stone*, these words were
circling her head as she tried to make sense of what was being
said, the female officer led her to a chair and advised her to sit,
Jake had returned to the games consul and was happily racing,
Lois looked up at the male officer,
"Are they okay, are they hurt?" she asked disconcertedly,
"I'm afraid that they both died at the scene, they have been
taken to the mortuary and we need a formal identification, I
understand that you are an only child is that correct?" The
officer asked Lois didn't hear him as *they died at the scene*, played
over and over again until the realisation hit her, and she fell to
the floor and wept uncontrollably.

As she stepped outside the main doors of the hospital she
paused for a moment, for fear of her trembling legs being
unable to hold her, "You got a fag?" a woman dressed in a
hospital gown asked aggressively,
"What? Sorry no, I don't smoke," Lois replied as she walked to
the carpark in a dazed manner. She climbed into the car and
rested her head on the steering wheel, she had always
imagined, dreamed, of the day when she would go to her
parents, hold them close, tell them that she loved them, and

catch up on life, but now that opportunity had slipped away, all at the hands of a drunk driver.

She trudged through the hallway of her house and could hear Mark and the children laughing in the lounge, thank goodness for Mark, who, as soon as she called him, came straight over to watch the children, she opened the lounge door and peered around, smiling a small smile,
"Right you two, it's time to hit the sack, give your Mum a big kiss and get yourselves into bed," Mark said forthrightly, Jake ran to Lois and threw his arms around her, "I'm sorry that your Mummy and Daddy are dead," he said, Lois held him tightly, she didn't want to let go, then Amber walked to her and hugged her, she kissed them both goodnight as they made their way up the stairs.
She slumped into the armchair and placed her hands over her face as Mark walked into the lounge and handed her a large mug of coffee, which she received gratefully,
"Thank you, Mark, I don't know what I would do without you," she said and smiled,
"That's what friends are for isn't it, besides, I hardly have a busy love life do I?" he said and sat on the sofa.

Work had given her two weeks of compassionate leave, which allowed her to organise the funeral and her parent's estate, the entire time became all but a blur as she lived a nightmare that she hadn't ever thought about. During the two weeks, there was still no sign of the big bad wolf, she was half expecting him to show up at the funeral, but thankfully he didn't, and now she was sitting on her bed, preparing herself for her imminent return to work, she took out her journal and flicked through the pages, she hadn't written anything for weeks, she sighed as she read the last two exerts, her thoughts had been so frazzled, she hadn't given Alex a second thought,

Wednesday 15th Nov 95,

Dear Lois,

I could not find the strength to write to you since the devastating discovery that both my parents died in a car accident, to be honest, I have been worse than useless, thank goodness for Mark, who has been my rock throughout, he took his last two weeks holiday so that he could help me, I will be forever in his debt! I have found it incredibly hard to come to terms with the fact that I will never have the chance to tell them how much I love them, how much I have missed them over the years, and how I thought about them every single day, but hey ho.

Tomorrow is the beginning of the rest of my life, and I have decided that now they are no longer here, I should seize the opportunity to get the hell out of my marriage, this town, and my life as it is now!

And now I get to Alex, who, I ashamedly have to say, has not entered my thoughts during my horrific ordeal. Is that bad? Does that mean that maybe I am not as attracted to him as I first thought? I thought that he was my knight in shining armour, well who wouldn't, when you are married to a pig like Kevin any form of attention is most welcoming.

I shall summon up the courage to see him in the first available moment tomorrow and see how I feel then,

Until then Xxx

She walked into the department the following morning to be met with melancholy looks of sympathy from all of her colleagues, she smiled and walked to the station to await her instructions, luckily, the A&E was pretty quiet for a Thursday and at half eleven, Jackie sent her for a break. She slowly and hesitantly climbed the stairs to the floor of the HDU, she walked through the double doors and walked to room 2 where she walked in and jumped back as a man in his sixties lay in the bed attached to a variable amount of machinery. After a short apology, she stepped out of the room and to the nurse's station,

"Hi, could you tell me where Alex from room 2 is please?" she asked a student nurse, who idly sighed and checked the transfer list,

"He transferred to Medical on Monday," she huffed and continued reading the magazine sitting on the desk in front of her. Lois didn't feel that a reply was necessary as she ran down the stairs and to the nurse's station in the medical ward, scanning the boards for his name as she did,

"Lois! We don't often see you in this neck of the woods," Diane the ward sister said as she smiled, Lois had spent a year training under the watchful eye of Diane, she learned so much from her and would always look up to her,

"No, you know how it is in A&E, don't get a minute, I'm looking for a patient," Lois replied,

"The name?" Diane asked,

"Oh, er Alex," Lois replied as she still looked at the name boards,

"What's the surname?"

"Oh, I er, I'm not sure," Lois replied, she could feel the burning feeling of embarrassment spreading across her cheeks,

"Really? What is he in for?"

"Oh he had a fractured Femur, he would have been transferred from HDU," Lois replied as Diane looked through the notes,

"Oh, hang on, Alex Gardener, he was discharged yesterday," Diane said as she looked up at Lois, who was showing signs of bitter disappointment from the expression that she now wore, "I don't suppose there is an address for him is there?" Lois asked in desperation,

"No, doesn't seem to be, hello what's this? It's addressed to you," Diane said and frowned, Lois snatched the small white envelope from her hand and sprinted along the corridor, placing the envelope into her pocket, she was already five minutes late back, which left her no time to read it.

The afternoon shift seemed to last for days, and Lois silently cheered when it came to the end of her shift, she swiftly made her way to her car, and as she climbed in, she took out the now crumpled white envelope and opened it, it read:

Dear Lois,

Your ward manager came and told me about your parents, I cannot imagine what you are going through, I only wish that there were some way to make things better for you. I cannot thank you enough for all the care and affection you have shown towards me during my stint in hospital.

The doctors were amazed at my speedy recovery, hence the sudden discharge, which I argued, of course, in the hope that I could see you one last time, unfortunately, they were insistent, even threatening security if I didn't leave!

I hope that life is kinder to you than it has been of late, you truly deserve to be happy, you are a wonderful nurse and a beautiful person,

Enough of all this sloppy talk, I am beginning to feel a little nauseous myself! I wish the very best

Dear Lois...

in life for you, and you will be forever in my
thoughts,
All my love
Alex xxxxxx.

CHAPTER FOUR

She wiped the tears from her eyes and composed herself as she started the engine and then looked at her sad reflection in the rearview mirror, she sighed and drove towards Julie's house, as she climbed out of the car, she heard her name being called, she turned and saw Kevin's older sister Janette running towards her, "Hey, how's things?" Janette asked breathlessly, "You got a couple of days?" Lois asked and chuckled, "I'm sorry Lois, Mum told me about your parents, I was absolutely gutted for you," she said sincerely, Lois, had always had a good relationship with Janette, in fact, she was the only member of Kevin's family that she could get along with, Lois smiled a small smile, "I'm glad that I have bumped into you, I was going to give you a call this afternoon, Tony is going away on a business trip and the girls have been bugging me to see Amber and Jakey, so I was wondering if I could have them to stay over tonight?" Janette asked and smiled, Lois wasn't keen on the idea of the children being away from home, especially on a school night, but she knew that it would do them both the world of good, and she could catch up on chores that had been overlooked for the past fortnight,

"Sure, but what about the school run in the morning?" Lois asked,

"I can drop them off at school before I take the girls," Janette replied, Lois nodded, "I'll pop in at five, is that okay, I'll take them all out for dinner," Janette said as she began to jog back to her car, Lois walked up the path and knocked on Julie's front door.

"But I don't want to go to Aunty Janette's it's boring!" Jake shouted from the back seat of the car, Lois looked at him in the rearview mirror, sighed and shook her head,

"What about you Amber, do you want to go?" Lois asked as she turned her gaze to Amber, who miserably shook her head, "No not really," she sighed.

They ran in through the front door, both children pushing past Lois to race up the stairs, Lois stopped in her tracks when the dank aroma of stale cigarette smoke filled her nasal cavity. She pushed the door to the lounge open and cringed when she saw Kevin sprawled out on the sofa, at that very moment, every emotion that she had pushed back came racing forward showing itself in a torrent of rage, she raced over to the sofa, ripped the newspaper from his hands and stood beside him with her hands on her hips in a show of self-confidence,
"I'm sorry, but what gives you the right to flounce in and out of my house, whenever you feel like it," she seethed, he began to laugh,
"Keep your knickers on," he said as he pushed himself up,
"Keep my fucking knickers on? You have been gone for over a month now, what happened, did your latest conquest finally realise what a fucking pig, you actually are?" Lois screamed as fury coursed through her veins like white water rapids, Kevin climbed to his feet and grabbed her face in his hands,
"Shut your mouth! I haven't been near another woman, I was looking for work," he sneered, saliva flying from his mouth as it began to foam,
"LEAVE MY MUM ALONE!" Jake bellowed from the doorway as he took a run at Kevin, bounding into his legs and causing them to buckle beneath him, he quickly jumped to his feet and pulled his arm back, releasing Lois as she jumped in front of Jake, blocking Kevin's way, he brought his hand down and slapped Lois forcibly across the face, sending her flying into the wall, Jake, and Amber both began to scream as Amber ran to Lois, who was knocked out cold,

"What have you done?" Amber cried as she lifted Lois's head, at the moment when Janette stepped into the room and gasped,
"KEVIN! What the hell is wrong with you, get out quickly, I need to call an ambulance and the police will attend," Janette said as she shooed him to the door and picked up the telephone.

She opened her eyes to bright light, "Argh!" she cried as pain shot through her head like someone had taken a drill to her brain,
"Sorry, it's good to have you back in the land of the living," the paramedic said and smiled, Lois looked around her living room, Jake and Amber were huddled together on the sofa, Janette was standing beside them, the lounge door opened, and a strange woman walked in,
"Where is the lying bastard?" she asked, her heavily made-up face and overbleached hair displaying signs that she was beyond the years that she was desperate to portray, Janette stepped forward,
"He is not here as you can see, if I were you I would go home and forget about him," Janette said as she frantically edged her towards the door,
"You could have warned me that he was a lying, cheating bastard, you were all saying what a lovely couple we made the other night in the pub," the woman fumed as Janette pushed her out of the front door and closed it. The paramedics were happy that there were no signs of serious or permanent damage, safe in the knowledge that Lois was an A&E nurse, they were happy to leave her and began to pack their equipment away, Lois looked at Janette,
"You knew? You knew and yet you invited my children for a sleepover? Get out of my house!" Lois said sternly, albeit quietly,

"But"

"GET OUT!" she shouted causing pain to soar through her head, a police officer who was waiting to take a statement stepped forward and looked at Janette,

"You heard her," he said as he walked Janette to the door.

The following morning, Lois dropped the children at school and headed off to work, her head was still a little tender, but in all honesty, she needed the distraction. She sat at the nurse's station, Mark took one look at her and grabbed her hand, leading her to the nurse's room,

"What happened?" he asked as he trembled, Lois spent a few minutes filling him in with the gory details, when the door opened, and Jackie peered her head around,

"In case it had escaped your attention, I am trying to run an incredibly busy accident and emergency department, why are you in here?" she asked sternly, Mark climbed to his feet, looked at Jackie and then Lois as he slowly shook his head, he left, and Jackie approached Lois and gasped when she saw her bruised and grazed face.

The morning flew by incredibly quickly, the department was busier than usual, Isobel another staff nurse, made Lois laugh when she blamed it all on the full moon! Lois and Mark were standing at the nurse's station, waiting to go to lunch, when security rushed past the doors and into the main hospital, which was slightly unusual, they were mainly called to the A&E department. They looked at one another both wearing an expression of surprise and then walked to the canteen to grab a bite to eat,

"Why don't you and the children come and stay at my house for a while, you know, just until the dust settles," Mark suggested, Lois, who had a mouthful of cheese roll, shook her head, chewing frantically so she could answer,

"No, we are fine Mark, they have placed a restraining order on him, so he cannot come anywhere near us," Lois said as she gulped her food down and smiled,

"I would feel much happier if you would, just for a few days," he said, now his tone was rather insistent, again Lois smiled and shook her head,

"Okay, why don't you book a viewing for that sweet little cottage then?" he asked, Lois rolled her eyes,

"Will you stop nagging me if I do?" she asked, Mark nodded, somewhat over exaggeratedly causing Lois to laugh, Mark winked and took out his address book,

"I'll go and give him a call now, should I book it for Saturday?" he asked, Lois nodded.

Back in the swathe of yet more admissions, there didn't seem time to think as staff members hurried around relentlessly, she was relieved when it came to the end of the shift and she and Mark walked out to the carpark, Mark stopped outside the main entrance, his innate curiosity caused him to ask one of the security officers what had happened earlier that day,

"Some nutter was in HDU, ransacking the place," he replied, Mark looked at Lois and raised an eyebrow,

"I take it that he is in police custody now," Mark said nervously, the security officer shook his head,

"Nah, he ran off before we had time to alert the police," he replied as he walked back inside the hospital, Mark turned to Lois and shuddered as they walked to their cars,

"OI!" they both heard as Kevin charged towards them, Lois winced,

"You're a fucking turncoat, filling her head with all kinds of shite, and you, where is the wounded soldier now then, your knight in shining armour, WHERE IS HE?" Kevin roared in

Lois's face, Mark jumped on his back and dug his nails into Kevin's eyes as two security officers ran to them and grappled Kevin to the ground.

"How did he know?" Lois asked after they had given their statements to the police and were driving to collect the children in Mark's car, purely because there had been reports that someone fitting Kevin's description was seen tampering with Lois's car earlier in the day and the police had taken it in to inspect it,

"I have no idea. Have you spoken to any of your friends?" Mark asked, Lois chuckled,

"You are my only friend," she replied, "My journal! He must have been back to the house and read my journal!" Lois exclaimed.

Fri 17th November 95

Dear Lois,

It seems weird writing this from a strange bed, in a strange house, but after the complete chaos of the last couple of days, I have been left with no other choice. The big bad wolf came back with a vengeance, hit me, and then created no end of havoc at the hospital! My car is now being tested as they believe that it has been tampered with and the children and I are staying at Mark's house tonight before our big adventure tomorrow. I have had to book a hire car, but still, it adds to the adventure doesn't it? It turns out that Kevin had been staying with a woman called Sharon, and once he had cleaned her out, decided to come back, looking for money, luckily I hid it well, but in the process, he found you! So now he knows my plan, he knows that I am going to disappear, luckily I wrote that we were thinking of moving to the lakes, which I hope beyond hope he thinks is the Lake District, anyhow, tomorrow morning at six thirty, Amber, Jake and I are driving to 'A Lake' in Wales.

I had a letter from Mum and Dad's solicitor today, it was an appointment for the reading of their will and a letter addressed to me written by Mum, I have never felt so utterly heartbroken when I read the words, the same words that I have longed to say to them for many years, but the strange thing is, I feel them around me, I know you will think that my marbles have gone on a short trip, but it's true, when I read the letter I could feel a hand touch my shoulder as if to comfort me, I just knew that it was Mum! Even with all this happening I still cannot get Alex to leave my thoughts, he is always there, I just wish that I knew where to find him,

I am going to attempt to sleep now in preparation for the impending adventure, so I will bid you a goodnight, As ever Xxx

It was a wonderful drive, they had a few pit stops and soon were driving ever higher into the mountainous landscape, Lois was thrilled to hear the gasps of the children as the mountains towered over them as they drove. Lois found the small office where Mark's brother worked, and she and the children walked along the narrow pavement and into the office. There were two women perched behind desks, one of whom smiled at the children as they walked in and the small bell above the door rang out,

"Can I help you?" she then asked Lois,

"Yes, I have arranged a viewing," Lois replied, the woman opened the diary,

"For what property?" she asked,

"Drift-end cottage," Lois replied as she read from the brochure and the two women erupted into laughter,

"Drift-end, are you sure?" the woman asked as she wiped the tears of laughter carefully from her eyes in an attempt not to smudge her thick eye makeup, Lois frowned and nodded,

"I'm sorry, I hadn't realised that I said something humorous," Lois stated sternly,

"No, sorry, it's a private joke, never mind us!" She replied as she made a call, she spoke for a few moments replaced the handset and looked up at Lois,

"Kyle wants to meet you at the edge of Coltsfoot Coed, it is clearly signposted, the cottage is a little off the beaten track you see," the woman said as she stifled the desire to laugh, Lois nodded,

"Well, thank you for your help, I'm glad that I was able to bring a little joy into your lives," she sneered as she guided the children towards the door.

The drive, well it was something of an experience, driving along single-track lanes that had more potholes than tarmac, and Lois sighed with relief when she noticed the large green signpost for the forest carpark, she pulled up alongside a Land Rover, which had a man in the driver's seat. He climbed out and walked to the driver's side, Lois opened the window,

"Lois?" he asked, she instantly recognised him, the family resemblance was remarkable, she nodded,

"If you follow me, it's a bit of a bugger to get to," he said as he walked back to his vehicle and climbed in, Lois turned to look at the apprehension on the children's faces,

"Are we ready?" she asked excitedly, they both slowly nodded their heads,

"No, ARE WE READY!" she asked again, hoping this time for a little more gusto!
"Yeah!" they both squealed as she pulled off and carefully followed the Land Rover in front.

After what felt like a thousand dirt tracks later, they pulled up outside, what appeared to be an abandoned property, Lois screwed up her nose and looked at the children,
"That's not it, is it?" Amber asked,
"Only one way to find out, come on, out you get," Lois sighed and climbed out of the car.

It had once been loved, that cottage nestled in a valley, cocooned by the giant mountains which surrounded it, she stepped inside, which was like stepping back in time, odd pieces of furniture which had surely dated back to the 1920s were scattered around, the curtains had most definitely seen better days, along with the carpet, but, and it's a big but, standing in the centre of the spacious living room was the most beautiful inglenook fireplace, which for Lois was its selling point, the kitchen was dated but workable, and there was another standout feature, a beautiful powder blue Aga. She walked up the small staircase to find the children who had disappeared up there upon entering the cottage, she found Amber in one of the front bedrooms,
"This is my room, can I put posters up?" Amber smiled and asked, Lois grinned and nodded, they found Jake in the small back room, he was standing at the window looking out at the many sheep in the field behind,
"Well Jakey, what do you think?" Lois asked, he turned and smiled,
"Can I ride the sheep?" he asked, causing Amber and Lois to laugh,

"No sweetheart, I don't think that the sheep would appreciate that, maybe we can find somewhere close by that gives horse riding lessons," Lois suggested as the three of them made their way down into the lounge,

"Well, what do you think?" Kyle asked apprehensively,

"Would I be able to decorate it?" Lois asked, Kyle smiled and nodded,

"I am sure that Old Mrs Hughes would be over the moon if you did, she is the owner, but it is a little too remote for her now, so she moved closer to civilisation," Kyle said as they walked outside, Lois looked up at the wooden sign, suspended on two rusty chains as it blew back and forth in the brisk, icy, northerly wind, that had the name of the cottage painted on,

"Drift-end, that's a strange name for a cottage, don't you think," Lois said as still she studied the sign, Kyle nodded,

"If you follow me, I'll show you," he said and Lois followed as he walked down into the valley, "You see, after significant snowfall, the valley becomes completely filled with drifts, this place is susceptible to blizzards you know," he smiled, his smile turned to a frown and he looked solemnly at Lois, "Mark told me about your current situation, will you be all right out here by yourselves, it can be rather isolated, especially when the bad weather sets in?" he asked, his voice full of concern.

CHAPTER FIVE

They were lying on the king-size bed in the hotel room after having a scrumptious pub meal, Amber and Jake had insisted on watching a movie, so Lois thought it would be the ideal time to report back to Mark, who had been clucking like a mother hen ever since they had set off on their adventure.
"I spoke to Kyle earlier, and he seems a little apprehensive, apparently the location is pretty isolated," Mark said, Lois shook her head in annoyance, they had made their decision and on Monday morning she would happily waltz into work and hand over her written resignation she was thinking as a smile grew across her face,
"Well, you will be able to see for yourself soon, won't you," Lois said and winked at Amber, who was watching her,
"So, you are taking it then? What about your house?" Mark asked as the phone line crackled,
"I'll fill you in on all the details when we get back tomorrow okay," Lois shouted as the fizzing on the line became louder,
"Lois, make sure you call me before you head off," Mark managed to say hastily before the line went dead, Lois placed the receiver down, walked to the window and gasped as she watched the snow falling from the sky, blanketing the road with an icy white layer.
They huddled up together in bed, "Just think, we will move into the cottage a week before Christmas, how exciting!" Lois stated as she looked at Jake, whose heavy eyelids were closing, she kissed them both and then snuggled beneath the warm duvet.

Dear Lois...

Sunday 19th Nov 95,

Dear Lois,

I am writing this at 4.30 in the morning! Firstly I need to tell you about the weird dream I had which woke me up and now I find myself writing to you. I was in a building, an old building, no not the cottage that we are moving into, no, it was a large building, and I was serving hot drinks from behind a counter, everyone inside was wearing old-fashioned military uniforms. There was a loud sound, coming from outside and we all ran out to watch a plane falling from the sky above, crashing in the field beside us, that's when I woke up with a jump, it was so real, I have never experienced anything like it before!

Now that I have got that off of my chest I can reveal all! We arrived at the cottage this afternoon, the scenery is breathtaking, this is my first visit to Wales, and now I ask myself why, why have I never been before? The cottage is <u>very</u> dated but has an air of I don't know what about it, the feeling I had the entire time we were there, was one of family life, a happy, contented family. I signed the lease, Kyle, Mark's brother is insisting that I buy a more suitable vehicle before the move on December 18th, so my to-do list for Monday is to give a month's notice at work, instruct the estate agent about the sale of mine and Mum and Dad's houses, and then go on the hunt for a 4x4! The children are so excited, I did ask Kyle about the local schools, unfortunately, they are mostly Welsh speaking, so I am considering teaching them myself at home, I think that we could all learn together. I have just looked out of the hotel window and the earlier snowfall seems to have disappeared, so I think that I will wake the children

*and begin the journey back, there is much to do and not a
lot of time to do it!
Until tomorrow,
xxx*

The drive back seemed to take forever, the children were both
miserable at the prospect of the impending return, but Lois
promised that she would make a tick chart to count down the
days before they left their old lives behind and began a new,
Lois was more than relieved when she pulled up on the drive
to Mark's house. He ran out to the car, helping the children to
carry their belongings into the house, desperate to hear all
from Lois.
She washed and dried the school uniforms while Mark cooked
dinner and once the children were tucked up in bed, they sat
together in the lounge, and she revealed all.
"Don't you think that it would be better to hire the services of
a removal company from up there? You know what people this
end of the country are like, one snowflake and the whole place
shuts down?" Mark suggested, Lois nodded and wrote it on
her ever-growing 'to-do' list.

The smug look that she wore the following morning was a
sight to behold as she strolled into the department five minutes
late, ready for the look of disapproval and strong words from
Jackie, she skipped to the nurse's station, envelope in hand,
Jackie looked up from the paperwork and smiled, which threw
Lois somewhat, spoiling her announcement, she
apprehensively handed the envelope to Jackie,
"What's this, it's not my birthday yet," Jackie said and
exaggeratedly laughed,
"It's my letter of resignation," Lois said quietly,

"It's your what? For a minute there I thought that you said letter of resignation!" Jackie stated loudly as she once again howled with laughter, looking at her growing audience of staff as they gathered around.

"That's exactly what I said," Lois said and blushed as she heard the gasps and groans of her fellow workers, Jackie scowled and began to tear away at the envelope, making her feeling of disappointment clear for all to see, she mumbled each word as she read it, which caused Lois to now turn a shade of scarlet,

"I see," Jackie said as she folded the envelope and placed it into her pocket, stood and walked to the whiteboard, where she began to scribble incessantly, Lois looked around, the area had now cleared as her colleagues realised that Jackie's mood had now taken a turn and they would all be in for a royal rollicking if they were not doing as they should.

The days flew by, which, when time is against you is not ideal, Lois had booked a local Welsh removal firm and purchased a second-hand 4x4, and now she was left to pray that the sales on both houses would go through without a hitch. With only two weeks before the big move, Lois was en route to collect the children from Julie's and head over to the burger bar, where she had arranged a goodbye party for Amber and Jakes's friends. The restaurant was full of excited children, Amber and Jake were in their element as they sat at a table, unwrapping all manner of keepsakes, which their friends had brought, Lois looked over her coffee cup at Julie, who seemed to be pre-occupied, "Is everything okay Julie?" Lois asked as she blew on the still molten liquid in her disposable cup, Julie smiled and nodded,

"Yes, why?" she asked awkwardly,

"You seem to be miles away, that's all," Lois replied and smiled, a smile which soon turned to a deep frown as she watched a large familiar figure walk past the glazed restaurant gazing inside as he did, Lois looked at Julie, wearing an expression of utter disbelief,

"I had to tell him, he threatened me," Julie said regrettably as the door to the restaurant flew open and Kevin marched in and headed towards Amber, who he grabbed forcefully by the wrist, lifting her out of the chair, Lois ran and grabbed his arm, which he threw backwards sending her across the restaurant, Jake began to scream as Kevin dragged a screaming Amber towards the door, "GET OFF OF MY SISTER!" Jake screamed as he then sank his teeth into Kevin's leg, clamping his jaw in refusal to let go, Kevin roared out in pain as Lois pulled herself to her feet and ran to Amber,

"Let her go!" Lois seethed,

"You are not taking them anywhere! YOU HEAR ME!" he roared as flashing blue lights appeared from the car park and two police officers ran inside, cuffing Kevin as soon as they reached him, once the dust had settled and the multitude of tears had relented, the last of the parents had collected their children, hearing the offering of apology from Lois as they did, she sat at the table and sighed as she looked at her troubled children,

"Two weeks, that's all, then we will be free of him forever," Lois said as she wiped the still-running tears from Amber's face,

"But what if he finds us?" Amber asked as still she trembled, Lois smiled,

"Amber, it was a nightmare for us to find and we were following someone who knew the location, I haven't told anyone the new address, so he will never find us," Lois said as she cradled her distraught daughter in her arms.

Saturday December 4th 95,

Dear Lois,

Sorry, it's been a while, I have been so busy there are just not enough hours in the day to fit everything in! So, today I did an extra shift at work, they have all been so lovely, and they are so short-staffed, how could I refuse, anyway, I planned a party at Snappy Jack's burger bar for the children, as a way of saying goodbye to their friends, and the inevitable happened, yes you guessed it, Julie told the big bad wolf, and he turned up. He grabbed Amber by the wrist and began to drag her out, I was thrown across the restaurant, which lately is proving to be a common occurrence, and my Jakey, bless him, ran to Kevin, and sank his teeth into his leg, which brought enough time for the police to come in and arrest him.

I spoke to Mark this evening and I have decided that the children will not be going to Julie's again, Mark's new partner Will has kindly offered to watch them here at Mark's house, the man is a legend, Jake keeps asking them both if they will move to Wales with us, Bless.

I keep having the same dream, you know, the one I wrote about, it is always exactly the same, weirdly. I don't know why, but I feel that it is connected to Alex, every time I have the dream, upon waking, he is there at the forefront of my mind, I wish that I could see him before we leave. I find myself drifting away with my thoughts, to a place where I imagine that he will turn up out of the blue and whisk me up into his arms, he knows where to find me right? So why doesn't he? Maybe his feelings for me were strictly platonic, and my companionship was welcomed to dull the boredom of a hospital stay.

Never mind, it's okay to dream, it sometimes keeps me going. Tomorrow I am off to the city on a Christmas shopping excursion while Mark and Will take the children to watch a movie at the cinema, I am absolutely dreading it but as we are moving so close to the big day, I need to be organised,
Sleep is a calling, so I will bid you a good night,
As always
Xxx

The alarm rang out, causing Lois to almost fall out of bed, she groaned loudly as she switched it off and climbed sluggishly out of the warm, comfort of the bed, after her hectic weekend, she felt as though she had had no break and exhaustion was slowly creeping up on her. She arrived at the department at least twenty minutes before her start time so she walked down the main foyer to grab a coffee from the coffee shop, the lattes they served were nothing short of perfection, so she paid the disgruntled-looking woman behind the counter and walked away, frantically blowing on the hot coffee, not watching where she was walking, she collided with someone, who shouted loudly as her latte escaped from the cup and covered the person in incredibly hot coffee,
"Oh! I am so sorry!" Lois gasped and looked up to meet the eyes of the man she had been dreaming of for what seemed an eternity, "Alex!" she gasped as he grinned, rubbing his wet shirt with a paper napkin,
"Lois," he said as she gazed at him, her eyes wide, her heart now thumping like a big base drum,
"What.. what are you doing back here?" she asked when she realised that she was staring at him longingly, her cheeks now burning with sheer embarrassment,

"I have my follow-up appointment with the Orthopaedic surgeon at nine, and then I was going to come and find you," he said as sighed, he looked so well, so fit!

"Oh, I see," Lois replied awkwardly, now lost for words, "Well that is if you want me to," he said and frowned, her reaction not being one that he had imagined, her cheeks were reddening by the second, the colour deepening more so when she looked into his eyes, she was mesmerised, "Er, Lois?" he asked, she quickly shook her head, to bring her back from dreamland, and laughed,

"Yes! Yes sorry, of course, yes I'd love for you to come and find me," she said as she laughed, mainly at herself and her ever-growing stupidity,

"Great, I'll come to your department as soon as I'm done," he said, Lois nodded and looked at her watch, realising that her shift was about to start, she began to step backwards,

"I have to go, my shift is about to start," she said as she turned and jogged back to A&E, where she was met by no end of chaos as the festive season kicked in in true A&E fashion. Her head was all over the place as she desperately tried to concentrate on her job, but found herself, forever watching the doors, looking towards the nurse's station, waiting to see if an approaching colleague was the announcer of Alex's impending visit, but until now, there had been no sign of him.

"Lois, go and take your break," Jackie said as she strolled past her, with arms full of folders, Lois turned and smiled and then looked at the clock, it was eleven thirty, there was no way that Alex was still waiting to be seen, clinics were known to overrun, but by two and a half hours, no, he must have been seen and then left, Lois was thinking as she ripped off the plastic apron and ventured out of the doors and along the corridor towards the canteen, all the time, endlessly looking all around to see if she could catch a glimpse of him. She sat at the table and stared out of the window, watching as the air ambulance landed and many staff members ran towards it, there had been no red telephone, so obviously the patient wasn't heading for her department,

"Do you mind if I sit here?" she heard, then turned to look at the inquirer, she smiled and nodded, pulling the chair out for Fiona, whom she had known for years since they started their nursing studies at the same time,

"How're things?" Fiona asked as she sat down,

"Not too bad," Lois replied,

"You still in the throes of the A&E department then?" Fiona asked, Lois nodded,

"Yes, well I have two weeks left and then I am out of here," she replied,

"You're leaving? Have you been poached by another trust then? Or are you braving the private sector?" Fiona asked, discretion never being a strong character trait of hers,

"Yes I am leaving, no I have not been poached, I am leaving because the children and I are relocating," Lois replied as she finished the remnants of coffee in her cup,

"Ooh, anywhere nice?"

"The Lakes," Lois replied as she stood and pushed her chair in, she trusted no one and was not going to share any information with the in-house gossip.

"Lovely, well I'll think of you while I am sawing off plaster casts in the clinic," she replied and smiled,

"Wait, you work in orthopaedics?" Lois asked as her mind began to work overtime, Fiona nodded,

"Did you happen to see an outpatient this morning a Mr, er, Gardener," Lois asked her voice full of relief that she had managed to remember, Fiona sat in deep thought, then smiled,

"Yes! That man from Surrey, a bit of all right, he was," Fiona said as Lois scowled, then nodded, "Yeah he was about to be discharged but then he took a call and ran out!" Fiona continued,

"A call from whom?" Lois asked agitatedly,

"I don't know, I'm not in the habit of prying into other people's business," she said and shook her head,

"You could have fooled me," Lois said under her breath as she began to walk away,

"Are you having a leaving do?" Fiona shouted across the canteen,

"Saturday in the clubhouse," Lois replied as she ran back towards A&E.

The afternoon flew by and before she had time to think, her shift had come to an end, she slowly walked out of the main doors and headed towards the car park, the sky was dark with looming rain clouds promising a deluge of rain, the icy wind whipped around her causing her to wrap her jacket closely around her body, she put her hood up as large droplets of rain began to fall from the sky and she jogged towards her car, "Lois," she heard as a hand grabbed her arm, blinded by the side of her hood, she pulled the hood down to see Alex standing beside her smiling a small smile.

CHAPTER SIX

"Quick, let's get to the car," Lois said as large hail stones began to fall from the heavy clouds, they both ran, Lois, fumbling in her bag as she ran in search of her car keys, quickly unlocked the car and they both jumped in,

"Sorry about earlier, I had to go somewhere urgently," Alex said as he swept the rainwater from his combat trousers,

"Hey, you weren't under any sort of obligation," she replied shortly, she was now in self-survival mode and believed that she should put up her guard as a way of protection, Alex looked at her, holding his gaze as once again, she began to blush, how could she give him the cold shoulder when her mannerisms were telling a tale all of their own, she was silently thinking,

"I know, I had a call, my Mum had taken a fall and landed herself back in hospital, I had to drive there to see her," Alex said as he watched the rain fall down the window of the car, Lois turned to look at him, then she sighed, what was it about him that made it so hard to be angry? She asked herself before she replied,

"I'm sorry to hear that, is she okay?" Lois asked, his hand moved up and gently stroked her cheek,

"She has to have surgery on her hip, she is being moved to a London hospital this evening," he said and smiled.

"Oh how awful, mind you she will at least be in good hands, I suppose you had better get your skates on then," Lois said as she attempted to smile, trust had become quite an issue recently and she tended to sit on the 'not sure that I believe this' side of life,

"Oh, no, my Dad will be there with her, I told him that I would travel up in the morning," Alex replied awkwardly as his face now began to redden with embarrassment, "I, er, was wondering if I could take you out for dinner, as a way of thanks for taking care of me," he then asked, inside her soul was skipping about like an excitable five-year-old, but she, as always was edging on the side of caution,

"Hmm, I'm not sure if I can get a sitter at this short notice," she lied, knowing full well that Mark would happily watch the children, Alex frowned and sighed,

"That's a shame," he mumbled as he stared out of the car window, Lois was now wondering if she had somehow acted a little too hastily and began to panic as she desperately needed to backtrack,

"I'll just give my friend a quick call and ask if he will watch them, I'll be back in two minutes," Lois said as she opened the car door, jumped out and ran back towards the hospital, where she stood inside the foyer for a few minutes and then ran to the car,

"Sorted, my friend Mark and his partner are going to take them out for food," she said breathlessly as she smiled,

"Brilliant, I'll pick you up at seven thirty if that's okay?" he asked as he grinned, Lois nodded and Alex climbed out of the car, closed the door, and began walking towards his car,

"YES!!!" she said as she glory punched the air, her heart skipping away like a new-born lamb until she heard a tapping on the car window, she slowly turned and cringed as Alex stood beside the car laughing as he witnessed her self-celebration, she wound down the window, her face felt like it was on fire, and she awkwardly smiled,

"I don't have your address," Alex said as still he laughed, she opened the glove box, grabbed her small notepad, and scribbled down Mark's address, which she handed to him, trying to avoid eye contact, however, Alex had different ideas and leaned in and kissed her gently on the lips, the most longing, zealous, tender kiss, before he turned and headed back to his car.

Her head was spinning, she had to have a moment before she drove the car, she needed to digest what had just happened, she had kissed many frogs before, but this frog was most definitely a prince in disguise, she had never, ever felt anything like it and she was still in a state of euphoric shock, and then the laughter began, uncontrollable, unbridled laughter.

She must have tried on five different outfits, every time she paraded around the lounge, both Mark, Will and Amber would give her the thumbs up or thumbs down, Jake was taking no notice whatsoever as he was completely enthralled in the world of Mario! she was now onto the final outfit, a pretty black crochet dress, which she dressed down by wearing with a pair of torn jeans, she walked into the living room and beamed a wide smile as she received three thumbs up from the panel of judges and glided back to her room, to finish getting ready. A little later there was a tap on her bedroom door and Mark peered around the door,

"We are off now, have fun and stay safe," he said as he blew her a kiss. She waited until she heard the front door close and the car engine start, then she walked to the kitchen and poured herself a large glass of wine, Dutch courage was most definitely in order, which she swallowed down in three large gulps, she wiped the remnants of wine from her lips and walked to the lounge to watch out for unfamiliar vehicles, every few seconds checking her watch, it was now seven thirty-five and the road outside was deserted. By seven forty she had resigned herself to the fact that she had been stood up, so she walked back to the kitchen growling as she poured herself another glass of wine, well and truly drowning her sorrows and as she gulped down the wine, the doorbell sounded and she choked on the wine as it slipped down the wrong hole, she stumbled to the door, coughing, and spluttering and opened it, Alex looked at her despairingly,

"Are you all right?" he asked, his voice full of genuine concern, and all that Lois could do was nod, once she stopped choking, she began to laugh, the effects of the wine had now kicked in and she howled with laughter as she wiped the tears from her eyes, hoping that she hadn't spoiled her make up.

Monday 6th December 95,

Dear Lois,

What a fucking day! Tonight I possibly had the best night of my life to date! I was going to write this in the morning, but excitement got the better of me, and after only two glasses of wine, I can actually see to write, to cut a long story short, I literally bumped into Alex this morning at the hospital café, and when I say bumped I mean bumped. After covering him in my latte, he eventually asked to take me for dinner. We went to a beautiful riverside restaurant, and our table was beside the window, where we had a full view of the river, which was alight with small fairy lights, it was magical. We spent the evening talking about our lives and things that had happened since our last meeting, he is divorced, has no children and is an architect, which may come in handy if

Dear Lois...

I decide to put an offer on Drift End in the not-too-distant future.

He has to drive to London in the morning, so I chose not to invite him in for a nightcap, even though I desperately wanted to, he kissed me like I had never experienced before, it felt almost familiar, it was beautiful, anyway, I digress, he has agreed to come to my leaving party on Saturday night, which is exciting, however, if I had the choice, I would rather spend the evening with just him and me, but I'll take what I can get. I feel as though I am drifting high up in the clouds, my mind is full of him and him only, thank God I only have a few days left at work!

Well, my eyes are closing as I write, so I will bid you a good night,

Until tomorrow

As ever Xxx

She looked at the clock on the A&E department wall and sighed, it was shift end, her very last shift end and unexpectedly she began to feel an overwhelming sense of sadness, she had worked in the same hospital since her nurse training began all those years before, and now, this would never be her place of work, her familiar department ever again. She looked all around, every single member of staff was either busy with a patient or on their break, the place was deserted, she sighed as she slowly walked to the nurse's room to collect her coat and belongings, she grabbed her mug from the drainer and placed it into her bag, then turned and had one last look around as tears filled her eyes. She wiped away the rogue tears and walked to the exit doors, she pressed the green button to release them, but they would not budge, she pushed and pushed to no avail, and then she heard the voices of her colleagues,

"And where do you think that you are going, young lady?" Jackie called out, she turned and saw the gathering crowd of colleagues, huddled around her ward manager, Lois smiled as once again rebellious tears began to fill her eyes, she had assumed that they were busy and didn't care enough to say goodbye and those that did care would be at the party to say goodbye, Jackie beckoned to her to join them as they then gathered all around her showering her with affection and gifts.

Once she had recovered from the emotional goodbyes she walked out of the exit doors for the very last time, she said goodbye to the security guards and wrestled with arms full of gifts as she made her way to her car. She was shoved hard from behind into the path of an oncoming ambulance, the gifts scattered all over the road as the ambulance ground to an unexpected halt as a booted foot then went into her side and she cried out in pain. The two security guards ran to where she was lying face down, quickly they turned her over as Kevin made a run for it, "Christ are you all right?" One of the guards said as he watched blood run from her swollen lip, the paramedics ran to her aid,

"I'm fine, go after him, the police are still looking for him," Lois cried as the paramedics helped her to her feet, she reassured them that she was fine as she hobbled to the safety of the pavement after picking up the gifts which were strewn everywhere. The security guards returned breathless and empty-handed, and Lois sighed and shook her head, in the distance, she could see Kevin being frog-marched towards her by none other than Alex!

The security guards ran to them and restrained Kevin, marching him to the holding room beside A&E,

"I'm coming for you Bitch, you will never escape me, DO YOU HEAR ME!" Kevin roared as he struggled to break free,

"How did you know?" Lois asked as Alex gently touched her swollen, bleeding lip,

"I had just parked my car, and I wanted to surprise you when I looked over here and watched as he pushed you, he was running in my direction, so I put my foot out and he went arse overhead, and then I grabbed him," he said humbly,

"You really are my knight in shining armour aren't you," Lois said as she stroked his face,

"Nonsense. Anyone would have done the same," he replied as he relieved her of the many gifts and helped her to her car.

As she closed the boot, she turned and looked at Alex, "So why the surprise visit? I thought that I was seeing you tomorrow?" Lois asked and attempted to smile,

"Well, I was wondering if you would allow me to treat you and the children to a meal and bowling?" he asked hesitantly, thinking that she was most probably not in the mood for a fun-packed evening, Lois grinned despite the pain,

"We would love to," she said as she stepped closer, he pulled her in close to his body and she inhaled his scent deeply, at that moment she was lost, lost in him,

"Fab! I will pick you all up at half six," he said and kissed her, the pain soured through her face as his stubble rubbed against the painful grazes, which embedded deep into her skin, and yet, she made no utterance and relished in the moment.

There was a definite awkward silence when Alex arrived to take them out, Amber sat glaring at him as Lois was left with no other choice but to bribe Jake to turn off the confounded games consul, as they readied to leave, Will whispered something to Amber and then to Jake, who in turn looked at Alex and grinned, Jake took hold of Alex's hand as they walked out to his car.

It turned out that Alex was somewhat of a whizz when it came to bowling, however, he did take the time to show Amber and Jake how to play, which left Lois trailing behind miserably on the scoreboard, after Alex scored yet another strike, Lois admitted defeat and walked to the bar to grab refills when she returned they all smiled widely at her, she looked down, wondering if she had perhaps, unknowingly spilt something down her hoodie, but it seemed fine,

"Come on then, what's the joke?" she asked as she placed the drink-filled tray on the table, they shook their heads, resembling the three stooges and Lois frowned, "Well, why are you laughing at me?" she asked as she dropped her swollen lip,

"We're not fucking laughing!" Jake shouted in full voice, Lois gasped,

"Jake! Why on earth are you using language like that?" she scorned as she looked around to see if any of the other bowlers had heard him, then turned to Alex who was stifling a laugh,

"You say it all of the time, especially when you are driving, today you called the man in the blue car a fucking idiot, didn't she Amber," Jake said in his defence, and Amber burst out laughing, Lois looked at Alex who could not fight the compulsion to laugh any longer as his shoulders bobbed up and down involuntarily, which in turn caused Lois to chuckle as very soon they were all howling with laughter.

As he parked the car, Lois turned to look at the children in the backseat, who were both yawning and sleepy, she then turned to Alex, "Do you fancy a coffee?" she asked with a glint in her eye, Alex checked his watch,

"I could have a quick one, the B&B locks its doors at eleven," he said and wore a look of sadness.

She jogged into the kitchen and put on the kettle as she then rounded up the children and marched them upstairs to bed, the house seemed pretty deserted, meaning that either Mark and Will had gone out for the evening, or had decided on a peaceful early night.

They sat in the warm lounge cradling their hot coffees, chatting about the children when the front door closed, and Mark and Will walked in.

Friday 10th December 95

Dear Lois,

Wow! Just Wow! Alex is everything you could imagine in a man and more. Today not only did he manage to restrain Kevin after he had yet again assaulted me, but he took the children and me out for a wonderful evening of bowling and food, I lost miserably, but I don't even care. Jakey seems very taken with him, Amber I'm not so sure, but given what she has had to witness over the years I think her level of trust is the same as mine, she did talk to him and laugh at his jokes, and she never laughs at mine, instead she huffs and rolls her eyes, like I'm so embarrassing, ha-ha.

Dear Lois...

This evening I did invite him in for coffee, I know, I know, what you are thinking, but it wasn't like that, not of course through choice, he had a curfew at his B&B, anyway, we were chatting away when Mark and Will returned from their weekly 'date night.' Alex told them that he had to go because of the curfew, and Mark asked him about tomorrow, after a discussion, it was decided that he would stay on the sofa, of course, tomorrow night, so that he wouldn't have to leave the party early.

I am going to drop the children at Tina's house mid-afternoon so that I can go dress shopping, I have to look my best don't I, the party is in my honour after all. Jake and Amber are as excited as I am, Tina's mum has hired a children's entertainer, so that should keep them out from under our dancing feet, for a while anyway, Mark, Will, Alex and I are getting a cab, and Mark has arranged a minibus collection for after, so, fingers crossed nothing should go wrong, especially as there was a message on the answer machine from the police to say the Kevin is now on remand and will hopefully stay that way until the trial!

I savoured two of Alex's amazing kisses today and my head is still swimming in sweet thoughts, so on that note, I shall bid you a good night and swim away,

Until tomorrow,

As ever Xxx.

CHAPTER SEVEN

What a night! They danced, they sang, they consumed lots of alcohol and they laughed, my, how they laughed. The night was drawing to a close and the obligatory smoochy slow song blared out from the speakers, Alex grabbed Lois by the hand and led her onto the dance floor, as they held each other close Alex gently whispered in her ear, "I wish that we could stay like this forever," Lois smiled and nodded, she would love nothing more, "When you move, can I come to visit?" he asked,

"I should bloody well hope so," she replied and smiled radiantly,

"When? When can I come?" he asked with a sense of urgency in his tone,

"Are you free on Saturday?" she slurred, the copious amounts of Jack Daniels had now affected her ability to speak somewhat, Alex nodded enthusiastically, "Good, you can help us move then," she said as she hiccupped,

"Would you come and meet my parents before then?" he asked,

"I'd love to!" she said as she moved in closer to him.

And now it was Wednesday, and she was nervously waiting for the arrival of Alex's car to drive her to meet his parents. After her awful relationship with Kevin's family, she was dreading it, she couldn't believe that she had agreed to it, mind you she was blind drunk and in a loved up state of euphoria at the time, the car stopped, she kissed both the children and then slipped out of the front door.

"All right," Alex said as she climbed in, she nodded confidently, however, she wasn't totally convincing as Alex could feel the anxiety oozing from her. The drive took just under an hour and Lois was shocked when Alex pulled up at a hospital carpark, she turned and looked at him, and he smiled,

"Mum's still an inmate I'm afraid, and Dad has booked a private relatives room," he stated cheerfully as he unclipped his seatbelt. They walked hand in hand toward the hospital entrance and just before they reached the doors of the main entrance, Alex stopped and turned to face her, grabbing both her hands in his, "They will love you, I just know it, don't look so worried," he said reassuringly, Lois nodded, smiled and they walked inside.

Alex tapped on the door and stepped in, Lois following him, his Mum was sitting on a chair beside her bed, and memories came flooding back of when Alex was in the same position, and their likeness was incredible, upon seeing Lois, his Mum attempted to stand,

"No please, don't stand," Lois said as she walked to her and kissed her cheek,

"You must be the wonderful, mysterious Lois that he keeps talking about, thank you for taking good care of my boy," she said kindly, Lois grinned,

"You are more than welcome," she replied,

"Well, come on, sit yourself down here beside me, Alex get Lois a drink will you, oh and I'll have a nice cup of tea, what about you Norman, do you want tea or coffee?" she asked and looked at a chair in the corner containing who could only be Alex's Dad, he looked up from the newspaper and grinned,

"I'll have a cup of tea if you're making one son," he said cheerfully, he had such a kindly face,

"Now Lois, I'm Treena and that oaf over there is Norman," she said and beamed a wide smile,

"It's lovely to meet you both," Lois said, neither of them was at all as she imagined, she thought that Alex must be from a middle-class class upbringing, Alex was well-spoken with an excellent career, yet his parents seemed so down to earth, so sweet and welcoming,

"Hello love, it's good to put a pretty face to a name," Norman said and smiled,

"Alex, Trevor will be here in a minute, he wants to have a chat with you," Norman said as Alex handed him a cup of tea, Alex nodded,

"What about?" he asked as the door opened and a man a little older than Alex, who bore a striking resemblance to him walked in and smiled, he walked to Treena and kissed her cheek,

"How are you today Mum?" he asked as he turned his gaze

towards Lois,

"I'm feeling much better Trev, this is Lois, Al's friend," she said and grinned at Lois,

"Hello," he greeted Lois rather abruptly, "Al, could I have a word?" Trevor asked, Alex nodded, and they both left the room,

"Take no notice of our Trev, he's overprotective of his little brother, especially after what that other thing did to him, she almost broke him, didn't she Norm?" Treena said angrily as Norman nodded,

"I'm sorry, did she break his heart?" Lois asked now filled with curiosity, he told Lois that he could not stand his ex-wife, that he began to loathe her two weeks after they had married,

"Break his heart, no my love, she broke his bank balance, took him for everything, he has only just managed to get back on his feet, she had five credit cards that he had to pay off, didn't she Norm?" Treena said wide-eyed, again Norman just nodded,

"That's dreadful," Lois replied, not knowing what to say, she felt as though she were delving into things that were none of her business, Treena nodded an exaggerated nod,

"And it's still not over yet, she is trying her hardest to take half of his business, even though the lazy cow hasn't done a decent day's work in her life, has she Norm?" Treena stated and looked at her long-suffering husband,

"No love," Norman replied as Alex and Trevor returned, Alex looking somewhat put out,

"Well? what do you think, we think that it's a wonderful idea, don't we Norm?" Treena said and looked at Alex,

"If it makes you happy Mum then it makes me happy," Alex replied not very convincingly, Lois looked at him and frowned, she had a distinct feeling that she may have just stepped into the middle of the beginning of a family feud.

"Good well that's settled then, once I'm out of here we'll have to have a get-together to celebrate, won't we Norm?" Treena said, and yet again, poor Norman smiled and nodded.

After just short of an hour, Alex made his excuses and they left, as they walked through the hospital corridors, he seemed agitated, like his thoughts were elsewhere, Lois grabbed his hand and squeezed it,

"Are you okay, you have been awfully quiet?" she asked and smiled.

"Sorry Lois, it's just that, Trevor wants to sell Mum and Dad's house and move them in with him and his wife, who is not a very, how can I say this without sounding rude, she's not a very compassionate person, and with Mum's early onset of dementia, I feel that it could end up a complete disaster," Alex explained sadly,

"Oh I'm sorry Alex, I had no idea," Lois gasped, Alex chuckled,

"Really?" he asked with raised eyebrows,

"I just thought that she was a little quirky," Lois replied and smiled,

"Hmm, anywhere, that leaves me in a slight predicament, now

I will have to find somewhere else to live," he muttered as they walked through the busy car park towards the car,

"I didn't realise that you lived at home," Lois said,

"I don't, well, I do but only temporarily, it's just that because of the divorce I had to sell the house to pay her off, I was staying with Mum and Dad until I decided where I wanted to lay down my roots so to speak," Alex said as he climbed into the car,

"I shouldn't think that it would be for a while though, it takes weeks if not months for a sale to go through," Lois replied, thinking how lucky she was to have sold both properties in such a short space of time.

Wednesday 15th December 95,

Dear Lois,

I cannot tell you just how busy I have been, Alex has gone to collect the Indian takeaway with Mark, and I have just had a lovely soak in the bath and have a few minutes to kill, so I thought that we could have a catch-up. The leaving party was wonderful, I paid for it on Sunday, I had so much packing to do, the furniture that I selected from my house and Mum and Dad's is due to go on Friday, and the rest was being collected by a house clearance place on Sunday afternoon, and of course, I had the mother of all headaches due to the vast amounts of JD that I consumed at the party! The children have been great, they both came back to the house with me and sorted through what they were taking and what they were donating to charity, Jake completely surprised me as he packed up so many of his plush toys for children who were less portunate (his words not mine) than him, which threw me somewhat, Jake being Jake and having a slightly possessive nature over anything which he deems belonging to him, but he did and that made me very happy, he is growing into such a beautiful, thoughtful lad.

As you have probably guessed, Alex has been here since Friday, and today he took me to meet his parents, but I will save that for next time as the front door has just closed and the aroma of tandoori chicken is wafting up the stairs. I probably won't write again until after the move on Saturday, I am sure that I will have lots to share with you then,

Until Wales, Xxx.

Saturday morning 5.30 am…

They loaded all three vehicles with as many boxes and bags as they would carry, loaded the children into the 4x4 and began the convoy. Mark was driving his car, Will was driving Alex's car and Lois was driving her car as they pulled away, ready to embark on a new chapter in their lives. Lois made a detour and drove past her parent's house, her childhood home and sighed as she parked outside, in the darkness, she could almost see Dad struggling to pull the lawnmower out of the small shed, as Mum hung out the washing in the back garden, she felt the sting of tears when she realised that this was truly goodbye to the past and the only way to look now was indeed forward, Alex looked at her and tapped her leg reassuringly as she wiped the tears away and inhaled deeply, "Are we ready?" she turned and asked as she grinned,

"YES!!!" Amber, Jake, and Alex shouted at the top of their lungs.

By four that afternoon, the convoy finally pulled up on the uneven driveway behind the removal truck which had finished unloading and one of the men closed the back doors,

"All done for you then," he said and grinned,

"Thank you very much," Lois said as she breathed in the fresh mountain air and watched as tiny flakes of snow began to fall from the grey clouds above,

"We had better get this monster out of here, don't want to get caught in a blizzard," he shouted to his team as they all jumped into the truck and manoeuvred it away from Drift End Cottage. The night sky was ever-darkening and the view had disappeared beneath the blanket of clouds, Mark looked around and then began to unload his car as Alex and Will unloaded the others. Lois set to work, making all of the beds and then she walked into the lounge, she approached the inglenook fireplace, where there was a basket of logs, a bucket of coal and a note from Mrs Hughes,

I hope that you will be as happy here as me and my family were for many years, I took the liberty of asking Kyle to provide you with a starter set for the fire, which will bring you much warmth on these cold dark winter nights,

All the best,

Elsie Hughes.

Lois grinned and began to place kindling down as she set about building the fire, the men were wondering in and out with boxes and bags a plenty and as soon as the fire was lit, Lois pulled the kettle from the box marked in big bold writing **KITCHEN** and filled it, making them all a well-deserved mug of coffee.

CHAPTER EIGHT

She crept up the small creaking staircase a little after eight and peered around Jake's bedroom door, earlier, Alex had set up his portable TV and games consul, which made Jake a happy boy indeed, the big bad wolf would not allow them to have televisions in their rooms, bedtime was exactly that, time for BED! He would continuously growl at them, Lois on the other hand, never saw it as a problem, so long as they turned them off at a reasonable time, then why shouldn't they? Jake was yawning as he raced around another circuit on his game, "Hey, you might want to turn that off now," Lois whispered as she entered the room, looking at the many unpacked boxes which Jake had earlier insisted that he wanted to unpack, Jake yawned again and nodded as he turned the TV off and pulled back the covers, Lois tucked him in and kissed his head, "Tomorrow, before you play your games you need to unpack Jakey, yes," she said gently, he nodded as his eyelids closed, she switched off the light and pulled the door to, she then walked to Amber's room, she had already unpacked everything, hung her posters up and was lying on her bed, reading a book with her favourite album playing on her portable cassette player, Lois smiled as she perched on the bed beside her,
"Your room looks amazing," Lois said as she looked around, Amber grinned,
"I love it!" she sighed as she turned her gaze back to her book,
"I'll leave you to it," Lois said, kissed her head and walked back down the stairs into the lounge.
"Where are Mark and Will?" Lois asked Alex as he placed more logs on the fire, she looked at her Mum's beautiful,

chunky oak coffee table and saw two large glasses of wine poured as Gladys Knight sang out from the record player, "They headed back to their B&B, they didn't want to get stuck out here, have you seen it outside?" Alex asked, Lois shook her head and then followed Alex to the front door. He turned on the outside light, which didn't work, and they both stood in the porchway watching snowflakes fall to the ground, everything was so still, there was not a sound to be heard, it was wonderful.

A little later as they both sat on the fireside rug, Alex sighed, "You definitely made the right choice, getting out I mean, this place is idyllic," he said and smiled, Lois grinned, she knew the moment that she entered the house, it had such a lovely warm glow to it, she knew that it was meant to be,

"I think that once I have decorated and put my stamp on the old place, it will be wonderful," Lois replied as Alex yawned,

"Right, where did you put the spare bedding?" he asked, Lois side glanced at him and grinned,

"In my bedroom," she replied, Alex lifted himself up and crept up the stairs, and then she heard him whispering her name and she began to chuckle, she climbed to her feet and slowly crept up the stairs to her room,

"I can't find it," he said,

"It's right there," she replied and glanced at her bed,

"Where?" he asked in bewilderment,

"There!" she said and pointed to her bed,

"What, you mean that I can sleep there, with you?" he asked humbly as Lois burst out laughing and walked to where he was standing,

"We are both adults, aren't we?"

The following morning she could hear loud rapping coming from the front door, she rubbed her eyes and turned to see

Alex sound asleep beside her, she gently stroked his face as
memories of their first night together filled her mind, the door
opened and Jake ran in, stopping in his tracks when he noticed
that Lois was not alone,
"Mum, Mark and Will are here," Amber called up the stairs,
"Ok, I'll be down in a minute," Lois called back as she climbed
out of bed, grabbing her robe as she continued to look at Jake
and his blank expression, Alex woke up, and could feel eyes
boring into him, he turned and jumped when he noticed Jake
standing beside the bed, glaring at him,
"Do you love my Mum?" Jake asked forthrightly, Lois gasped
and looked at Alex wide-eyed,
"Yes Jakey, yes I do," he replied confidently, Lois's face was
now glowing like the embers of the fire,
"Well that's all right then," Jake said as he turned and marched
out of the bedroom,
"I am so sorry Alex, how embarrassing," Lois gasped, Alex
climbed out of the bed and walked to where Lois was standing,
"I meant it, every word," he said as he leaned in and kissed her.

The day was pretty chaotic as they all set about to unpack and
Christmas the fuck out of everything,
"Lois, where is your tree? I have found the boxes of
decorations, but no tree," Mark shouted from the outbuilding.
If you hadn't guessed already, Lois loved all things Christmas,
every year without fail, she went above and beyond to make
the festive season extra magical, even though they shared a
house with a miserable, drunken arsehole, who hated
Christmas and relished in that fact, by spreading his misery.
"Oh, I can't remember seeing it if I'm to be honest," she said
as she thought back to packing,
"Right kids, grab your coats, we're going on a tree hunt," Mark
shouted as he put on his coat and threw Will's at him, Alex
walked to the coat stand and grabbed his as Lois frowned,

"Where are you going?" she asked as Amber and Jake skipped past her excitedly and grabbed their winter coats,
"I am going shopping, tonight I will cook for you all, if that's okay?" Alex asked, Lois smiled and nodded.

Sunday 19th December 95,

Dear Lois,

Even though we have moved over four hundred miles, I have to say that it was one of the easiest moves I have ever done, I think my helpers played a huge part in that! This place is amazing, I think that we are going to be very happy here. Last night was the first night that Alex and I shared a bed, don't worry I won't go into details! But suffice it to say, it was magical, watching his face this morning when he opened the curtains and saw the scenery was absolutely memorable.

The children seem to be in their element, Jake has even unpacked and made his bed! They are currently on a Christmas tree hunt with Mark and Will and Alex has nipped to the shops as he has volunteered to cook for us all tonight. I am currently sitting on my Mum and Dad's beautiful, incredibly comfortable sofa, (Thank god I managed to get rid of the other thing!) looking at box upon box of decorations, so without further ado, I will put you back in my bedside drawer and get cracking, it is the season to be jolly, after all,

Until then, Xxx.

She was in her absolute element as she placed the many boxes of decorations on the table and began to rummage through them, since childhood, she had lived in suburbia, in semi-modern homes yet she always had a deep yearning for an ancient cottage in the middle of nowhere, and now her dream had come true. She took out her hand-made garland which sat year after year on the modern mantlepiece, silently crying out to adorn a real fireplace, she decorated the mantle, then moved to the kitchen, where she placed garlands on top of all the kitchen cupboards, filling them with tiny, twinkly fairy lights. She stood back and admired her work so far, the door opened, and Alex walked in, his arms full of many bags of groceries, which he carried into the kitchen,

"You managed to find a supermarket then?" Lois asked as she began to help him unpack, he growled and then smiled,

"Yes, but I think that we should go early tomorrow to buy the Christmas food, it was carnage in that place," he said as he placed things into cupboards,

"Oh, so you are staying for Christmas then?" Lois said and frowned, slowly Alex turned to face her, wearing a look of horror on his face as Lois then laughed and pointed at him,

"Gotcha!" she said as she laughed, Alex wiped the beads of sweat from his brow and sighed with relief as he picked her up and swung her around.

They managed to squeeze in some smooch time before Mark and Will arrived back with an enormous real tree tied to the roof of Mark's car, Lois and Alex ran outside and Lois gasped when she saw the size of the tree,

"Will it fit in the cottage?" Lois asked as she gauged the height of the tree,

"I'm sure that we can chop some off if needs be," Alex said as he walked to the car and helped Mark and Will lower it to the ground,

"Jake chose it," Mark said as the three men carried it through into the cottage, Lois nodded it all made perfect sense, who in their right mind would allow a seven-year-old to select the

Christmas tree? She was thinking as they placed it into the holder and just about managed to stand it upright.

"Dinner smells amazing, what are we having?" Mark turned and asked Alex as Lois, Amber and Jake began to decorate the huge tree, it being their annual family tradition,

"Braised steak in a garlic and pepper sauce," Alex said as he gazed at Lois in admiration,

"Smells divine! Let's hope that it is better than Lois's attempt at roast," Mark said and laughed loudly,

"Hey!" Lois scowled,

"I'm only joking darling, no honestly Alex, we are all in for a treat come Christmas day, Lois's roasts are notoriously good," Mark said and winked a cheeky wink at his best friend, who laughed.

"What? So you and Will are staying for Christmas too, what about work?" Lois asked as she stepped off of the small stool,

"I didn't think it would be a problem darling?" Mark said as he dropped his lip,

"No, it's not a problem, I thought that you were rostered to work Christmas day," Lois replied and smiled sweetly, Mark had been so good to her and the children and he was the last person that she would want to upset, Mark grinned a wide grin and shook his head,

"No, I resigned, I couldn't bear to work in that place without my right-hand woman," he replied,

"Aww sweet! But what are you going to do?" she asked as she sipped her coffee,

"I am taking a leaf out of your book, a change is as good as a rest is it not," Mark replied and smiled at Will, "Will and I are making plans, we have put both our houses up for sale, we just have to decide as to where we want to go," Mark said,

"That's wonderful!" Lois said as she walked over and hugged him, out of every person that she knew, Mark deserved to be happy more than anyone else.

She opened her eyes, and breathed in the sweet aroma of coffee as Alex placed two mugs on the bedside tables and climbed into bed, shivering as he did,

"This is a nice surprise," Lois said and smiled as she pulled herself up to a sitting position,

"It is bloody freezing down there, I have put the heating on and lit the fire, I thought we could have a coffee up here until downstairs warms up a little," he replied as he pulled the duvet up to his neck,

"What time is it?" Lois asked as she sipped the delicious coffee, it always did taste better when it was made by someone else and served to you in bed she was thinking,

"It's five fifteen," Alex replied as he cradled the mug in his hands for warmth, Lois almost choked upon hearing the revelation,

"Why are we awake at such an ungodly hour?" she turned and asked, wearing a look of disgust,

"We agreed to go shopping early yesterday, remember?"

"When you said early, I thought you meant eight or nine, not five! Mark and Will won't be here for hours, and I am not taking Jake anywhere near a supermarket this close to Christmas," Lois fumed, just as the front door knocked, she turned her head and looked at Alex in disbelief,

"Sounds as though the cavalry have arrived, come on, up you get," he said as he climbed out of bed and pulled the duvet off of Lois.

Monday 20th December 95,
Dear Lois,
I feel as though I am having the best dream of my life, where everything seems too good to be true, and as pessimistic as ever, I am silently, fearfully waiting for the

proverbial shit to hit the fan so to speak. I cannot believe that I was in a supermarket in Wales at six a.m. this morning, what the hell? But yes I was, it felt weird, food shopping in an alien supermarket, but fun nevertheless, anyway four hundred pounds less in my bank, we purchased enough food to feed an army, the turkey is too big to fit in the fridge, so we have been resigned to store it in the outbuilding, I just hope that there are no resident furry friends with an appetite for poultry.

Mark and Will left when we returned, they were spending the day Christmas shopping, which left the four of us wondering what we should do with ourselves, I mean I would have happily spent the day baking and chilling, but Alex had other ideas and we all set off on a winter ramble around the valley, and I hate to say it, I am so glad that we did, the place is breathtaking, so many wooded walks, streams, and cute ravines, the children absolutely loved it! Amber became so excited when she found pine cones and now she is sitting at the dining table, happily covering them in glitter and fake snow, while Alex and Jake are constructing the Christmas train set, that I brought today.

Alex spoke to his Mum today, she is out of hospital and now living at Trevor's (Alex's brother), she wants to visit, which worries me slightly as the stairs are so steep and small, I am worried that she may struggle to get up and down, but I am sure we will come up with a suitable arrangement. They want to come for the new year, I wonder how the children will react.

The plan for this evening is, a delicious curry for dinner and then we are all going to curl up and watch Scrooge, and I for one cannot wait, so until tomorrow, I will bid you a good night, as ever Xxx

Christmas afternoon,
They sat on the sofas with full tummies, yawning as Judy Garland belted out somewhere over the rainbow, Lois looked at each one of them in turn, "Right, that's it, I have had enough of the Bloody Wizard of Oz, let's wrap up warm and go for a walk," she said as she fought hard to push herself up from the sofa, Jake looked at her and frowned,
"But we don't have a dog," he said as he scowled,
"What? What has a dog got to do with it?" Lois asked as she pulled her new jumper on,
"On all the Christmas movies, people only ever go for a walk on Christmas day if they have a dog to walk," Jake stated, as he folded his arms across him in a show of defiance,
"Well Jake, this is not a movie, and we are going to walk off our Christmas dinner, dog or no dog," Lois exclaimed as they all began to gather at the front door,
"Does that mean that I can have a puppy?" Jake asked as he walked through the door and began sliding on the icy path,
Lois looked at Alex despairingly,
"We'll see," she sighed as she grabbed Alex's arm,
"That means no then," Amber said and laughed as Jake began to wail, Lois shot Amber a look of disdain,
"I promise Jake that I will think about it," Lois said still scowling at Amber.

After the best Christmas ever, the 27th came and it was time to bid farewell to Mark and Will, who for a time seemed to have become fixtures and fittings of the place, Lois wrapped her arms around Mark and squeezed him tightly, she was going to miss him so much,

"Promise that you will call me every day," Lois said as still, she squeezed, once Mark was able to remove himself from Lois's bearhug, he nodded and smiled,

"I promise, we will be back before you know it," he replied and kissed her cheek, then turned to Alex,

"You promise me that you will take good care of my girl," Mark said as he hugged Alex, who nodded,

"I most certainly will, well until I have to return to work anyway," Alex replied as Lois's ears pricked, he was leaving, he was going back to Surrey. Whatever would she do? she asked herself as she watched Mark, and Will hug the children, climb into the car, and head off into yonder.

CHAPTER NINE

After a quiet discussion away from prying ears, Lois discovered that Alex was indeed returning to work the following day. She sat and stared into the flames of the fire silently contemplating her next move,

"Say something, Lo," Alex said anxiously,

"I'm fine, it's fine, it just took me by surprise, that's all," she replied and mustered a smile,

"As much as I want to stay here like this forever, there are some loose ends which I need to tie up, and I need to bring Mum and Dad here on Thursday, I'll only be gone for two days," Alex said as he held her face in his hands,

"By loose ends you mean Cassie, don't you?" Lois sighed,

"Sort of, I am going to close the office and move all my paperwork, there is no way on this good earth that she is getting another penny out of me!" he replied,

"Where am I going to put your parents?" she asked as she sat up, now fully composed,

"I was thinking, you know the study, how about this, we pop out today and order a bed, and temporarily make the study a guest room, that way neither of them will have to climb the stairs," he suggested,

"Wait, I have a spare double in the outbuilding, but we could go and grab some paint, that way I can keep myself busy while you are away," Lois beamed, but then a dark cloud loomed over her and she frowned,

"I must come across as really needy," she sighed, Alex chuckled,

"Not at all, Lois, I am madly in love with you, and I never want to be apart from you, ever, I have been wanting to ask if I could bring my computer and office equipment here so that I can work, but didn't want to seem as though I was jumping the gun," he said as he leaned in and kissed her,

"Really! Get a room," Amber huffed as she walked into the lounge and switched on the TV, Lois looked at her in bewilderment, since when had she turned into a sulky teenager, she was ten years old! Lois thought,

"You can turn that off, we are going out," she said as she climbed off of the sofa and wandered off in search of Jake,

"Does it bother you?" Alex asked Amber,

"Yeah! I wanted to watch Buffy," she sulked causing Alex to burst out laughing,

"Not the TV, the fact that I am here," he said as the smile left his face,

"No, you're nice, you don't shout at Mum or us or hit us, you're all right," Amber said as she walked to the coat hook and grabbed her coat.

Dear Lois...

Dear Lois,

I am knackered, I thought that nursing was hard, but my god, painting and decorating certainly take a toll on the body! Alex left this morning!!!! I know, I know, you can put the violin away now, and since the tearful goodbye.... Only joking, I have been decorating non-stop. I have already done two coats, one more in the morning should do it, I am surprised how much it has brightened the room, it looks ten times bigger now, well ten is a slight exaggeration. It's funny isn't it, when I was clearing Mum and Dad's house, I almost gave all the contents of her very full linen cupboard away to charity, but then something inside said, no, keep it, it may come in handy, which it has because I can completely kit out the spare room for Alex's parents and spend not a single penny.

The children and I had sausages and chips for dinner, Jake was over the moon, but after decorating all day the last thing that I felt like doing was cooking a huge meal, and it meant that I could have a lovely soak in a hot bath and write to you. Today while I was painting, Amber asked if she and Jake could go for a walk, at first I said no, but after twenty minutes of whingeing from them both I caved and agreed, giving them a boundary and a time to return.

Amber was breathless and incredibly anxious when they came back, Jake disappeared up to his room, and when I asked what was wrong, she told me that they had seen a man in the woods, he appeared to be watching them, and she could have sworn that he looked like Kevin. I immediately called the officer in charge of the case, and he assured me that Kevin was still locked up at Her Majesty's pleasure, so now I am wondering, who it was that they saw if it wasn't their overactive imaginations. Certainly, food for thought eh!

I am going now as Alex promised to call at nine, I have already had my daily call from Mark, and guess what? He and Will are relocating to Liverpool, which means they will be closer, happy days, well that's all for now,

As ever Xxx.

After an hour-long phone call with Alex, completely exhausted she slowly walked through the cottage locking all the doors and securing all the windows. She stepped into the study to check the paintwork, and she jumped back as a figure crossed the outside of the window, she walked slowly and looked, but could see nothing, so she left the room, turning out the light and closing the door before she made her way up to her lonely, empty, bed. As she tossed and turned in the darkness she could hear the rustling of the bare branches of the trees as they bent in the strong northerly wind, occasionally tapping against the window, she continued to fight the compulsion to get up and look out of the window, thinking that it was her overactive imagination after what the children had said and eventually dropped off to sleep.

She opened her eyes, the room was still in complete darkness, yet in the corner she could see what looked like an old man standing in the corner of her room, she rubbed her eyes and looked again, he was still there, still glaring at her, quickly she sat up and turned on the bedside lamp, but the same as all good stories, the corner was empty, except for her mannequin which she could have easily mistaken for a figure. She gave herself a good telling off, checked the time, smiled, realising that she had at least another four hours of sleep and turned off the light, drifting quickly back into the land of nod.

Screaming! She sat up as Jake ran into her room screaming hysterically, she jumped up and held him, softly soothing him until eventually, he stopped as she rocked back and forth with him in her arms, she swept the hair from his face, "Did you have a night terror?" she asked as she wiped the tears away,

"There was a man in my room, the man from the woods, he was looking through my books," Jake whimpered,

"Looking through your books? Why did you scream if he was just looking?" she asked,

"Because he looked at me and smiled and then he walked towards me with arms like this," Jake said as he demonstrated, walking like a Mummy from a 1950s movie,

"Do you want to sleep in my bed?" she asked, Jake shook his head,

"No, I want to sleep in my room, in my bed," he said as he yawned, she walked him back to his room and tucked him in,

95

as she walked to the door, he turned and looked at her,

"Leave the light on, Mummy," he said as he snuggled down beneath the warm quilt.

The howling wind whistling through the bedroom window roused Lois from her sleep, she rolled onto her side and looked at her digital alarm clock, which was flashing large green numbers 9.06. She jumped out of bed and raced down the stairs, expecting to see both children waiting for their breakfast, but the downstairs was pretty much as she had left it the night before, she dragged her slipper-encased feet out to the kitchen and filled the kettle, rubbed her tired eyes and walked back to the stairs, she peered inside Jake's bedroom and smiled to see him still sleeping soundly, she then walked to Amber's room and witnessed the same thing, it had to be the first time in forever that either of them had slept past half seven, she thought as she again smiled and returned to the kitchen. Coffee made and steaming in the mug, Lois opened the back door and embraced the winter air, which blew like a hurricane through the door, thus rapidly changing her mind, she pushed against the wind and managed to eventually close the door. She walked through to the lounge, where she set about lighting the fire and as she did thoughts of Kevin filled her mind, he was the reason that the children never slept in, they were always so on edge when he was around. Even when he disappeared on one of his away days, they were still on edge because of his constant unpredictability. One day he was there, only to disappear for weeks on end to then turn up out of the blue and act as though nothing was different, bastard, Lois was thinking, she then heard footsteps coming down the stairs,

Amber walked through and grinned,

"Hello sleepy head, what time do you call this?" Lois asked and grinned,

"I had the best sleep ever," Amber replied as she yawned and stretched,

"Amber, Alex's parents want to come and visit on Thursday, how do you feel about that?" Lois asked awkwardly,

"Are they old?" she replied and screwed up her nose,

"Well, they are not exactly spring chickens, why is being old a problem?" Lois asked and frowned, Amber smiled and shook her head,

"They are not like Gran and Grandpa are they?" she asked, neither of the children had a good relationship with Kevin's parents, who were under the misapprehension that children should be seen and not heard, the rows that Lois had with *her* over Jake and his apparent appalling behaviour, ' a bloody good smack is what he needs, not the bloody doctors' is what she said when Lois tried to explain that Jake was in the process of an Autism assessment. Lois shook her head,

"No they are nothing like them, they remind me a little of my parents," she replied and smiled sadly,

"That's good, isn't it? Oh but what about Jake? Do they know that he is disabled?" Amber asked as she wore an expression of horror on her face and Lois frowned,

"He is NOT disabled, he is just different that's all, why on earth would you say he was disabled?" Lois scowled,

97

"That's what the teachers at school said about him, especially when he was noisy in assembly, they would tell him off and then say, take no notice of Jake, he is disabled," Amber stated,

"Did they now!" Lois fumed as she walked into the kitchen swearing like a trooper under her breath. A few minutes later a sleepy-looking Jake appeared silently out of nowhere, causing Lois to jump out of her skin when she turned and saw him, after yesterday she was still a little nervous.

Wednesday 29ᵗʰ Dec 95,

Dear Lois,

It seems as though I do not get a minute to myself at the moment, although I am thrilled to say that I have finished the spare room and it looks lovely, well except for the ancient carpet, Mum had some lovely rugs which I have laid down to hide the grim pattern. I had a nightmare trying to move the double bed in from the outbuilding, I tried to move it by myself, failed, then asked Amber to help, failed, then Jake, failed, but as luck would have it, Kyle turned up to make sure that we had settled in and he gave me a hand, although he seemed quite put out that I had asked him, ha-ha.

But tomorrow, Alex is coming home, and I am so excited! It feels like he has been away for weeks not days, even the children miss him, aww, however, I have had some weird telephone calls, three today, and when I answer, it remains silent, so on the third call, Amber answered and a woman asked to speak to Alex, so I will be having words about who he gives my number to, it is probably his ex-wife Cassie, all legs, and no brains, you know the type!

I don't know why, but since the children and I have been in the house alone, I keep seeing things out of the corner of my eye, twice today I could have sworn I saw the old man standing in front of the fire, my overactive imagination I guess, but I saw him in my room last night and Jake saw him in his room, are we both suffering from cabin fever? Maybe I should take them both for a long walk tomorrow, that way I will not be pacing back and forth waiting for Alex to return.

My bath has now run, and I am going to jump in and have a soak before Alex calls,

So I will bid you a good night,

Until tomorrow, Xxx.

There must have been significant snowfall during the night, the ground was blanketed in the stuff, Lois wrapped the children up and all three of them looked like Michelin men as they embarked on their first lone trek in their new surroundings. They had walked through the valley, down to the ravines, then stopped to rest a while, Jake looked up and pointed to a building which stood at the top of the steep hill which surrounded the valley,

"What's that up there?" he asked as he pointed, Lois squinted as the said building was in the same direction as the sun,

"I'm not sure, probably an old farm building," she replied,

"Can we go up and see?" Jake asked sweetly, Lois nodded, Amber huffed, and they set off on the steep incline, stopping every so often, to enjoy the view, well Lois was trying to find the last breath in her lungs, but she told the children it was all about the views! Halfway up Jake was still fixated on the building,

"Do you think there are ghosts inside?" he asked wide-eyed, Lois chuckled, and Amber huffed,

"Don't be stupid Jake, who would haunt a place all the way up there!" she exclaimed and shook her head. They finally reached the top and Jake ran as fast as his legs would carry him towards the building, Lois and Amber hurried to keep up with Jake and he scowled when he turned to face them,

"It's closed!" He huffed,

"What do you mean closed?" Lois asked breathlessly,

"It says so on the door!" Jake replied, Lois approached and gasped, up there on the mountainside, in the middle of nowhere was a bookshop! A fucking ancient bookshop!

"Why on earth would anyone have a bookshop here?" Lois thought out loud as she walked the perimeter of the building, which from afar looked like a disused barn, but on closer inspection, the Georgian-type windows and door looked like something out of a Dickens novel. Lois peered through the windows, there were floor-to-ceiling shelves stacked with hundreds of books and a small counter with an old wooden chair neatly tucked in behind.

"Maybe it is full of books about Mountains, you know for the people that climb mountains," Amber suggested, causing Lois to chuckle,

"Maybe, well, it's closed, and we know that it's here now, so maybe we should come back and buy some books for learning, what do you think?" Lois suggested as they both smiled and nodded and then turned to begin the walk back to Drift End Cottage. They walked along the top for a while and took the path which led them down to the valley when they saw a figure in the distance walking towards them, both children clung to Lois as the figure of a woman approached. She was a middle-aged woman wearing leggings and a winter coat, with a large scarf wrapped around her head and neck to keep out the biting wind, she stopped when she reached them,

"Hello," she said gently, Lois smiled and nodded,

"Hi,"

"I don't often see folks around this part of the Mountain," she said and looked at the children, who then hid behind Lois,

"Sorry, they are both a bit shy,"

"That's all right, why shouldn't they be, I am a stranger after all, and all good children know, not to speak to strangers, isn't that right," she said, Amber nodded fearfully,

"Well, we had better get a move on the sun seems to be disappearing rapidly," Lois said as she looked in the direction of the ever-lowering sun,

"So it is, you don't want to be out here in the darkness when goodness knows what is lurking in the shadows of the moonlight," she said and grinned menacingly,

"Yes indeed, well it was lovely to meet you," Lois said as she guided the children downwards on the path,

"Lovely to meet you, Lois," the woman said as she walked away, which sent shivers crawling up and down Lois's spine as she hurriedly pushed the children forward desperate to get back to the safety of the cottage.

"How did she know your name?" Amber asked nervously,

"I have no idea, maybe one of the locals told her, that's how Country people are," Lois replied trying to play down the situation,

"Look! Mum, Alex's car is outside! Yay!" Jake exclaimed excitedly, Lois grinned full of relief as they all began to jog back to the cottage.

CHAPTER TEN

"Mum, Dad, this is Jake and this is Amber," Alex announced as he touched each one on the shoulder, Treena walked to where they were standing and pulled her glasses over her eyes, smiling as she did,

"Hello Jake, Hello Anna, my name is Treena and him over there is Norman," she said still smiling,

"Hello," they both said in unison,

"How old are you Jake?" Treena asked,

"I'm seven," Jake proudly announced,

"Seven, seven, my goodness you are a big lad for seven isn't he Norm?" Treena stated, Norman looked at Jake, smiled and nodded, "And what about you Anna? How old are you?" she asked as Jake burst out laughing, Amber blushed and scowled at Jake,

"I am ten," she replied bashfully,

"She's called Amber, not Anna, are you deaf?" Jake shouted as Amber nudged him causing him to fly across the room, landing at Norman's feet,

"Jake, that's rude!" Lois scorned as she walked into the lounge carrying a tray of hot drinks,

"He's all right Lois, our Alex used to be exactly the same, didn't he Norm?" Treena replied still grinning like a Cheshire cat, Lois shook her head at Jake, who in turn stomped off towards the stairs in a sulk,

"Jake has autism Mum, sometimes he doesn't realise what he's saying," Alex explained,

"A bit like me then, eh Norm," She replied and chuckled, causing Amber to giggle and Norman to nod his head once again.

Dinner time was slightly awkward, every time that Treena spoke, she would automatically bring Norman in on the conversation, which was irritating Amber somewhat, but amusing Jake, to no end. After a lovely spaghetti Bolognese, Lois stood and began to clear the plates, Alex jumped up and frowned,
"Let me, the children can help, you cooked," Alex said and gently pushed her back in her chair, Lois smiled, she had never been treated in such a considerate manner,
"Do I have to?" Jake sulked as Amber jumped up and began to carry the plates out, Lois nodded,
"Yes Jake, yes you do,"
"Yes Jake, many hands make light work, don't they Norm?" Treena said and smiled, causing Jake to burst into fits of laughter once again, Norman was stifling the compulsion to laugh, and a little while later Jake skipped into the dining room,
"Do you want some chocolate cake for pudding?" he asked as he looked at them, Lois shook her head after a severe case of eyes bigger than the belly when she dished up the food and was now fit to burst,
"Ooh, I'd love some, wha.."
"What about you Norm?" Jake finished her sentence, causing both Treena and Norman to laugh loudly,
"Yes, young Jake I'd love some, what about you?" Norman and Jake said in unison as they all laughed.

Later that night with children and parents safely tucked up in bed, Lois and Alex sat together in front of the roaring fire, and as the wind howled through cracks and crevices, it made them both appreciate the protection of the stone walls and the glorious warmth of the fire, "A woman called here three times, asking for you, did you happen to give Cassie this number?" Lois asked as she cradled a glass of red wine in her hands, Alex frowned,

"No, I most definitely did not, I haven't given your number to anyone," he replied as he scowled, Lois smiled, realising that she had now jumped the I'm not sure that I believe this fence and was on the I am beginning to trust you wall, she leaned in and kissed him,

"Sorry about Jake and your parents," she said as they broke from the long-lasting embrace, Alex chuckled,

"No need to apologise, earlier Dad was saying what a breath of fresh air Jake is," he replied and Lois rolled her eyes,

"I have heard him called many things, a breath of fresh air is most definitely a new one," Lois chuckled.

Friday 31st December,

Dear Lois,

This being the final day of 95, I thought that I had better write to you before the festivities kick in, and I'm too drunk to see. This has to be the first New Year's Eve, where I am a little sad to say goodbye to the year, I know that for the most part, it has been a year fraught with misery and great sadness, but on the other hand, there is the part when Alex crashed into my life (literally!) and life changed forever. I can honestly say, hand on heart that I have never felt as happy in my life, the man is a godsend, and I would happily spend every waking hour with him if life permitted, which of course, it doesn't. It's a beautiful thing when you watch two children who grew up petrified of men because of the behaviour of their own father, absolutely adore and yearn to spend time with Alex, Jake in particular, loves the very bones of him, and even Amber, who had her reservations about him, now hangs off of his every word! At times I feel that we are all vying for his attention, poor Alex.

Mark and Will arrived this afternoon, they are staying at Kyle's house, so, of course, I had to invite him, especially as he is a teetotal and allocated driver, and he in turn, has invited a few of the locals as a you know meet and greet type of thing, I just pray that Jake behaves himself.

Saying that Treena and Norm absolutely love him, constantly laughing with him, today, Jake took Norm for a walk down to the woods, and they came back laughing and joking, I have never seen Jake so happy.

I had a slight shock last night, I woke up and saw the figure in my room again, I quickly woke Alex and he put the light on, we both jumped out of our skins, only to find that Treena had got up to visit the loo and got lost, finding herself in the corner of my bedroom! (So much for her not managing the stairs!)

Well, the front door has just knocked, signalling that guests are arriving, so I had better go and be the hostess with the mostest, HA!. I want to thank you, for always being there for me, for lending an ear when I need to vent, never judging my decisions. Thank you!

I wish you all the best for 1996,

As ever,

Xxx

The cottage was filled with people, the music was playing, the food was laid out and all seemed to be having the most

wonderful time, Lois walked to the kitchen to grab another
tray of chicken when a woman followed her and smiled,
"Lois, isn't it?" she said, Lois instantly recognised her, she was
working in Kyle's office that day, Lois smiled and nodded as
she held her hand out to shake,
"Ruth, Pentre-Llwyn's one and only spinster," she said as they
shook hands,
"You work with Kyle don't you?" Lois asked,
"For my sins, yes," she replied and laughed, Lois nodded as
she began to walk back to the lounge, "Lois, I must apologise
for our behaviour the day that you came to view Drift-End,"
Ruth called out, slowly Lois turned to face her, "We had an
ongoing bet you see, when Old Mrs Hughes put the house up
to rent, both Ellis and myself bet Kyle that he would never
rent it," Ruth explained, Lois nodded, waiting for an
explanation as to why,
"Lois, I am exhausted, would you be a dear and help me into
bed, Norm's been drinking," Treena asked as she appeared in
the kitchen,
"Of course," she replied and turned to face Ruth, but she had
returned to the throes of the party.

On her return she looked all around for Ruth, but couldn't see
her anywhere, so she joined Alex who was chatting with a
couple, "Here she is, Lois, this is Gareth and Bronwyn Jones,
they own the village shop," Alex announced,
"Pleased to meet you, Lois, we have heard so much about
you," Bronwyn said and smiled, Lois was then puzzled,
nobody knew her, so how could they have heard about her?
She was thinking,
"Really? I had no idea that anyone here knew who I was," Lois
replied and looked at Alex,
"Kyle has been telling the entire village about what a
wonderful nurse you are, you might want to have a chat with

Glenda over there, she is the Practice nurse at Fobey's Surgery, but she is due to retire in the spring, it would be wonderful if you were to be the replacement," Bronwyn said and winked, Lois smiled and nodded, if she were to be perfectly honest, she hadn't even thought about returning to work, she had the children to consider, but on reflection, the money that she inherited from her parents was never going to last forever, she pondered as Gareth spoke to Alex about an extension on the shop.

The party drew to an end a little after one a.m. and the last of the guests finally departed, Lois walked up the stairs to check on Amber and Jake, while Alex warmed the milk for bedtime cocoa, Lois opened Amber's door and walked in when she realised that Amber was awake and sitting up in bed,
"Hey, you, it's late, you should be asleep," Lois said as she perched on the edge of Amber's bed, Amber smiled a beaming smile,
"I really love it here Mum, and I have made a friend already," Amber said proudly,
"Really, who?" Lois asked,
"Tiggy, her Mum and Dad own the village shop,"
"Tiggy? What an unusual name," Lois replied, Amber chuckled,
"Her name is Amanda, but she was obsessed with Tigger when she was little, she used to call him Tiggy, so her parents gave her that nickname,"
"Right, well that's all very nice, but you need to snuggle down now, we have a huge dinner to cook tomorrow as Alex decided to invite half the village!" Lois said and pulled up the duvet and began to tuck her in,
"Mum! I'm not two!" Amber huffed, Lois laughed and walked to Jake's bedroom, smiling when she watched him sleeping soundly.

She woke with a jump, her dream forcing her to wake, she sat up and looked to her right and exhaled with relief as she watched Alex, still sleeping, she opened the drawer of her bedside table, and found an empty notebook, Lois was a sucker for stationary of any kind, she had pens, pencils, and notebooks everywhere, and began to jot the details of her dream down, after having the same recurring dream now for weeks, she needed to keep a journal as this particular dream was slightly different.

She heard footsteps out on the landing and concerned that it could be Treena again she climbed out of bed and crept to the door, she opened it and peered around, the landing was deserted, Lois stepped out, now in need of the toilet and walked quietly to the bathroom. Whilst in the bathroom, she heard footsteps yet again, she hurriedly finished and quickly opened the door, the old man was standing by her bedroom door, he placed his finger over his lips and pointed to her bedroom door as Lois froze to the spot in complete terror, unable to move, not quite believing what her eyes were seeing, she continued to watch as he then walked to the top of the staircase and completely vanished.

She climbed back into bed, she was chilled to the core as she snuggled behind Alex for warmth and reassurance, closing her eyes tightly for fear of seeing another apparition.

She heard the bedroom door close and the aroma of coffee filled the room, she opened her eyes and watched as Alex placed the two full mugs on the bedside tables, she smiled and sat up.

As they sat side by side in bed sipping the hot drinks, Lois sighed and turned to look at Alex, "Do you believe in ghosts?" she asked, Alex moved the mug from his lips and sighed, "I believe that people truly believe that they see them, but I think that it all results from a sense of longing," he replied, causing Lois to frown,

"Well, I have no sense of longing for the man that I keep seeing in this cottage!" she scorned and huffed, Alex chuckled, "What man?" he asked,

"All the while you were away, he appeared in here and in Jake's room, Jake was terrified, and both Amber and Jake saw him in the woods," Lois exclaimed, wide-eyed and fearful,

"Who is he?" Alex asked,

"I don't know. He didn't leave a bloody calling card, he's just some old man, I saw him in the middle of the night when I got up to use the loo,"

"Are you sure it wasn't Dad?" Alex asked and chuckled,

"No it wasn't your Dad this ghost had hair," Lois scorned and shook her head, "Anyway, I don't wish to discuss it any longer!" she announced sulkily, Alex began to laugh as he took the coffee mug from her and pulled her into him,

"Ooh, I like it when you're angry," he said as he threw the duvet over the top of them.

She served the roast to the awaiting guests, she had the foresight to bring Mum and Dad's table which until now had been stored in the outbuilding, and she smiled as she looked at all of the happy faces sitting around the two long tables, every other New Year dinner consisted of Lois eating alone with the children, the big bad wolf either sleeping off his hangover or in the pub and now she was hosting a huge New Years dinner party. After the meal, Alex, Gareth, and Mark cleared the plates, Will brought in a tray of coffee, and the children, including Bronwyn's two daughters, helped wash the dishes.

"Who is the Old man?" Treena asked as she sipped her tea, gaining the attention of all,

"Sorry Mum, what Old Man?" Alex asked and frowned at Lois, who was secretly smirking,

"Every night I see him, don't I Norm?"

"She does," Norm replied, Jake was now sniggering,
"Where?" Alex asked,
"In the kitchen, in our bedroom, I'll tell you this, I'll be glad to get home and have a decent night's sleep, won't you Norm?" Treena said, Norm nodded, but his face told a story of its own,
"Yes about that, Trevor and Alison will be here at four tomorrow, he can't make it any earlier as she has a hairdresser's appointment," Alex stated disapprovingly,
"Four, four, we won't get home til the early hours, will we Norm?" Treena shouted, and again Jake laughed, which made Norm smile.

Sunday January 2nd 96,
Dear Lois,
Man! It has been so hectic here, the last few days, were wonderful, nonetheless, New Year was brilliant, I met some of the locals and Alex and I have been invited to dinner next weekend at Bronwyn and Gareth's, the local shop owners, they both seem nice. Amber has become firm friends with Tiggy their eldest daughter, and the youngest daughter Jess has taken quite a shine to Jake, who pretends to vomit, every time her name is mentioned, which shows that he does in fact like her.
Bronwyn told me that there is a children's club, which runs every Friday night in the community hall, it's aptly named the Little Monster's Club! Both Amber and Jake are eager to go, I am just hoping that they understand Autism, so many people do not have a clue.
Alex is down the stairs with his parents waiting for his brother to collect them and take them home, I have only met his brother once and he seemed slightly standoffish, so as you can imagine, I can't wait for their imminent

arrival. I will be sad to say goodbye to Norman and
Treena, the children adore them, which is lovely to watch,
but hopefully, they will return soon.
Alex has set up his temporary office in the spare room/
study, just until he finds a suitable office to rent, he's
looking at Liverpool, Mark and Will have offered him their
spare room Monday to Friday, which worries me somewhat
when Alex isn't here strange things begin to happen, mind
you saying that I have seen the old man a couple of times
while Alex has been here.
I have just heard the slamming of car doors outside so I am
guessing that Trevor is here, so I'll sign off for now and
get back to you soon,
As ever Xxx

As the car pulled away and the children waved sadly, Alex
placed his arm around Lois's shoulder as they walked back
inside the cottage, "I get the distinct impression that your
brother doesn't like me," Lois sighed as she walked to the
kitchen to prepare the dinner, Alex following closely behind
her,
"Trevor's always stuffy around new people, take no notice,"
Alex said as he began to peel the potatoes, Lois sighed,
"His wife didn't seem too keen either," she huffed as she
shaped the minced steak into burgers,
"Alison, she is a stuck-up cow anyway, I never have liked her,"
he replied,
"Well I hope that it doesn't cause problems with your parents,
I'd hate to think that Trevor's opinion of me rubbed off on
them, what with them living with Trevor and Alison," Lois
sulked, Alex placed the knife down and walked behind her,

"My parents adore you, just as I do, stop worrying about them, they are not worth it," He said and kissed her neck as Jake walked into the kitchen and began to gag loudly,
"Urgh! That's disgusting!" he shouted in utter disgust,
"So you don't want to kiss Jess then, I bet you do," Alex teased him,
"No, I don't!" he replied, screwing his face as he left the kitchen,

"They are not used to shows of affection," Lois sighed as she placed her arms around his neck and kissed him.

CHAPTER ELEVEN

Lois spent the following week decorating, starting with the lounge, she worked night and day, eager to finish it due to the fact that everything was turned upside down and for Lois, being the creature of tidiness that she was, this was beginning to grate on her somewhat. Amber and Jake had spent the week entertaining themselves on the promise that Friday, Lois would take them out for a burger before Monster Club, and now Friday had arrived and Lois found herself completely exhausted. She placed every piece of furniture back into its rightful place and then stood back to admire her work, pleased with her achievement, she took herself up the stairs to shower before she fulfilled her promise and took the children out. She stood under the hot, steaming water, enjoying the refreshing sensation when a thought popped into her mind, it was the dream she had the night before, it was not dissimilar to the others, yet this one weighed heavily on her mind. Once she had showered, wrapped in a large towel, she took out her dream journal and began to read:

Jan 1st 96,
I was yet again behind a counter serving drinks to servicemen in wartime uniforms. He walked to the counter and I instinctively knew that it was Alex, he asked for tea and a bun, gave me a wink, and walked out to the aircraft outside, which I can only think was a spitfire. The woman who was working beside me then asked me when the big day was?? And unfortunately, I woke up before I could answer!

Jan 3rd 96,
I was in an old-fashioned hospital, a nurse led me to a room and told me to wait there, and then Alex's Mum and Dad walked in and asked me if there was any news. Then I woke up!

Jan 5th 96,
I was back behind the counter, with the same woman, who looked strangely similar to my Mum, was speaking to me and from what she was saying, it appeared as though we were sisters! *He* came in again and ordered a tea and a bun, told me he would pick me up at seven and then left. I walked outside and the ground was covered in purple flowers??? I watched him walk to an aircraft hangar.

Jan 6th 96,
I was behind the counter waiting for him, but he never came, then the sound, the sound of a falling aircraft, we all ran outside as the plane came crashing to the ground, then a figure, engulfed in flames walked out from the wreckage and walked towards me, again the purple flowers were everywhere, I then woke up.

She read through, what did it all mean? Why was she having recurring dreams? "Mum, come on," Jake called out impatiently as he stood in the doorway of her bedroom, breaking her chain of thought, she turned and smiled, "I'm just coming sweetheart, wait for me downstairs," she replied as she gently closed her door and dressed. She walked into the lounge, looked at Jake and shook her head,

"Shorts and a T-shirt are not suitable clothing for a cold January afternoon Jake, go and put something warmer on," she said and smiled as Alex walked into the lounge, and then the telephone began to ring,

"Hello," Lois answered, after a long pause, the caller cleared their throat,

"Could I speak to Alex please?" a woman's voice asked, Lois frowned,

"May I ask who is calling?" she replied as she scowled,

"You can ask but I'd rather not say," Lois shook her head and handed the receiver to Alex, who took it from her wearing a look of bewilderment,

"Hello," Alex said reluctantly, then looked at Lois wearing an expression of perplexity, "They hung up," he said and handed the receiver back to Lois who put it to her ear and listened to the whirring tone of an ended call, Lois shook her head,

"Did they say who they were?" Alex asked, Lois shook her head,

"She said that she'd rather not say," Lois replied bluntly looking at him suspiciously,

"I promise you, hand on heart that I have not given this number to anyone," Alex stated despairingly, Lois smiled sarcastically and sighed when Jake returned wearing the same T-shirt, shorts, and now a woollen jumper over the top,

"Jake for goodness sake," Lois said agitatedly as she ran up to Jake's bedroom and chose a more suitable outfit, throwing it at him as she returned, "Put those on quickly or there will be no time for burgers," she said as Jake huffed and slouched up the stairs to change.

Lois was miles away as she and the children sat in the burger restaurant, thoughts of the mystery caller filled her thoughts as Jake and Amber chatted amongst themselves about all things Goosebumps, the woman's voice did have a sense of familiarity about it, she had most definitely heard that voice before, she thought to herself,

"Amber, do you remember when we had those calls and a woman asked for Alex?" Lois asked it was a long shot, but what did she have to lose,

"Yeah,"

"Did she sound like someone you know?" Lois probed, Amber shook her head and then continued to talk to Jake, Lois huffed and sipped at her coffee, well it was supposed to be coffee, but it slightly resembled coffee.

"Are you sure that you are going to be all right, I can stay if you want me to," Lois asked Jake as they stood in the doorway of the community centre,

"I'm all right Mum, I don't need you to stay!" Jake huffed as Jess ran up to him, grabbed his hand, and pulled him into the hall,

"Amber, make sure you watch him," Lois said as Amber and Tiggy walked away giggling with one another, Bronwyn laughed,

"Girls eh!" she said, Lois smiled, paid the fee, and left the building. She paced up and down the tiny high street not having a clue what to do, when a shop door opened and she heard her name being called, she turned and saw Ruth beckoning to her from the estate agent's office. Lois walked to her,

"How goes it then?" Ruth asked, Lois sighed,

"The children have gone to Monster Club and I'm at a loose end, I'm not sure what to do with myself," Lois replied,

"Could I interest you in coffee and cake?" Ruth asked as she held the door wide open and beckoned for Lois to step inside,

"Thank you," Lois said as she walked in and sat at Ruth's desk.

Ruth placed the coffee on the desk with two cream cakes,

"Tuck in," she said as she took a huge bite from a cream slice,

cream shot out of the sides and hit Lois on the cheek, Lois laughed as she took a tissue from her pocket and wiped the remnants of cream from her face,
"Why didn't you think that Drift End could be rented out?" Lois asked as she slowly savoured the chocolate-covered choux bun, "I meant to ask you at the party, but you vanished,"
"Well, it sounds a bit daft, but the locals think that it's haunted by the spirit of Mr Hughes, died in there he did," Ruth said as she licked the cream from her fingers, Lois frowned,
"Really?" Lois asked wide-eyed, maybe just maybe Mr Hughes was the mystery spirit that appeared now and then, saying that he had been elusive since Norman and Treena had left, Ruth nodded,
"I've never seen him mind, and I did the inventory on the cottage by myself and there was no sign of anything spooky, it's all local chit-chat, scare themselves silly they do superstitious lot!" Ruth replied and laughed, then looked at Lois and noticed that there was an air of seriousness about her, "You don't want to take any notice of it like I said they're a superstitious bunch around here," she added, Lois did not wish to share the fact that she had more than likely seen the infamous Mr Hughes, owing to the fact that she hardly knew Ruth and from what she could gather, she seemed to be a bit of a gossip, so she laughed it off and changed the subject.

Saturday January 8th 96,
Dear Lois,
We have only just got back from dinner at Bronwyn and Gareth's, we had a delicious meal, and the children seemed happy. Alex and Gareth were discussing the plans for the extension of the shop most of the night, boring..... and Bronwyn spent all evening talking about the children,

which is very nice, but when you spend every waking hour with them, surely the need to speak about something a little more adult-centred should be in order! Anyway, she told me that at the club on Friday, both Jake and Amber told her that they wanted to go to the local school but I had said no! This is not true, I told her it was because Kyle mentioned that the schools were Welsh-speaking and she told me that they do learn the Welsh language, but they spoke in English, so I will have to have a chat with them both tomorrow.

Alex is in the study as we speak, he said that he needed to tweak the blueprint for the shop extension, which allowed me to write to you, he has been a little off since that ominous phone call the other day, one that we still haven't got to the bottom of yet, so tomorrow, I think that I will put the beef in the oven and take myself off for a walk, maybe I can walk to the strange book shop. Sometimes it's good to disappear into nature and have a good think, it helps to put things into perspective. And now to the dreams... they are similar but the most recent has been haunting me, the vision of the man engulfed in flames is so lucid, but I just can't seem to understand the meaning of them, maybe the walk will help,

On that note, I will bid you a goodnight,

As ever Xxx

She placed her journal back inside the drawer, pulled back the duvet, and climbed beneath, very quickly slipping into sleep, she was however rudely awoken by the loud entrance of Alex when he eventually made his way to bed, Lois growled and turned over, pulling the duvet over her head to shield her from the bedroom light which Alex had switched on, and within a few minutes the light was off and he deliberately threw himself into bed heavily, causing Lois's small frame to lift slightly into the air. He turned his back on her and sighed loudly, all the time, Lois pretended that she was asleep.

After half an hour of loud sighs, tossing and turning, she could take no more, she pushed herself up and switched on the bedside lamp,

"Argh! Turn it off will you," Alex groaned,

"Not until we have had a conversation," Lois stated adamantly, glaring at him, Alex growled and sat up,

"What?" he asked wearing a look of disbelief,

"I cannot go through this again Alex, I thought that we had something special, but now, all of a sudden, you have your boots under the table and things have changed, I've seen it all before," she said as she sat upright with her arms folded in a show of self-reliance, he shook his head,

"I cannot believe that you are blaming me for this, you have been acting strange since that bloody phone call the other day," he huffed, clearly not backing down,

"I've been acting strange, that's rich coming from you, you haven't given me the time of day since the call!" she shouted,

"Shh, you'll wake the children,"

"Don't you shh me!!! I'll shout if I fucking well want to!" she shouted, Alex shook his head as footsteps could be heard outside of the bedroom door,

"See, what did I tell you," he whispered as Lois crept out of bed and opened the door, peering along the landing, Alex was soon standing behind her and they looked at one another in disbelief as the old man stood between the two bedroom doors of the children and placed his finger over his lips before he vanished into thin air.

"What the fu…." Alex said as they crept back inside the room and ran back to the safety of the bed,

"Now do you believe me?" Lois asked as she scowled, slowly Alex nodded his head,

"It's not that I didn't believe you, but I am a naturally sceptical person, and seeing is believing,"

"Anyway, where were we?" Lois asked and attempted a small smile,

"We were in the process of our first row, I think," he replied and grinned, Lois sighed,

"I never want to row with you, but on the other hand, I cannot go back to life in a non-existent relationship, I love you too much," she said quietly, he gently held her chin and looked deep into her eyes,

"I love you with all my heart, the minute I saw you, I knew that we were meant to be, Lois, will you marry me?" he asked earnestly, she threw her arms around him and held him tightly, never wanting that perfect moment to end,

"I'd love to!"

The following morning the four of them were sitting around the breakfast table, owing to a new lease of life, Lois had crept down the stairs early and began to prepare pancakes for breakfast,

"So, Amber, how do you fancy being a bridesmaid?" Alex asked and winked at Lois,

"Ooh! I'd love to be a bridesmaid, who for?" she asked as she frowned,

"Me!" Lois chirped and grinned widely,

"Really!" Amber asked as she jumped up from her seat, ran to Lois, and threw her arms around her,

"What about me, can I be a bridesmaid?" Jake asked sulkily, causing Lois and Alex to laugh,

"No Jake, we have a special job for you," Alex said smiling,

"What? What am I going to be?" Jake asked excitedly,

"Well it is tradition for the father of the bride to give the bride away," Alex replied and winked, Jake scowled,

"But I am not a father and I don't have a bride!" Jake sulked, Lois looked at Alex,

"No Jakey, what Alex meant to say was that Mummy and Alex are getting married, which means that I will be the bride," Lois said trying to make it a little easier for him to understand,

"I am not you father!" Jake scowled again, Lois could not fight the compulsion to laugh,

"I know that you're not sweetheart, but my Dad died not so long ago didn't he?" she asked, Jake nodded his head,

"So I have no one to give me away," she continued,

"Alex you can have my Mum, I give her to you, now can I be a bridesmaid?" he asked seriously as they howled with laughter.

As Alex washed the dishes and Lois prepared the roast he looked at her and smiled,

"One thing," he sighed, and she nodded, "Do you have to get a divorce?" he asked, Lois smiled and shook her head,

"Yes unfortunately so, but I can contact a solicitor first thing on Monday," she replied and grinned,

"Cool, we can start planning then," he said as he walked to her and kissed her.

A little later, Jake and Alex were in the process of building a big train set in the study, one of Jake's Christmas presents from Alex, and Amber had gone swimming with Tiggy, Lois had prepped the dinner and decided that she was going to go for a lone wander, she put on her coat and hat and peered around the study door, "I'm just going out to grab some fresh air okay?" she said and smiled, Alex looked up from the many lengths of track he was holding, smiled, and nodded.

She walked down to the ravine, the sun was shining, illuminating the morning dew which sat on the bare branches of the trees, the air was fresh, and white puffs of cloud glided gently through the blue sky in the gentle breeze, it felt good to be alive. She sat beside the stream watching as the water slowly trickled forth, and looked up, it was still there, the bookshop in the middle of nowhere, or was it? Maybe they had been slightly delusional? Maybe she had put the idea into the children's minds? She thought as she climbed to her feet and began the arduous walk up. She stopped a few times to catch her breath and finally reached the top, she walked to the ancient building, it was still very much a bookshop, and much to her surprise today the sign read OPEN. A bookshop in the middle of nowhere was open on a Sunday! Really! Lois thought as she placed her hand on the door handle and turned it, hesitantly she stepped inside as a small bell rang out above the door, she closed the door and looked to the small counter, she jumped when she saw the same woman that they had met the day that they discovered the bookshop, sitting on the chair behind the counter,

"Greetings Lois, I have been waiting for you to return," she said and smiled,

"I, er, I'm sorry, I didn't catch your name," Lois said awkwardly,

"That's because I didn't throw it to you," she replied and chuckled,

"What do you seek?" she then asked,

"I, er, I'm not sure,"

"There must have been a reason behind the trek surely?" Lois was lost for words, "you can speak your mind here, no one will hear you, nothing goes past me," she said as though she was reading Lois's thoughts,

"Well, I just needed to walk, to clear my head," Lois eventually replied, the woman nodded,

"But why here, the stream would have given you clarity, why the ascent?" she asked, Lois blushed,

"I, er, I, the shop was in my thoughts, I er, .."

"You doubted yourself didn't you, you were seeking affirmation," the woman said and smiled, she climbed to her feet and walked to a door at the back of the shop, "Take a look around, see if anything jumps out at you," she said as she walked through the now open door.

Lois's legs began to tremble, who was this strange woman and how did she know her name? she thought as she looked at the shelves, skimming through the thousands of titles, she jumped when the woman returned, clearing her throat loudly as she did, she walked to the counter and placed two steaming mugs down, "Come and drink, before it gets cold," she said, Lois slowly walked to the counter, where she reluctantly grabbed the mug and lifted it, imagining that the liquid inside could be all manner of things, but as it neared her nose, the distinct aroma of tea wafted, Lois smiled and sipped at the amber liquid.

The woman bent down, grabbed something from under the counter, and passed a dust-covered book to Lois, who wiped the dust off and revealed the title: 𝕾𝖜𝖊𝖋𝖓 𝕬𝖓𝖉𝖌𝖎𝖊𝖙, she looked at the woman in dismay, not understanding the title, and the woman smiled, "Not everything is as it seems, take it home, study it, and return it seven days from now. It is time for you to leave now," she said as she smiled, Lois smiled and placed the book inside her jacket,

"Thank you, er.."

"Cerys,"

"Thank you, Cerys, for the book and the delicious tea, I will return it in seven days," Lois said as she then hurried out of the shop.

CHAPTER TWELVE

After discovering that the children did in fact wish to attend the local school, Lois made it her priority to sort that out the following week. As she, Amber, and Jake were shown around the tiny school, Lois watched Jake's expression as they stepped into the small class that would be his. With only twelve children, a friendly-looking teacher, and an equally friendly-looking TA, Jake grinned when the teacher spoke about the new class project, namely, Steam Travel. The children went out to the small courtyard playground at break time, giving Lois the opportunity to speak to the staff about Jake's additional needs, and happy with what she was told, it was arranged that the children could start the following day. From the school, they drove to the nearest town in search of a new school uniform.

Thursday 13th January 96,

Dear Lois,

What a week! The children started at their new school on Tuesday and three days in Jake is still loving it, I think that the smaller class size suits him, we have had no episodes of sensory overload, which is wonderful! Amber of course is happy, she is sitting beside Tiggy, they are inseparable, and she seems to have slotted into life here incredibly well. So what have I been doing with myself I hear you ask, I have divided my time between decorating the kitchen and reading the book lent to me by Cerys, the strangest bookshop owner ever! Now you are probably going to think that I have finally lost all sense of reason

125

when I tell you, that the book which is titled Swefn
Andgiet is about dream analysis, and I have been
researching my dreams, which may not seem any way
out of the ordinary, but, when Alex picked up the book and
flicked through the pages he asked what language it was
written in, I laughed and said English of course, but he
said that he could not understand a word of it! I asked
Amber if she could understand and she couldn't either,
but going back to the dream meanings, the book suggests
that maybe I am reliving past life memories, the flowers
are forget-me-nots, which is pretty significant.
If that is true, it suggests that Alex and I knew each other
in that life, which I find fascinating, we both felt a certain
familiarity when we met the day of the accident, so I truly
believe that there could be some truth in it. What I don't
understand is, how did Cerys know about the dreams and
my desire to interpret them?
I will ask her when I return the book on Sunday! Alex has
been busy overseeing the shop extension, so I only see him
in the hours of darkness, but he is so excited about the
prospect of getting married, we are going to a wedding fair
soon. We have had three phone calls this week, where the
same woman asks for Alex, only to hang up when he
speaks. He became so irate the other day, that he phoned the
police, who have now put a trace on the phone line, it does
unnerve me somewhat, I trust Alex implicitly, and yet I
feel that whoever is doing this, wants me to distrust him.
Well, whoever it is can get fucked, they are not ruining
my chance at happiness, no way Jose!

Okay, well, the children will be home soon, Bronwyn gives them a lift, bonus! And I need to write in my dream journal, I had a very strange one last night!
So I will say cheerio for now,
As always, Xxx

Just as she placed her journal back inside the drawer and took out her dream journal, the phone began to ring, she waited for five rings, just like the police officer had instructed, and then answered,

"Hello,"

"Mrs Parker?" An unfamiliar man's voice asked,

"No, it's Ms Stone," she replied as she frowned,

"Oh, I do apologise, I was given this number by the officer in charge of the case," he replied as the penny then dropped,

"Oh! Sorry, I used to go by the name of Parker," she said quickly, she heard the man chuckle,

"I am head of the remand unit, and as you are down as next of kin, it is my duty to inform you that Mr Kevin Parker has been transferred to the hospital, he was found in his cell this morning and it is believed that he has suffered a stroke," the man said, Lois looked out of the window and watched the children waving to Bronwyn as they ran to the door,

"So, will he recover?" she asked,

"It's a little too early to say I'm afraid, but it does mean that the case against him will have to be postponed, and I will keep you updated on the situation," he said, the door slammed and Jake, followed by Amber ran through to the lounge, ready to tell all about their day.

"Listen, your Dad is very poorly in hospital," Lois said quietly,

"What? The big bad wolf is dead?" Jake shouted and cheered,

"No, not dead but very poorly," Lois replied and looked at Amber, who shrugged her shoulders,

"Good! At least he won't come here and be nasty," she said and smiled, "Can we have milk and biscuits now?" she asked as she skipped towards the kitchen.
Making it so much easier than she had anticipated she smiled and led the children out to the kitchen for food, while they were taking their fill of the freshly baked double chocolate chip cookies, she grabbed her dream journal and wrote the previous night's dream down.

Jan 13th,
I was on a mountainside, I instinctively knew that it was in Scotland. Alex was with me and we walked to the loch and sat with one another as we gazed into the water, but then we heard gunshots and hundreds of horses' hooves, so we ran and hid in a thick gorse bush. Soldiers in red coats came charging forth, searching the area, we were so afraid, a hand reached into the bush but I woke up! Grrr!

The sound of the front door closing alerted her that Alex had returned as too did the smile on her face, when she cast her tired eyes upon him, god how she loved him, there were no words to express just how much! She walked to him and wrapped her arms around his neck,
"I have just had a visit from the local constabulary, it turns out that they have identified the mystery caller," he said and smiled,
"Really? Who?"
"Janette,"
"What? Kevin's sister Janette?" she asked, Alex nodded, and Lois frowned, "But why? And how did she get the number?"
"Kent police questioned her, and she said that she got the number from Jackie, your Ward manager," Alex replied,

"Jackie? Jackie, why would she do that?" Lois asked in bewilderment, Alex shook his head.

Later that evening, following a call to Mark, who did some digging, she and Alex sat in front of the fire listening to music and she explained,
"Mark spoke to Jackie, it turns out that apparently since Mark and I resigned the department had semi-collapsed, she bumped into Janette who fed her some cock and bull story that I was really unhappy here, coercing her to give her my number, telling her that she could persuade me to return," Lois said and frowned,
"What a bitch!" Alex growled, Lois nodded in agreement,
"But that's not all, she told Jackie that I was the violent one in the relationship, that I would continuously attack Kevin and he would only retaliate in self-defence," Lois stated in disbelief,
"Surely that must have raised alarm bells," Alex said, "Surely she could see what a good nurse, and good person you are," Alex continued, Lois nodded,
"Yes, that's when she became suspicious of Janette's motives, but she had already given her the number, Mark said that she was in tears when he spoke to her,"
"How did the children take the news?" Alex asked as he stared into the dancing flames of the fire, Lois sighed,
"It's sad really, Jake thought that he had died and did a celebratory dance and Amber said that she was happy that he couldn't come here and be nasty,"
"Well, he's only got himself to blame for that, I cannot honestly understand how he could have been so vile to you all," Alex said as he leaned in and kissed her.

The following morning was utter pandemonium, it was Friday and both Jake and Amber were overly excited, after all, it was Friday, meaning that it was Monster Club! As Lois fumbled through her purse looking for the entrance fee, Alex emptied his pockets, giving them not only the fee but also two pounds each for drinks and snacks, which Jake celebrated loudly. Alex then hurried them out of the door and into the car as Lois watched and waved from the front door as they happily drove away. She looked at the surroundings, how things had changed so rapidly within such a short space of time, she thought and grinned as she looked out at the giant hills that snuggled around the cottage, offering protection from the wind and icy rain, she turned to walk inside when she saw him, the old man, he was standing in the kitchen doorway. Lois jumped back as her heart began to beat out of her chest,

"Who are you? What do you want?" she asked, her voice breaking through the fear that was coursing through her, he smiled, nodded, and walked through the closed back door. Now a quivering wreck, Lois wasted no time in throwing her clothes on, locking the door, and driving into the village, she parked on the village square and walked to Kyle's office, relieved to see that Ruth was there. She walked in and Ruth smiled as she looked up from a large pile of paperwork,

"Hello Lo, how goes it?" Ruth asked, Lois slowly approached the desk,

"I need to ask a favour?"

"Go on then,"

"I need to speak to Mrs Hughes, where can I find her?" Lois asked barely above a whisper,

"Why?" Ruth asked Lois assuming that she would, being somewhat of a gossip,

"It's about the water inlet tap, we can't seem to find it anywhere,"

"Hang on," Ruth said as she stood and walked to the filing cabinet, she then pulled a file, sat back at the desk, and scribbled the address on a piece of paper, "are you sure it wasn't in the inventory?" she asked, Lois shook her head and Ruth handed her the paper,

"Do you know where it is?" she asked, Lois shook her head, "Go past the school, at the end of the road you will see a large white building, she lives there in a ground-floor apartment," Ruth said, Lois smiled, thanked her, and made a quick exit as she walked in search of Mrs Hughes.

Lois inhaled deeply before she pressed the buzzer to apartment 5b. "Hello," a croaky voice said through the intercom,

"Mrs Hughes?" Lois asked gently,

"Yes,"

"It's Lois Sto.." the door buzzed open before she had finished, Lois walked along the light and airy hallway and when she reached apartment 5b she gently tapped on the door, within a few seconds she heard the shuffling of feet and the door opened, revealing a small elderly woman,

"Come in," she said and smiled kindly, Lois stepped inside, the apartment was bright and airy, beautifully furnished with the distinct aroma of freshly baked bread wafting throughout. Mrs Hughes guided her into the spacious lounge and asked her to take a seat on the pretty chintz sofa, Lois had the distinct impression that Mrs Hughes had been expecting her,

"You are here about Emrys aren't you?" she asked as she sat in the armchair,

"Is that your late husband?" Lois asked and smiled a sad smile, the thought of losing Alex was unthinkable, Mrs Hughes nodded, Lois sighed,

"I take it that he has made himself known," Mrs Hughes said with an air of sadness in her voice, Lois nodded, "Oh my dear, I am so sorry," Lois frowned,

131

"Why are you sorry?"

"After he passed I stayed in the cottage, everything was a permanent reminder of him, which of course I loved, but then he appeared to me one evening when I was sitting next to the fire, he said nothing just placed his finger to his lips and then vanished," she said, her eyes wide as she relieved the memory, Lois nodded,

"Yes, that's what he does when I see him,"

"He appeared every day for weeks, always the same thing, except for one night, when I woke up and he was standing at the foot of my bed, tears falling from his eyes. The next morning there was a knock on the door, it was Peters, the local policeman, he came to tell me that my son Elwyn had been involved in a car accident and died at the scene," she said as tears fell from her eyes, Lois leaned forward and gently touched her hand,

"I am so sorry," she said quietly,

"After that, I stayed at the cottage, that was until he began to appear again, same thing, and then the night that tears were shed, my son's widow gave birth to her son, who then died in her arms a few hours later," she explained, Lois shook her head, "I had to leave then you see, I was so afraid for my other children, I left the cottage and moved here," she said as she wiped her eyes and blew her nose,

"So you understand what it means when he appears?" she asked as an air of severity washed over her, Lois nodded,

"Keep them close my dear, very close indeed," she said as she looked at the tall window and grinned,

"Well, thank you ever so much for your time, but I really must get going," Lois said as she stood, every hair on her body standing to attention, the entire apartment was filled with a sinister atmosphere, she quickly walked to the door,

"Listen to your dreams Lois," she said as Lois opened the door, quickly closed it, and ran along the hallway, the need for air was intense.

She sat in the 4x4 and placed her head on the steering wheel, did this mean that one of the children was going to die as Mrs Hughes had implied? Or was it because Kevin, who had suffered a stroke was going to die? She asked herself over and over again, until there was a loud tapping on the window, causing her to jump, much to her relief it was Bronwyn,

"Are you all right Lois?" She asked and frowned, Lois nodded as she opened the car door, "Come on, let's grab a coffee and have a chat," Bronwyn said, she could see that Lois was distraught and in need of a shoulder.

For an hour they sat in the small café and Lois poured out her heart to Bronwyn, who was more or less a complete stranger, "I think that you shouldn't read too much into what Mrs Hughes said Lois, I have been told by many locals that she creates stories to get attention," Bronwyn sighed as she said, "Yes, but it was true about her son and grandson was it not?" Lois asked, Bronwyn nodded,

"Yes, Lois that is just utter bad luck, nothing more," Bronwyn replied as she placed a hand on Lois's hand, "The spirit that you see may not be Mr. Hughes, have you seen a photo, did she show you a photograph of him?" Lois shook her head, "Well then, the cottage is ancient, there could be all manner of spirits dropping in, if she were that sure that it was Emrys, surely she would have shown you a photo of him?" Bronwyn said being the edge of reason that Lois needed at that moment in time.

CHAPTER THIRTEEN

Then evening drew in quickly and the children were tucked up in their beds as a storm raged outside, wind whistling through gaps in the windows and doors and the sound of driving rain against the windows gave the cottage somewhat of a sinister feel about it, Lois shuddered as an icy breeze whipped around her and on noticing, Alex placed another log on the fire, "You're not coming down with something are you? I think that it's toasty in here," he said as he wrapped his arms around her in an attempt to warm her, Lois placed her hand on his and smiled, what she had learned from Mrs Hughes earlier that day was weighing heavily on her mind, but she didn't feel comfortable sharing it with Alex, him being the master of scepticism and all, she sighed and kissed his hand, "Maybe, I had a coffee with Bronwyn today and she was full of cold," she replied, Alex walked to the kitchen and returned with two glasses of whiskey, handing one to Lois, "Kill or cure eh?" she said and chuckled, and then sipped gently from the glass, "I spoke to Dad today, he is worried about Mum, she forgot who Alison was this morning and told her to get out of her house," he said and laughed, Lois almost choked on the mouthful of whiskey, "I bet that went down well," she said after eventually swallowing the burning liquid, Alex frowned as a look of deep concern swept across his face, Lois stroked his face, "I am worried, I mean let's be honest here shall we, Alison is not the most compassionate woman on the planet is she? Trevor has gone to Florence on an apparent business trip and she is left in the house with Mum and Dad," he sighed,

"Why don't you go and get them, you can set up the office in our bedroom," Lois suggested,

"But it's a lot for you to take on Lo," he sighed,

"I am not doing much at the moment am I, maybe if I get your Mum involved in the wedding preparations, it might help with her short-term memory, I think that when someone's mind becomes a little inactive, it somehow spirals if you know what I mean," Lois replied, trying to ease his troubled mind,

"Would you? Would you do that for me?" he asked,

"Of course, it really isn't a big deal is it, besides, it eases my yearning for my parents when your parents are here," she said as the last remnants of whiskey slid from the glass onto her tongue,

"There are no words to describe how I feel about you, I am honestly the luckiest man alive," he said as he took the empty glass from her hand and walked to the kitchen to refill it,

"Alex, bring the bottle," she called out, her troubled mind now eased by the soothing sensation of the whiskey.

Saturday 15th January 96,

Dear Lois,

It's Saturday morning, and my head is splitting, but it is self-induced, too much JD again I'm afraid, when will I ever learn? It's just so nice to drink in the company of someone and not have to worry about a random explosive outburst, we laugh a lot! Alex this morning has driven to Surrey to collect his Mum and Dad from Trevor's house, it seems that Alison is not coping with them and Trevor is away on business, which has been worrying Alex. The children are very excited, they love having them here, so this morning it is my job to turn the study back into the bedroom for them. I am waiting for David (Foreman of local builders) to come and take a look at the utility room, which is huge and we were thinking that we could maybe make a small bathroom in part of it, to save Treena from getting lost when she needs the loo, also I have made an offer for Drift End cottage and Kyle has just called and told me that Mrs Hughes has accepted the offer, which is wonderful news, now all I have to do is work out how to deal with her husband! But that's another story that at present I do not wish to think about or discuss.

We are off to the wedding fayre in a few weeks, which I am so excited about, when I spoke to the solicitor the other day, he said that the divorce should not be a problem all things considered, but now that Kevin has had a stroke, I wonder if that will change things in that respect? I should call the solicitor on Monday I suppose.

I have read the book from cover to cover and I am slightly apprehensive about returning it tomorrow, she is rather strange, but what I have learned from reading the book has helped me immensely in interpreting my dreams and given me a new level of understanding.

I must go because the builder is knocking on the door,

So until next time,

As ever Xxx

"They're here!" Jake called out excitedly and rushed to the front door, he had been watching out of the window since they had returned from the supermarket, Lois put down her oven gloves and walked to greet them, secretly worrying that Treena might have forgotten who they were, much to Lois's relief, she hadn't and gave both children a big hug when she walked inside.

Lois and Alex took their belongings to their room, while they sat in the lounge with Amber and Jake, having a catch-up. Back in the kitchen, Alex put his arms around Lois's waist and muzzled into her neck,

"Er you have a job to do Mr," she said as she turned to face him and smiled,

"Do I?" he asked,

"Yes, there is a matter of a rather large train set which at present is in pieces in Jake's bedroom," she said and grinned,

"Oh but Lo, I have been driving for hours!" he said and swept his brow,

"I know but I have been working like a pack horse to get things sorted, so off you go," she said and patted his bum.

After dinner, Treena, Norman, and the children were playing cards at the table, Alex was building the train set in Jake's bedroom and Lois was finishing cleaning the kitchen when the phone rang,

"Hello," Lois answered from the kitchen extension line,

"When are you taking the children to visit Kevin?" The mother-in-law from hell scowled,

"I'm not and how did you get my number?" Lois replied sternly, taking great pleasure in actually having the ability to say and act how she now pleased,

"What does that matter, those children need to see him, he is in a bad way and has been asking for them," she replied,

"I couldn't give two shits what he needs, he didn't give a toss when he physically and mentally abused them both for years could he?" Lois roared.

"I am telling you now, either you bring them back here to visit their father or there will be hell to pay!" she replied as she swiftly ended the call, denying Lois the pleasure of telling her what she could do with her threats, Lois growled as she placed the phone on the worktop, all manner of thoughts filled her mind as feelings of guilt began to creep in, unnecessary guilt I might add, but when you have been in a toxic relationship for years, and are constantly told that everything is your fault, sometimes no matter how hard you try, you cannot break that cycle, Lois told herself as she headed for the stairs, needing to speak to Alex.

"Lois, the man is a bastard, stroke or not it doesn't change the fact that the children were terrified of men because of him, and you endured years of abuse, fuck him, he does not deserve to see them, can you imagine what it would do to them both if they had to be faced with him?" Alex stated angrily while Lois nodded, fully agreeing with everything he said, yet there still in the back of her mind, was that ever-lingering pot of guilt, waiting to take over her thoughts.

Sunday morning greeted Lois with bright sunshine pouring in through the cottage windows, which was an unexpected, albeit pleasant change from the wind and rain. She walked down to the kitchen, put the kettle on, and stood at the open back door with her coffee. The birds were in full song, enjoying the rays from the sun, she smiled, but then the dark clouds in her mind appeared, namely the beast that is guilt, and began to rage through her thoughts. Then one by one, they all began to descend into the kitchen, Lois busied herself and her mind by preparing the breakfast and the meat for roast dinner.

She sat beside the stream, studying the trickling water, searching for clarity, was she justified in denying him the right to see his children? Or did that make her as bad as him, selfish and uncaring? She asked as she placed her hand into the water,

the iciness crept up her hand and into her arm as she swiftly
pulled it back and tucked it up inside her coat, trying to bring
life back into her blue-tinged fingers.

She edged towards the top of the hill and walked towards the
bookshop, where the open sign swayed back and forth in the
gentle breeze. She placed her hand inside her coat and
removed the book from her inside pocket, before opening the
shop door and entering, the shop was deserted, with no sign of
Cerys anywhere, Lois walked to the counter placed the book
down, and hit the service bell, all the time looking around at
the hundreds of book, all calling out to her to read. Within a
few minutes, Cerys walked through from the back of the shop,
carrying two steaming drinks, she walked to the counter and
smiled at Lois as she passed her a mug,

"Thank you, how did you know that I would be here at this
time?" Lois asked as she cradled the mug to warm her still-icy
fingers,

"Assumption, you being a creature of habit," Cerys replied
shrugging her shoulders and smiling, "How did you find the
book?" she asked as she sipped from her mug,

"Brilliant!" Lois said as she blew on the liquid, desperate to
take a sip, it tasted like nothing she had tasted before, "How
did you know? About the dreams I mean?" Lois then asked as
she sipped at the delicious amber liquid,

"If you listen very carefully, you can hear, especially things that
are carried on the breeze," Cerys replied and again smiled,
"Come, let's step outside for a moment," she said and walked
to the door, Lois reluctantly placed her mug on the counter
and followed, they walked to a viewpoint on the hill and
looked all around at the amazing landscape which commanded
attention, Cerys closed her eyes and breathed in deeply, "Close
your eyes and breathe, all the while listen," she said, Lois
closed her eyes, but all she could hear were the calls from gulls
flying above,

"What do you hear?" Cerys asked,

"Seagulls," Lois replied frustratedly,

"Listen to the gulls, what do they say?" Cerys said, and again Lois closed her eyes and listened intently,

"Have your say?" Lois replied in bewilderment, Cerys smiled and led her back to the shop, and once inside, sitting at the counter Cerys paused for a moment,

"Who is Mark?" she asked, Lois frowned,

"He is my closest friend," she replied, Cerys nodded,

"That is what I heard the gulls call, Mark, Mark," she said as she mimicked seagulls, Lois chuckled,

"So what about what I heard?" Lois asked,

"Now that, only you can answer, go to the shelves and feel the energy of the books, take the one that calls to you more than the others," she said. Lois finished her tea and walked to the shelves, passing her hand over the many ancient titles that nestled upon the shelves waiting for their words to be ingested, she ran her hand over the shelf above and felt a sensation completely different from that of the others, she slowly pulled the book out and looked at it, all the time Cerys sat watching intently, Lois read out the title: **The ladder of life**, she read, Cerys nodded,

"Now this one should take a while, so I will give you three weeks to read," she said, Lois frowned,

"Does that mean that I cannot return for three weeks?" she asked sadly, Cerys smiled and nodded her head,

"You have much to do, as do I, so take the book and return to your family," She said as she stood and gestured to the door,

"But I wanted to ask you something," Lois said pleadingly, Cerys nodded, "Mrs Hughes, she said that my children are in danger is that true?" Lois asked despairingly,

"Again this is something that I cannot answer, look deep inside of *you* and reach for the answer," she replied as she walked out of the shop, grabbed the sign, nodded to Lois then closed the shop door and locked it.

The journey home was one fraught with angst as Lois tried to unravel Cerys's words, why was everything a riddle? Why couldn't there be answers? She thought as she walked past the stream which was now flowing faster, she paused for a second and looked into the frothing water as it jumped over rocks, she closed her eyes and listened intently, and then there were three, to her complete astonishment, that is exactly what she heard, the cottage now coming into view, she hurried back to the heart of her life.

Sunday 16ᵗʰ January,

Dear Lois,

I returned the book today, I am not sure what it is about the strange woman who runs it, but I feel very safe whenever I am near her, she sometimes, no mostly, speaks in riddles, yet I trust her 100%, does that sound strange to you? Anyway, she told me to listen, which I did, and heard the seagulls calling out HAVE YOUR SAY! She asked me who Mark was and I chose a book called The LADDER OF LIFE, I have flicked through the first few pages and feel that it is going to be an interesting read. When I returned home Alex said that Mark had called so of course instantly I called him back, it turns out that we have both been selected to receive an award at the national nursing conference! I was blown away, so next week Mark and I are heading to London for a posh do, eek!

I fear that Treena's dementia is worsening rapidly, after dinner, we all sat in the lounge watching Antiques Roadshow and she asked me what time we were going to have dinner, I explained that we had already had it, but she became very distressed and when Alex tried to calm her, she hit him, Norman then shouted at her which made her even more distressed and resulted in her locking herself in the bedroom! Suffice it to say that is why I ran myself a bath and am now hiding in here writing to you because I can hear raised voices coming from the lounge! I do wish they would keep it down, Jake told me earlier that he is frightened of Treena, she shouted at him for reading his book too loudly! I mean, it is hard enough getting him to do his reading at the best of times!

Will has very kindly offered to take the children to Liverpool next weekend, which I think will do them both the world of good to see a different part of the world and I can relax knowing that they are having a good time!

I shall go now as the voices are getting somewhat louder and I do not want the children to be disturbed, so until tomorrow,

As ever Xxx

Treena was standing in front of the fire with her hands on her hips, demanding to know who had taken her money, when Lois walked into the room, she looked at Alex for clarity, he shook his head,

"Nobody has taken anything Treena, look, there is your money, in your purse where it always is," Norman said wearing a look of hopelessness,

"That's not my purse," she roared as she hit it out of poor
Norman's hand,
"Mum! Please, stop this," Alex jumped up and said,
"Stop this, you, you drag me up here, just so that you can steal
my money!" she roared in Alex's face, Lois walked to her and
placed her hand gently on Treena's arm,
"Maybe we should take a look in the kitchen, maybe someone
has hidden it," Lois suggested, Treena looked at her vacantly,
then nodded as she grabbed Lois's hand and was led to the
kitchen, where Lois began by emptying every single cupboard,
showing Treena that her money was not there,
"How about a nice cup of cocoa before bed?" Lois asked,
Treena, who had now forgotten about the money, smiled, and
nodded as she walked to the fridge to take out the milk.

Later as they sat in bed, Alex looked at Lois and sighed,
"How did you know to do that?" he asked exhaustedly,
"It's not dissimilar to Autism you know, and I learned very
quickly that the way to diffuse a situation is distraction, your
greatest weapon!" Lois said as she valiantly held up an
imaginary sword, causing Alex to laugh.

CHAPTER FOURTEEN

Monday afternoon Lois was waiting outside of the tiny school for Amber and Jake to finish as Bronwyn joined her and frowned, "I thought that I was dropping them off," she said as she wore a puzzled expression, Lois sighed and then smiled, "Well, I was in the area," she said, Bronwyn raised her eyebrows in suspicion,

"You mean you needed to escape more like," Bronwyn said and chuckled,

"Is it that obvious?" Lois asked, now horrified,

"Alex was telling Gareth all about it this morning," Bronwyn replied as she nodded her head,

"I mean I don't want to come across as uncaring, in my line of work you have to have the patience of a saint sometimes, but my goodness, being in the house with her all day is just way too much," Lois said, Jake walked out with his classmates and teacher and spied Lois,

"MUM!" he roared happily and ran to her almost knocking her off of her feet, "Mrs Partridge wants to talk to you," he said as he began to forcefully drag Lois towards his teacher,

"I'll be back in a sec," Lois called to Bronwyn as she reached Mrs Partridge,

"I just wanted you to know how thrilled we are with Jake, he has settled in so well and is a true joy to have in the class," Mrs Partridge said and smiled widely at Jake who was brimming with pride,

"I cannot tell you how wonderful that is to hear, I have never seen him so happy to go to school in the morning," Lois beamed, she returned to where Bronwyn was standing with her girls and Amber,

"Can we go to the park?" Jake asked as he tugged on Lois's coat,

"It's a bit cold Jake," Lois replied as she told Bronwyn what the teacher had just said,

"PLEEEEEEASE," Jake implored, Lois looked at Bronwyn and rolled her eyes,

"All right, but not for too long, I have a large pot of stew simmering," Lois said,

"We'll come with you," Bronwyn said and together they walked a few hundred meters to the small park, where Lois and Bronwyn sat on the bench watching as the children played.

"You know, maybe you should consider the practice nurse post at the surgery, at least you won't be at home all day," Bronwyn suggested, Lois shrugged,

"I couldn't do that to poor Norman, besides, I have to work around the children," she replied,

"Well I do happen to know that there is a part-time nursing role at the cottage hospital, Agnes McBride placed an advert in the shop window," Bronwyn said, "Take a look when we go back," she continued, Lois smiled and nodded her head.

Chaos was not a word that could be used to describe the turmoil when they returned to the cottage after the trip to the park and a coffee at Bronwyn's, there were two cars parked outside, which Lois did not recognise, learning that one belonged to the local community police officer when she stepped inside. She convinced the children to change out of their uniforms as she listened to what the officer had to say,

"Of course I had to come and investigate, she sounded as though she was incredibly upset and in danger," he said after he had explained that Treena had called 999 and told them that she had been kidnapped and was being held hostage.

"I am so sorry that your time has been wasted," Lois said earnestly,

"Yes indeed, maybe you should consider some extra help," he said as he nodded to poor Norman who sat in the chair, head in hands, utterly distraught, and left the cottage,

"What on earth happened Norm?" Lois asked as she passed him a mug of tea, the poor man was trembling uncontrollably,

"I was up in Jake's bedroom, Alex asked if I would like to work on the train set see, Treena was watching an old movie and was happy knitting, so I thought that I would pop up there for an hour. Then I heard her shouting, so I hurried down to see what had happened, she was on the phone to the police, then she began to scream at me, telling me to stay away, that we had kidnapped her and she needed to get home to her children, I tried to tell her Lois, but she wouldn't have it, she just kept screaming at me," he explained as he sobbed. The GP walked into the lounge and sighed,

"I have given her a mild sedative, but I think that as a family now would be a good time to discuss Treena's future," he said sombrely,

"You mean to put her in a home, don't you?" Norman sniffed,

"It may be worth considering, her condition is likely to deteriorate rapidly," the GP replied as Norman sat and shook his head in despair, "I must be off now, you know where to find me if you need me," he said and handed Lois a card, she smiled and nodded then walked the Doctor to his car,

"Do you think that she will deteriorate that quickly?" Lois asked, The Doctor nodded,

"Looking at her medical record, this seems to be rather aggressive, her condition had worsened in a matter of weeks, which although not unheard of, is rather rare," he said as he climbed into his car, as Alex pulled up on the drive.

She then spent twenty minutes standing on the porch telling Alex what had happened in the freezing cold, desperate to get back inside to the children, what if Mrs Hughes was right, what if Treena had another delusional episode and killed them, these and many other irrational thoughts were now racing through her mind.

Monday 17th January 96,

Dear Lois,

You know when you feel that life has struck a balance and then wham! Something happens to tip it and all manner of shite gets thrown in your direction, well, yep you guessed it, it just did! For years, living with a violent alcoholic, having to adapt to Jake's autism, which at times was challenging, to then meeting the perfect man, moving to a wonderful part of the world, where the children are happy, Jake is loving school, and Amber has found her bestie, as she refers to her! Then there is Treena, who for the most part, is a wonderful, funny, loving woman, but is struck down by an incredibly harrowing, personality-changing condition, and I feel that I am back to square one! Tiptoeing on eggshells, we're all back to that, just at a time when I believed that we could be free, and act however we like, we have now resorted to stepping on those bloody shells again. I know in part that I am to blame, I suggested that they come here, but in hindsight, I hadn't realised the severity of her condition, and I couldn't have Alex fretting all the time, and now I feel that I have made the entire situation worse for all concerned, what a to do!

Dear Lois...

Yesterday the beast from the east, namely the ex-mother-in-law from hell dared to call here and demand that I take the children to see her ailing son! Not happening! And after she had hung up on me I began to feel guilty, I mean what the fuck? But I started to read the book and it showed me how to find my centre, which I did earlier today when Norman and Treena were having a row about the name of a distant cousin. I sat on the rug in my room and did as the book instructed, I found my centre and could feel a strange pulling sensation, almost as though the ground beneath me had a magnet attached and was drawing me down, but after that, I felt uplifted like I was floating on air, wow! I feel that it is going to take time to heal my wounded soul and to stop feelings of misguided guilt, but I shall endeavour to continue regardless.

When I came home today and Treena had called the police, it made me reconsider my life plan, earlier Bronwyn gave me the number of the cottage hospital, they are looking for a part-time staff nurse, and the hours would suit me down to the ground, but what with the situation here, I really cannot abandon them, not at this present time, can I? Well, Alex is calling me so I will sign off for now, sorry about the moaning!

As ever Xxx

The week continued in the fashion that it started and Treena was worsening every day, to the point where Lois was at her wit's end, and of course, Alex could sense it. As they sat around the dinner table on Thursday evening, the atmosphere was dreadful, the children too afraid to speak in fear of being bellowed at by Treena, Norman too afraid to say anything, for everything he did say was wrong, Lois was lost in thoughts of travelling to London with Mark, how relieved she was of the escape, and Alex who was forever worrying not only about his poor Mum, but his Dad and the prospect of losing his newfound family. Once the meal was over, Lois and Amber set about clearing the table and upon noticing that Treena was becoming irritable, Lois grabbed her pills and took them into her, placing them on the table with a glass of water,

"What are those?" Treena growled,

"They are your tablets Mum, the ones that help you to sleep," Alex said as he looked anxiously at Lois,

"No they're not, you are poisoning me, you think that I don't know, well I do!" she said and threw the tablets and water across the room, she threw her chair back, stood, and walked to the front door,

"What are you doing Treen?" Norman jumped out of his seat and asked,

"I am going to pick my Trevor up from school," she shouted as she opened the door and stepped outside into a storm, Alex, and Norman both running to catch her up.

"What is wrong with her Mum?" Amber asked her eyes widened with fear,

"Sometimes, when we get old our brain does silly things and begins to forget everything that we have learned," Lois explained,

"What everything?" Jake asked,

"Well, no, not everything but many things," Lois replied,

"Good! Because I don't want to forget about Thomas Newcomen!" Jake announced,

"Who?" Lois asked in bewilderment,

"Thomas Newcomen," Jake replied, Lois shook her head,

"Who is that sweetheart?" Lois asked as she frowned, thinking that Jake had been communicating with the resident spirit, "He invented the very first steam engine, he was from Porn Wall," Jake replied as Lois began to laugh uncontrollably, "No, Jake, he was from Cornwall," Amber said as she giggled.

It took Alex and Norman just short of an hour to convince Treena to return to the cottage and in that time, Lois and Amber had washed the dishes and both children had chosen to have an early night, much to Lois's utter astonishment. Treena walked past Lois who was folding the uniforms in the kitchen, saying not a word, slamming her bedroom door loudly, Lois looked at Norman and Alex and winced, Alex made tea which they took into the lounge after he had ensured that every exterior door was locked.

"I am going to have to do it aren't I?" Norman said sadly, Alex slowly nodded his head, Lois said nothing after all this was none of her business,

"I think that it's for the best Dad, I know that it's hard but she needs to be in a place where they are trained to look after her," Alex said and sighed, Lois grabbed his hand and squeezed it,

"But where son? Where do I even begin to look?" Norman said despairingly as he placed his weary head in his hands,

"What you have to ask yourself is where you want to be," Alex said as Norman looked up at him, "Do you want to stay with Trevor and Alison, here with Lois and me or do you want your own little apartment?" Alex asked, Norman shook his head,

"I don't know son, I just don't know,"

"Why don't you sleep on it, you are more than welcome to stay here and call this your home, the children love having you around," Lois said endearingly, Norman smiled a small smile,

"That's very lovely of you to say Lois, but what if the same thing happens to me? You will be lumbered with me then won't you," he sighed,

"Dad, no one is lumbered with anyone, it's an awful thing that has happened to Mum, sometimes I look at her and she seems like a stranger, it won't happen to you, it would have started by now," Alex said sadly, Norman nodded as then a piercing scream could be heard from Treena's room, all three jumped out of their seats and ran to the small room, Alex walked in first to see Treena sitting up in bed, wearing a look of horror on her face as she pointed to the end of the bed,

"Mum, what is it, what's happened?" Alex asked as he rushed to her side,

"That man, he was there, right there, crying he was, real tears!" she said as she began wailing, a shiver ran down Lois's spine as the words of Mrs Hughes resounded in her head.

As much as she tried to sleep she found that it just was not happening as she tossed and turned with all manner of thoughts running through her mind. She turned and watched Alex, who was usually a sound sleeper, fidget, and groan in his sleep, giving her the realisation that it was taking its toll on him, so she sat gently stroking his hair, trying to soothe his troubled mind. At long last, her eyes grew heavy and she snuggled down beneath the duvet and began to drift off to sleep.

She opened her eyes and immediately took out her dream journal,

20th Jan,
I was walking through an unfamiliar corridor and all that I could hear was 'And then there were three'? I have no idea what this could mean, obviously, the number three is the catalyst, but for what? Anyway, I continued to walk until I came to a door, which I opened and walked into a

small hospital room, inside were three soldiers standing beside a bed. I slowly walked towards them when one of the soldiers stopped me placing his hand in front of me, "Do you have it?" he asked, I shook my head, not knowing what he meant, "Then I can't grant you access I'm afraid," he said, the door opened and a medical team rushed in, shouting at us to leave the room as the equipment began to bleep. I woke up and saw the old man walking towards my bedroom door, he turned and smiled then vanished!

In the kitchen, Lois sighed with relief that she had packed the children's weekend bags the night before, so all that she was left to do, was pack her own. She kissed them both at the door as she handed them their bags, "Have a great weekend, be good for Will and I will see you on Sunday," she said as they nodded before running excitedly to Bronwyn's car, "Have a great time in London, take lots of photos," Bronwyn called out from the open window of the car, Lois nodded and smiled, "Will do," she said and waved as the car drove away, she turned to step back inside when she jumped as Treena was standing directly behind her, "I know your game, seen it all before, you dirty little tart," Treena sneered as Lois gently moved her back inside the cottage, she smiled and nodded at Treena, refusing to acknowledge her vile remark, and returned to the kitchen to grab her clean washing, "She was the same, swanning off on weekends away, leaving my poor lad all alone, I knew it, the moment that I clapped eyes on you, you're nothing but a filthy slut," she sneered just as Alex had entered the kitchen, "Mum! How dare you speak to Lois like that!" he roared as he ran to stand beside Lois who shook her head and smiled,

"I'm going to pack," Lois said and hurried towards the staircase as Norman entered the kitchen, his attention aroused by the raised voices.

She sat on her small weekend case and struggled to pull the zip around, knowing that three pairs of shoes were probably excessive, but Lois being Lois simply could not make a decision, Alex walked into the bedroom and pulled the zip for her,

"See you're at it again, my knight in shining armour," she said and grinned,

"Lo, I'm so sorry for what my Mum said, please don't take any notice, you are nothing like Cassie," Alex said anxiously, Lois touched his face,

"I know," she said still smiling,

"You're not going to end it are you?" he asked, Lois chuckled and shook her head in disbelief,

"How shallow do you think I am Alex, trust me in my line of work, I have been called much worse!" Lois said and kissed his cheek,

"I know, but not by your prospective mother-in-law," he sighed miserably,

"Are you going to be all right here this weekend? Do you want me to cancel?" she asked,

"Absolutely not! I want you to go there and receive your award because you are the best nurse in the world!" he said and held her close,

"Only if you're sure," she said and kissed him gently.

CHAPTER FIFTEEN

Very soon she and Mark were on the train heading towards London, it had been an age since she had visited and the excitement was overwhelming, well it would have been, if it weren't for the worrying thoughts which continuously crept into the forefront of her mind, how on earth was Alex going to cope, the cottage was isolated, they were miles away from civilisation and Treena's violent outburst were becoming a regularity,

"I said, where should we eat tonight?" Mark shouted to gather Lois's attention, breaking her thoughts, she grinned,

"Oh, I'm not sure, what about that amazing little bistro we went to last year?" she suggested, Mark grinned and nodded, every year for the last five years they had made it an annual outing, spending the weekend in London, sightseeing, dining out and of course the annual conference, where they took the opportunity to chat to nurses from other regions and different fields.

After they had checked into the hotel, they wasted no time in walking to the tube station and heading into the centre of London, Mark stood and watched Lois on the busy train, she should be more relaxed, usually their trips to London were tainted because Julie was looking after the children and Lois would continuously worry about them, but this time it should be different, Will loved the children and the children loved Will, he had so many things planned for them to do and see, taking into consideration Jake's sensitivity to noise levels, lighting and people, yet she seemed miles away, still fretting.

In St James's Park, Lois was feeding a squirrel, happily chatting away to him, as people strode past, not giving anything a second thought, just their desire to get from A to B as quickly as possible,

"So what is it? What's wrong? Don't you trust Will?" Mark asked,

"Of course I do!" Lois scowled,

"So why are you so distant Lo, I feel like I am here on my own!" Mark said and frowned,

"Sorry Mark, I have been so excited about our trip, especially as I knew that Will was having the children, but I cannot stop myself from worrying about Alex being left at the cottage with his parents," Lois sighed,

"They are his parents, I'm sure that he will be fine, I mean do you honestly believe that your being in the house makes any difference to Treena's mood swings?" Mark asked, being as brutally honest as always, and that's why she loved him so, she could always rely on Mark to speak the truth, she had missed him terribly the last couple of weeks and now they had the entire weekend to spend together and she was marring it by worrying about Alex!

"Yes you are right as always, I am sorry Mark, I solemnly promise that from this moment on, I will be fun-loving, adventure-seeking Lois," she said as she grabbed his hand and marched him in the direction of the South Bank.

Friday 21st January 96,

Dear Lois,

Well here I am, writing to you from my hotel room in London, yes it's that time of the year again, the Annual Nursing Conference, doesn't time fly, I cannot believe that this time last year I was writing to you from the same hotel room, yet my life was completely different then and I was constantly moaning and fretting about the children! And now this year I have travelled from Wales, leaving my perfect man at our cottage and the children are having so much fun in Liverpool with Will. I have been a little absent-minded, as anxious thoughts creep into my mind about Alex and his parents, but after a short, albeit truthful telling off from Mark, I have managed to put it to the back of my mind and am enjoying the here and now, and my what fun we have had.

We spent the afternoon in the London Dungeons, which terrified Mark, especially when Jack the Ripper jumped out on him, (I have never laughed so much) him being a great woosie and all, we then took a stroll along the South Bank and had dinner on a riverboat, which was delicious and now I am well and truly stuffed.

Well, I shall sign off for now as I need to call the children and then Alex, so until tomorrow,

As always Xxx

She climbed out of the bath wrapped in a luxurious bathrobe, sat on the bed, and called the cottage number, she was buzzing after listening to the children on the telephone, telling her all about their evening in Liverpool and now as the phone rang, small butterflies began to flutter in her tummy as she anxiously waited for Alex to answer, "Hello," his familiar voice said upon answering,

"Hey you, how's things?" Lois gushed, her legs turned to jelly the minute she heard his dulcet tone,

"All the better for hearing your voice, God I miss you," he replied,

"I miss you, I wish you were here with me," she sighed,

"So do I, more than you'll ever know," he said as he chuckled,

"Oh sweetheart, has it been awful?" she asked,

"Nah, not too bad," he lied, having spent the afternoon in the minor injuries unit after Treena had attacked Norman with a knitting needle and ripped his arm to pieces, but she didn't need to hear that, he wanted more than anything for her to have some well-earned fun, "Anyway, what have you been up to?" he then asked, Lois spent the next twenty minutes telling Alex all about her and Mark's adventures, then the next ten minutes telling him how much she missed him, until Norman called for his assistance and he had to go.

Saturday 22nd January,

Dear Lois,

What a day, this morning we went to Covent Garden for breakfast, which was slightly overpriced but lovely all the same, spent the morning wandering in and out of museums, and had an early dinner before heading off for the award ceremony. We were both chuffed as punch to be honoured with awards and it got me thinking, that I should, when I return, apply to the cottage hospital, I shouldn't allow my experience to go to waste now, should I? After a wonderful evening catching up with colleagues from all over the country, we stepped out of the venue on a bit of a high, well that was until I was approached by none other than the Beast from the East and Janette just around the corner! After a full-blown row about me refusing to take the children to visit her son, and then her threatening to take me to court, Mark managed to drag me away before I completely lost it!

Dear Lois...

I have just spoken to the children and Alex and although I have had a lovely weekend, I cannot wait until I get back tomorrow, but now all this heavy city air has exhausted me and with a full day of travelling tomorrow, I will bid you a good night,
As ever Xxx

She woke the following morning early, the horrific dream that she had had, involving none other than the spectre of Old Mr Hughes, had unsettled her somewhat and when she realised that she had left her dream journal at home she searched the room for a piece of paper to jot down the details.
She smiled widely as they approached the lit-up cottage from the dirt track, she looked at Mark and grinned, "Thank you ever so much Mark, I have had the best weekend, are you sure that you won't stop for coffee?" she asked,
"No I want to get back to Will, I have missed him," he sighed, she kissed his cheek, climbed out of the car, took her case from the boot, and dragged it across the stony ground towards the front porch, where she found Jake sitting clutching onto his Sonic teddy, sobbing,
"Hey, what's wrong?" she asked as she lifted his chin from his chest, he looked into her eyes and then threw his arms around her tightly as still, he sobbed, the front door opened and a more than anxious-looking Alex sighed when he saw her,
"What's been going on? Why was Jake out here alone?" she asked and frowned, Alex let out a long exaggerated sigh,
"Mum," was his one-word reply,
"And... that doesn't answer my question does it, why was Jake out here alone?" Lois said sternly, demanding an answer,
"Mum shouted at him for playing too loudly, said that he would wake the children, Jake got upset and ran outside, he

refused to come back in until you were home," Alex said and winced,

"I see, so you all thought that you would leave him outside in the cold and dark while he sobbed his little heart out, do you have any idea how much damage this could cause him?" she shouted, her temper now spiralling out of control,

"Sweetheart, Amber, Dad and I tried to console him, but he told us all in no uncertain terms to get lost, we did try and Amber has been keeping watch out of the window ever since," Alex said trying to calm the raging fire that was Lois, Lois looked at Jake,

"Is this true?" she asked, Jake nodded as he wiped his nose on his sleeve.

She walked through the house, avoiding all contact with Treena, for fear of losing any remaining self-control and took Jake to his bedroom, where she sat him on the bed and once again tried to explain that Treena was not in control of her thoughts, which to someone who sees everything in black and white so to speak, was not an easy task.

Later that night with the children tucked up safely in bed, Lois sat in the lounge with Alex and Norman and it was then that she noticed Norman's heavily bandaged arm,

"What happened to your arm?" she asked apprehensively,

"Treena, she was knitting, I asked her if she wanted tea and she came at me, saying that I was trying to kill her as she stabbed the knitting needle into my arm," Norman replied as he looked at Alex, who once again winced, fearing Lois's reaction,

"When?" Lois asked,

"Friday, shortly after you left," Alex replied, Lois shook her head,

"I am sorry, Alex I know that she is your Mum, your wife Norman, but this cannot go on, she will end up causing someone serious damage and landing herself in trouble with

the police, dementia is not grounds for defence you know," Lois said as she shook her head in disbelief, "I mean, what did you tell the staff at the hospital?" Lois asked,
"We said that Dad fell onto them after he stumbled," Alex mumbled,
"What? And they brought that, did they? How many times did she hit you with them?" Lois asked in bewilderment,
"Well, I had to have stitches, a fair few times," Norman replied, Lois looked at Alex and shook her head.

That night as they sat in bed, the atmosphere was tense, neither of them having anything to say, thoughts of Treena ran around Lois's head as she desperately tried to find the words to say to Alex, she didn't want to come across as cold and calculating, but and this is a big but, she could not have her children in an environment like that again, she understood that Treena was not in control of her actions, but all the same, her children's safety and happiness had to come first, didn't it?
"I will take them back to Trevor's in the morning," Alex said as he turned over and turned out his bedside light, Lois said not a word, she threw the quilt over herself, turned out the light and closed her eyes.

24th Jan,
I had this dream on Saturday night, but being in London, haven't been able to write about it. I was in a field all alone, in the distance I could see a man, he was walking towards me, he was carrying a posy of flowers. At first glimpse, I did not recognise him, but as he got closer he resembled Alex, and I began to run towards him, but I stopped in my tracks when I realised that it most definitely was not Alex, but Mr Hughes! He pushed the

posy of forget me nots towards me as he began to laugh hysterically. He pointed all around and when I looked around the field had turned into a cemetery, a serviceman's cemetery, and I knew this because there was a plaque stating so. Mr Hughes began to run through the many headstones and stopped and pointed to one as he continued to laugh, I ran to where he stood and as I reached him he vanished, I looked at the headstone, it read: Benjamin Wright 1894-1916. I have no idea what this could mean, was it Mr Hughes's relative? And if so what has it got to do with me?

Treena scowled at Lois as Alex helped her into the car, Norman stopped and grabbed her hand,
"Thank you Lois, and sorry for everything," he said sadly as he walked to the car, his head bowed,
"Bye Norman, take care," Lois said as she fought the compulsion to cry,
"See you later," Alex said, not even glancing in her direction as he climbed into the car,
"See ya," she scowled as she walked inside and slammed the door closed. She spent the morning stress cleaning, something that she used to do quite often and since leaving the past behind this was the first time since then that she had. She took the ash bucket out to the compost bin and emptied it, desperate to light a fire as a strong northerly wind battered against the stone walls of the cottage, when she heard the phone ringing, and growling, she threw the ash bucket down and rushed inside,
"Hello," she answered,
"Lois, it's me, I just wanted to say that I am sorry, I have acted like an arsehole," Alex said, Lois smiled,

"It's fine, where are you?" she asked, "Alex, I said where are you?" she said again as she heard the whirr of call ended tone, she shook her head and replaced the receiver returning outside to the now empty ash bucket.

She was just about to light the prepared fire when the telephone began to ring once more, she ran to answer but this time it rang off before she had the chance to, she shook her head in frustration and lit the fire, stood up and turned to walk to the kitchen, she jumped back when she was faced with the spectre of Mr Hughes, standing in front of her sobbing,

"What? What do you want from me?" she whispered as she trembled,

"There were three, there were three!" he wailed as he vanished into thin air.

"What the fuck is happening?" she cried out walking to the kitchen in need of the calming effect of caffeine. She drank the coffee as she stood at the open kitchen door of the cottage, there was an eeriness inside which was making her feel on edge, she checked the time, hoping that it was time to collect the children, but it being only half one, she had a couple of hours to kill, so she finished the remaining dregs, put on her coat grabbed the car keys, locked the doors, climbed into her 4x4, and drove, having no idea where she was going.

She pulled up outside of Bronwyn's shop, climbed out, locked the car, and walked inside, Gareth was behind the counter and he smiled widely when he noticed Lois,

"Bad that is about Alex's Mum, isn't it?" he said, Lois nodded,

"Is Bronwyn about?" she asked, not wishing to talk about Alex's parents to anyone but Alex,

"She's out back, hang on I'll give her a shout," Gareth said as he walked through the back door and called her name, the shop door opened and Ruth stepped inside,

"Hello stranger, long time no see," she said and smiled as she joined Lois at the counter, Lois smiled,

"You know how it is, no time for anything," she replied hesitantly,

"What you doing here then?" Ruth asked suspiciously,

"Oh, I er, I need to speak to Bronwyn about the children," Lois replied and sighed with relief when Bronwyn appeared at the door,

"My two favourite ladies, what a treat, come on up girls," she called out as she headed towards the stairs, Lois looked at Ruth, who grinned and followed her up the staircase to the flat above. Lois followed Bronwyn into the kitchen with Ruth following closely behind,

"What brings you here Lois?" Bronwyn asked as she filled the kettle,

"She needs to speak to you about the children, ain't that right Lois," Ruth answered on her behalf,

"Oh really, they're not poorly are they?" Bronwyn asked wearing a look of concern, Lois smiled awkwardly and shook her head as Ruth took something out of her bag and slammed it onto the kitchen table,

"Brilliant, you remembered then this time," Bronwyn said as she looked at the deck of cards which were now sitting on the table, Ruth grinned, "Are you going to have yours done?" Bronwyn turned to Lois and asked, Lois shook her head in confusion, not having a clue what was going on,

"Sorry, what?" Lois asked in bewilderment,

"Your Tarot, I reads them you see," Ruth said,

"Oh, no, I never have been into anything like that," Lois replied meekly,

"Really? So you have never had a reading or your palm read, or anything?" Bronwyn asked wearing an expression of shock, Lois shook her head,

"No, never," she replied as Ruth handed her the deck of cards,

"Shuffle them for me will you," she said as she took a sip of the coffee that Bronwyn had placed in front of her,

"Oh, well, er, okay," Lois replied and did as she was asked, slowly shuffling the cards she could feel a strange buzzing sensation coming from them like they almost wanted to jump from her hands, she handed them back to Ruth who then began to lay them out on the table studying each one intently, "You have a gift, you're a dark horse aren't you, you have the gift of seership," Ruth said as she looked up from the cards.

CHAPTER SIXTEEN

"I haven't a clue what you are talking about, like I said I have never dabbled in anything of this nature," Lois replied and looked at them both despairingly,

"Well, your significator, the card that represents you is the High Priestess, which tells me that you do have a powerful gift," Ruth replied belligerently,

"Oh how exciting, what else do the cards say, Ruth, she is quite famous around these parts for her ability to read the tarot you know," Bronwyn said matter-of-factly, Ruth turned her gaze back to the spread of cards and the colour drained from her face,

"Oh shit, is that the time, I need to get going," Ruth said awkwardly as she gathered the cards up and placed them back into her bag,

"Really, where are you going Ruth, you are supposed to be doing me a reading," Bronwyn said disappointedly,

"I know, I'm sorry Bron, but I have an appointment that I must keep," she replied as she drank the last of her coffee and disappeared out of the door,

"What's got into her do you think?" Bronwyn mumbled, Lois, shrugged, if she were to be completely honest, she was relieved that she had gone, she never really knew how to take Ruth,

"Anyway, what did you want to speak to me about?" Bronwyn asked,

"Oh, I, Er, I just wanted to tell you that I am collecting them today," Lois lied,

"Oh, I see, is everything all right Lois, you seem a little distracted," Bronwyn asked kindly as she smiled her gentle smile, Lois desperately wanted to tell her about Alex and his parents, but she knew that she would tell Gareth and he would then tell Alex, so she thought better of it,

"Yes, I'm fine Bronwyn, I'm just feeling a bit tired from the weekend," Lois again lied.

After an hour of chatting about random nothingness, Lois and Bronwyn walked to the school to collect the children and Jake was ecstatic that Lois was waiting there for him, the journey home was wonderful as Lois listened to Jake singing in the back of the car, something he had never done before.

The children ran inside as soon as Lois unlocked the door, and Lois ambled in behind them, laden down with bookbags and lunchboxes, and no sooner had she placed them down on the kitchen worktop, did the telephone begin to ring, than she ran and lifted the handset,

"Hello," she answered breathlessly,

"Where the hell have you been? I have been trying to call all afternoon," an incredibly irate-sounding Trevor sneered,

"I'm sorry, but since when have I had to answer to you? Yes I'm fine Trevor, did you have a successful business trip," Lois scowled as she shook her head in disbelief at his blatant rudeness,

"Never mind all that, I have some rather terrible news," he said less angrily, and more sombrely,

"What?" Lois asked as she rolled her eyes, thinking that it was more than likely something to do with Alison breaking a nail,

"Earlier, Alex parked opposite the house, he, Mum, and Dad were crossing the road when an articulated truck spun out of control and hit them," Trevor said barely above a whisper, Lois lost her footing, landing on the back of the sofa,

"Where are they, what hospital did they go to?" she asked frantically,

"No Lois, you don't understand, all three died at the scene," Trevor sobbed, the receiver fell from her hands as the words resounded through her head and she slumped to the floor, Amber came skipping into the room, and took one look at Lois and ran to her,

"Mum, mum, what's happened?" Amber asked anxiously, she could hear a voice coming from the receiver, she lifted it and put it to her ear,

"I'm sorry, Trevor is distraught having just lost all three members of his family, you need to call DS Worth, he is the officer in charge of the case," Alison said snootily and ended the call,

"What did she mean lost all three members of his family, Mum, what did she mean?" Amber cried distraughtly, fearing the worst, Lois looked up from the floor, her tear-stained face told a story all of its own, "Did she mean Alex, Mum, is he dead?" Amber screamed hysterically, causing Jake to run down the stairs and upon hearing those words he too began to scream, Lois gathered them into her arms as all three sat on the floor comforting one another.

Monday 24th January,

Dear Lois,

I really don't know where to begin, as you now are my only confidant, and I really need to share my grief, I have once again turned to you for comfort. Alex took his Mum and Dad back to Trevor's this morning, Treena's violent outbursts had worsened so much that while we were away, she stabbed poor Norman with a knitting needle, and I must protect my children. When Alex parked the car opposite Trevor's house, a truck, whose driver had a cardiac arrest at the wheel, spun out of control and mowed all three of them down, killing them on impact. I still cannot believe it, I cannot believe that Alex is dead, the only man that has ever treated me with such love and respect and he is dead, what the hell am I going to do now? I feel so lost, so alone, I know that you will tell me that I have the children and this I am eternally thankful for, but I truly felt that we were soul mates, destined to be together for years and now, now that is all but a distant dream.

His face will forever be imprinted in my memory, and I will never forget him, for only knowing him for such a short space of time, I loved him so very much.

As always Xxx

The falling tears stopped her from writing more and she curled up into a ball on her lonely, empty bed and sobbed into the pillow, eventually sobbing herself to sleep.

She jumped from her slumber to the opening of her curtains and the stream of sunlight which filled the room, she quickly sat upright and sighed, it was Mark, he walked to the bed, sat down, and held her as again she sobbed uncontrollably,

"How did you know?" she asked once the tears finally abated,

"Amber called me last night and told me, she was pretty distraught, why didn't you call me?" Mark asked as tears ran down his cheeks,

"I was all over the place Mark after I took the call everything came but a blur, I had no concept of anything but utter hopelessness," she said as she wiped her eyes,

"Will is going to take the children out for the day, I have phoned the school and informed them, and you and I shall get on with contacting the police and such okay?" Mark said and smiled sadly, this being the second time that he had to pick her up after receiving devastating news, she smiled and gently touched his face,

"Whatever would I do without you," she said as she swung her legs out of the bed.

Down in the kitchen, Will had prepared the children breakfast and when they spied Lois walking towards them, both ran to her and held her tightly, it was at that very moment that she realised that she couldn't go to pieces, yes she loved Alex with all her heart, but her children depended on her to keep everything together and she could not let them down, they moved away to start a new life for themselves, just the three of them, and that was what this day signified a new beginning. She released them and smiled widely,

"So today, you guys are going to have lots of fun while Mark and I deal with the serious stuff, and then as soon as this is all over, we can start our new lives together properly, what do you reckon?" she asked over cheerfully, wanting to choke herself on the false, albeit necessary joviality,

"Yeah!" they both cried out enthusiastically as they danced around the kitchen, Lois wiped a rogue tear that was threatening to fall and glanced at Mark who smiled empathetically.

The day was filled with official things, Lois had no idea that Alex had named her next of kin on everything that he owned and sole beneficiary, which gave her the final say on when and where the funeral would take place, which displeased Trevor somewhat as he wanted all three of them to be buried at his local crematorium, but Lois was adamant that she wanted Alex as close as possible.

She sat in the window of the small café in the local town while Mark went to order the coffee, she watched as people dashed around, in and out of shops, and not one of them knew exactly how she felt at that moment in time, how lost she was, how alone she felt, the utter emptiness, but then again, why should they, for all that she knew, they could be suffering more than she,

"A penny for 'em?" Mark asked as he placed the tray on the table and sat beside her,

"There is something that has just dawned on me Mark, something weird," she sighed, Mark nodded and gestured for her to continue, "The policeman told me that the accident happened at 12.30, but that's not right, Alex called me at five to one, he told me he was sorry and then we got cut off," she explained, Mark scowled,

"Are you sure he called at that time? You said yourself that after taking that phone call everything became a blur," he asked as he frowned, Lois nodded slowly and exaggeratedly,

"Yes it most definitely was, because just after the call Old Mr Hughes app...." She stopped speaking as the memory of the old spectre sobbing filled her thoughts,

"What? What is it, Lo?" Mark asked as touched her arm to bring her out of her trance-like state,

"Old Mr Hughes appeared, he was crying, all he kept saying was, *there were three*, over and over again, which creeped me out, I looked at the clock, hoping that it was time to collect the children from school, but it was half one, so I drove to Bronwyn's instead," she said as still she remained deep in thought,

"So old Mr Hughes was trying to tell you about Alex and his parents, is that what you are telling me?" Mark asked, sceptical as ever,

"Yes! That's why he has been appearing to me. Don't you see, he was trying to warn me," Lois replied and smiled, "You see, he is not an old curse, he appears to warn people," she continued, Mark chuckled and shook his head,

"Drink your coffee it's getting cold," he said.

After dinner that evening, the children were tucked up in bed, Lois, Mark, and Will sat in the cosy lounge in front of a roaring fire, Lois watched as the flames danced in the fireplace, and slowly became mesmerised by the action,

"Lois, tell Will about Old Mr Hughes," Mark said and nudged her with his elbow,

"Why, so that you can both laugh at me, I understand that you are sceptical, everyone is entitled to their own opinion, but you never saw him, Mark, Alex was a sceptic until the night that he saw him," she said quietly,

"I'm not a sceptic Lois, I have experienced many supernatural occurrences, please tell me," Will asked sweetly.

She spent an hour or so discussing the spectre of Old Mr Hughes, told Will about her strange meeting with Old Mrs Hughes and then went on to tell them about the tarot reading with Ruth.

"So did she say what the cards were saying?" Will asked, his curiosity now pricked as he too for many years had read tarot cards, Lois shook her head,

"No, when Bronwyn asked her, she hurriedly packed the cards away and made an excuse to leave," Lois replied,

"Hmm, seems to me that she saw what had happened and chose not to tell you, many readers follow that ethos," Will said,

"And since when were you the all-knowing occultist?" Mark said teasingly, Will frowned,

"For years I read tarot cards, until one day a young man had booked a reading, I saw in the cards his death, I didn't tell him and he left thinking that everything was rosy in the garden until I discovered three days later that he had a heart attack and died, it was then that I made the decision never to read Tarot again," Will replied, Lois looked at him wide-eyed, not quite believing what she was hearing,

"So why have you never told me this before?" Mark asked feeling slightly disgruntled,
"It's not something that you drop into conversation, is it? Unfortunately, there is still a rather bigoted view of the metaphysical," Will replied and smiled at Lois.

26th Jan,
I was back at the airfield, in the same cabin serving drinks, and yes the same thing happened, we all heard the diving plane and ran outside. The plane crashed and the flaming man walked towards me, as he reached me, the flames disappeared and it was Alex, he held out his arms and I fell into him, *I'm so sorry for leaving you,* that's what he kept saying, but then screams could be heard and I was on fire as the flames reappeared on both of us, people scrambled to extinguish the flames and he lay on the floor lifeless, not breathing. It felt so real, but what does it mean? Maybe I should read more of the Ladder of Life.

She closed the journal and placed it back inside the drawer when she heard the telephone ringing down in the lounge, as she reached the lounge, she discovered that Mark had answered and taken a message,
"That was Kyle, apparently they are at the point of exchanging contracts on the cottage and you need to pop into the office and sign some forms," he said and smiled, after everything that had happened she had completely forgotten about buying the cottage, Lois nodded and walked to the kitchen,
"Where's Will?" she asked, Mark rolled his eyes disapprovingly,
"He has popped into the village to grab some milk," he sighed, Lois raised an eyebrow suspiciously,

"Is everything all right with you two?" she asked, Mark growled,

"You know when you think you know everything there is to know about a person and then you discover that you don't know the half of it," he said, Lois nodded hesitantly,

"Is this because he told you about Tarot?" Lois asked and rolled her eyes,

"Yes, Yes it is, laugh you might, but it shows that we are not as alike as I first thought, we have very different views on something that obviously has played a big part in his life, I mean, I had no idea that he followed a pagan belief, that he practices rituals and such if you ask me it's all a load of old bollocks!" Mark fumed, causing Lois to laugh, "What?" he then fumed,

"Don't you think you are being a little over dramatic?" she asked as she chuckled,

"No, I do not! Trust you to take his side," he sulked,

"I am not taking sides I just think that you are blowing things out of proportion, what does it matter what he believes in, as long as he loves you and you love him, surely that's all that matters," Lois said sadly,

"I do not want to discuss this any further, get ready and I'll drive you into the village," Mark sulked,

"I can drive myself thanks," Lois replied as she grabbed the keys from the hook and left the cottage.

She walked along the narrow pavement and entered Kyle's office, Ruth was sitting behind her desk and smiled a sad smile when Lois walked in, "Is Kyle around?" Lois asked,

"No, he's been called out but he has given me instructions on what you need to sign," Ruth replied gently, which was most out of character, Lois smiled and nodded as Ruth gestured for her to take a seat.

After signing what felt like a hundred documents, Ruth piled them up and placed them back into the file holder, Lois stood to leave,

"Lois, I have something to say," Ruth said her voice full of regret, Lois nodded, "I'm sorry, I should have told you about the curse, instead of laughing at you, you see, we thought that he would only appear to local people, I had no idea that something this awful would happen to you and your lovely family," Ruth said sincerely as tears ran down her cheeks,

"Ruth, you are not to blame for what has happened, it's not a curse, Old Mr Hughes just wants to warn people of impending heartache, that's all," Lois replied and placed her hand on Ruth's shoulder trying to comfort her,

"Saw it I did, in your reading, I should have told you," Ruth sobbed, Lois threw her arms around her,

"It wouldn't have changed things, would it? It had already happened," Lois said as she held her tight, the bell above the door rang out and Lois smiled as Will walked into the office.

CHAPTER SEVENTEEN

Wednesday 27th January 96,

Dear Lois,

It has been a strange couple of days, Mark and Will are staying until the funeral, they have both been wonderful, Will is sooo good with the children, and Mark as ever has always been the biggest shoulder that anyone could ever ask for, the only thing is there seems to be some angst building between them, which is causing the atmosphere in the cottage to become a little stifling. I had another call from the dreaded Trevor today, Christ the man is relentless! He continued to attempt to change my mind on the funeral, today, telling me that he knew Alex far better than me and that he would want to be buried with his parents in the family plot and I told him in no uncertain terms that it was simply not happening. Things got quite heated and suffice it to say I am no longer welcome at Alex's parent's funeral and Trevor and Alison will not be attending Alex's funeral here. If I am to be completely honest I am relieved, I was dreading having to play hostess to two of the most obnoxious people that I have ever met and was equally apprehensive about attending a funeral where I would be a complete stranger. Anyway, moving on, something rather strange happened today, I popped into the village to seal the deal on the cottage and Ruth and I were chatting when Will stepped into the office, he and Ruth then struck up a conversation about tarot and spiritualism and were very soon chatting away like they had known each other for years, which I thought was rather sweet, that was until Mark then came in and made it blatantly clear that he did not share the same affection as I for their newfound friendship. Long story short, Will and Mark are now not speaking and Will has set up camp in the lounge, which is why I have snuck up here to catch a few minutes to myself and avoid the dreadful atmosphere, I think that I might take myself off for a walk and maybe return the book, which was interesting but didn't really teach me anything, other than how to meditate.

The children are having tea at Bronwyn's tonight and she is not dropping them home until eight, so I will toddle off now and go for a wander, I need to clear my thoughts,
As always xxx.

She walked into the same air of contention that she had left not twenty minutes earlier, which was a decision maker, she walked to the coat stand and began to dress accordingly to the inclement weather,

"Are you going out?" Mark asked as he screwed up his face on seeing the trees outside almost bent double from the howling wind,

"Yes, I need some air," Lois replied as she placed her hat on and zipped up her winter coat,

"I'll come with," Mark huffed and rolled his eyes,

"No!" she snapped abruptly, "Really, I just want some time alone," she said and smiled as she hurriedly nipped out of the door and down the stony pathway towards the ravine below. She slowly pulled her scarf up around her face to shield her from the biting wind as she stopped at the stream and watched the icy water flowing rapidly away from her, jumping over

rocks and windfall which had found a resting place upon the
stream bed, relentless in its plight to reach its final destination.
"Is it me, am I cursed? Everyone that I love dearly leaves me,"
she sighed as thoughts of Alex, and her parents filled her mind,
she was fighting the compulsion to cry,
"What doesn't kill us makes us stronger, isn't that how the
saying goes," she heard a familiar voice say, she turned and
smiled when she saw Cerys wrapped up in a large, knitted
shawl,
"I don't know about that, I feel anything but strong right
now," Lois sighed, Cerys walked to her and placed her arm
gently around her shoulder,
"Come, I think tea is in order," she said as she led Lois up the
steep hill towards the old barn. She stepped inside the shop
and the warmth from the old stove in the corner welcomed her
in, she happily warmed her fingers in front of the glowing
embers behind the glass, all the while Cerys walked to the back
room and a few minutes later returned with two cups of
steaming tea, one which she passed to Lois, who gratefully
cradled it close to her now near frozen body, Cerys gestured
for her to sit beside the stove, which she did and once seated
she pulled the book from her coat and handed it to Cerys,
"You have returned it early, may I ask why?" she said as she
walked to the bookshelf and placed the book back in its former
home,
"It was really interesting, and I found that the grounding helps,
but apart from that I didn't learn much," Lois replied as she
blew on the hot tea, Cerys frowned as she returned to her seat,
"What did you expect to learn from it?" she asked as she
sipped her tea, Lois thinking that her mouth must be lined with
asbestos, the tea was still scalding hot,
"I don't know, I found the book on dreams was the same, it
never really addressed any of my concerns," Lois replied as
again she attempted to sip the tea very slowly,

"A book is just that, paper filled with words, a book does not or cannot solve or address your concerns, only you can," Cerys replied as she looked out of the window and watched as large flakes of snow began to fall from the grey sky above,
"But how can I if I have no idea how to?" Lois asked, Cerys smiled as she watched Lois drink down the tea,
"A book can show you the way, place you on the right path, it is just a matter of finding that book," Cerys said her eyes not averting from the now snow-covered ground outside,
"Can't you teach me?" Lois asked, Cerys smiled and shook her head,
"I can guide you, but only that, the answers are waiting for you, you just need to locate them. Walk to the shelves and as you do ground yourself, just like the book taught you, then see what happens," Cerys said her eyes now glistening with impending excitement, Lois placed her cup on the counter and inhaled deeply as she stepped forward towards the many shelves. She stopped and closed her eyes, feeling the energy of the earth below her, as though her legs had become the roots of a large ancient tree. Everything turned black she was surrounded by complete darkness and very soon was travelling through what appeared to be a vortex, at the end was an old key, which she reached out and grabbed, the darkness had gone and she could see a book which had pushed itself half out on the shelf, it had a keyhole in the centre. She walked to the book and placed the key inside, the book jumped from the shelf, into her hand,
"You should leave, the snow is falling thick and fast," Cerys said, causing Lois to jump, her hands were trembling and she reluctantly looked down at the book, it had no title, just an aged woven cover and the key was nowhere to be seen, all the while Cerys smiled and nodded, "Come, I'll walk with you, it appears to be the beginning of a blizzard," Cerys said as she wrapped the shawl around herself.

"But then you have to walk back, I'll be fine, stay here where it's warm," Lois said as she placed the book inside her coat put her hat on and walked to the door, despite her words Cerys followed, locked the door and together they battled through the blizzard. Once at the stream, Cerys stopped, "I will return now, keep the book for as long as you need it, but know this, you can come and visit whenever you like," she said as she turned and walked into the snow-filled wind, very soon disappearing within it.

As she reached the cottage she watched the headlights of Bronwyn's Land Rover coming ever closer towards her, she waited until it halted and then walked to the now stationary vehicle,
"Sorry we're early, didn't want to leave it too long, what with this horrible blizzard," Bronwyn said as Amber and Jake climbed out,
"That's absolutely fine," Lois replied as she steered the children in the direction of the front door,
"They have eaten," Bronwyn said as she began to drive away,
Lois nodded and then ran to the open door.

She tucked the children into bed and then joined Will in the lounge, Mark was in the kitchen preparing the evening meal, which once served, they sat and ate in silence. The lasagne was delicious, Lois didn't have it often as both the children preferred spaghetti, and yet the dining experience was spoiled by the awful silence. "That was delicious thank you, Mark," Lois said as she stood and began to clear away the plates, again no response, she marched out to the kitchen and put on the radio as she ran the hot water into the sink, all the while mumbling under her breath that she wished they would piss off home and continue their feud there, she stood at the sink, for once enjoying the usually arduous task of washing the

dishes, when a song began to play on the radio, Kiss from a
Rose, it was the song which she and Alex danced to at her
leaving party, she sang away as the beautiful memory replayed
in her mind, and at that moment she had stepped back in time
and relished being held in Alex's arms as they drunkenly
swayed to the melodic voice and haunting music,
"Lois," Mark shouted over the top of the loud music, dragging
her away from the beautiful moment and back to earth with a
jolt,
"What?" she snapped, now infuriated by the interruption,
"I just want to say sorry, we have disregarded your feelings,
wrapped up in our own pathetic problems, Will is going back
to Liverpool in the morning, is it okay if I stay with you?" He
asked as he edged towards her, her angry expression softening
as he did, she nodded her head and then wrapped her arms
around him.

Two weeks flew by and the day that Lois had been dreading
had finally crept up and was now commanding her to make an
appearance, she took one last look in the floor-standing mirror
and sighed, then walked to her bedside table, and took the only
photo that she had of the two of them and held it close to her
heart, the sensation of longing was overwhelming, the sting of
tears filled her eyes, then the door knocked and Amber walked
into the room. She could clearly see how heartbroken her
Mum was and quickly she walked to her and placed her arms
around her tightly, as they both began to sob.
They stood outside of the small crematorium waiting for the
hearse to arrive, Lois noticed a few of the locals had gathered
to pay their respects, she looked down at Jake and Amber who
were standing on either side of her holding onto her hands for

dear life, the landlady from the local pub approached them and
smiled a small smile,
"We have just come to pay our respects, I know that we are
not acquainted but that is the way we do things around here,
isn't that right Bryn," The large woman with long blonde hair
said to the man who was now standing beside her, Lois smiled,
"Thank you, that's very kind of you," she said quietly,
"Well that's settled then, where to is the wake being held?" she
asked brashly,
"Er, Bronwyn and Gareth kindly offered to hold it at the
community hall," Lois replied in bewilderment,
"We'll see you there then, one thing though, do you think that
it is appropriate for young children to attend a funeral?" she
asked as she looked at Amber and Jake disapprovingly,
"Yes I do, they were close to Alex and have more right than
anyone to say goodbye to him," Lois replied sharply, secretly
wishing that this woman would go away and bother someone
else, luckily the landlady took the hint and walked to a group of
strangers who were standing close by,
"Nosy bitch," Lois mumbled under her breath, Mark stepped
closer to where Lois and the children were standing, Will was
close behind, they both smiled,
"Everything all right?" Mark asked seeing the strained
expression on Lois's face,
"That fat bitch with the big nose upset Mum," Jake said loudly,
Lois inhaled with shock and looked directly at the landlady,
hoping beyond hope that she hadn't heard, both Mark and Will
stifling the desire to laugh.
After the emotional celebration of life ceremony, Lois needed
five minutes alone to catch her breath and gather her
emotions, so she took herself off to walk around the graveyard,
which seemed strangely familiar, she walked further and found
herself in a military burial ground, where the graves of the
fallen were beautifully dressed. Something caught her eye and

she turned and looked to see the spectre of Old Mr Hughes standing beside a nearby grave smiling, just like he had in her dream, she quickened her pace and walked towards him as he began to laugh as he pointed to the headstone, she inhaled deeply and as she reached him, he of course vanished, leaving Lois to read the inscription which read:

Here lies the fallen body of
Benjamin Wright
whose young life was taken
by the enemy in Belgium in the year 1916
leaving behind his heartbroken sweetheart
Doris Jones and his devoted parents
John and Deirdre
R I P
1894-1916

Lois had no idea what this meant, but it must bear some significance or why would she keep seeing this particular grave of this particular soldier? She was thinking as Mark took hold of her hand and gently pulled her away.

At the wake Ruth and Bronwyn had huddled around Lois, shielding her from the inquisitive locals who were desperate to gain some insight into the latest additions to the village, they were chatting quietly when an older woman approached them and broke through the human barricade, wearing the sternest of expressions she walked towards Lois and held out her hand, "I don't believe that we have been introduced, by name is Agnes McBride, administrator at the Cottage Hospital, I have been hearing great things about you," she said in a broad

Scottish accent as she squeezed Lois's hand with a vice-like grip and almost shook her arm out of its socket,

"Oh yes, Bronwyn showed me the ad in the shop," Lois replied and smiled,

"She said that she had, I was expecting a call from you," she said expectantly with her eyebrows raised in the fashion of a strict school teacher,

"I have been a little distracted recently," Lois sneered, trying her hardest not to be rude, she looked at Bronwyn and Ruth in disbelief,

"Oh he was your future husband, I am so sorry, I had no idea," she said as her face turned seven shades of red,

"It's fine, I would like to apply if the position is still available," Lois said and smiled sweetly,

"Wonderful! Pop in tomorrow morning for an informal chat," she replied and scurried back to the group of women who were edging ever closer.

"Funny woman that one," Ruth said as she watched her telling all to the WI,

"She's not that bad once you get to know her," Bronwyn said and chuckled,

"Look at her, she couldn't wait to get over here and find out gossip, they are nothing short of the SS that lot!" Ruth scorned as Bronwyn shushed her,

"They are not that bad, honestly Ruth coming from you," Bronwyn said just above a whisper,

"And what is that supposed to mean Bron?" Ruth asked angrily as she stood straight,

"It doesn't mean anything Ruth, come on, let's not blow it all out of proportion," Bronwyn said nervously seeing that Ruth was about to lose it,

"Ladies, shouldn't we do this some other time, it is Alex's wake after all," Lois said bluntly, as she too was losing all self-control and was ready to tell the lot of them to politely Fuck off!

Wednesday 10th February 1996,

Dear Lois,

Oh My! I cannot tell you how glad I am to be back in the cottage, after the day that I have had. The funeral went as well as could be expected, the celebrant did a wonderful celebration of life ceremony, I am so glad that I had the chance to spend time with Treena and Norman, who would tell me many things about Alex, when he was a child, teenager, and adult, so I had quite a substantial amount to tell the celebrant. The children and I met the local pub landlady, who on first appearance I could not stand I called her a nosy bitch, which Jake overheard and spent the entire day telling everyone! But on chatting to her at the wake, I find myself a little too quick to judge, both she and her husband are really nice, Trudy and Bryn, asked me if I wanted to go to the monthly quiz night and now back at home, tucked up in bed, I find myself considering the offer.

I walked around the cemetery today and I found the grave in my dream, Benjamin Wright, he died in battle in Belgium and left behind his sweetheart Doris Jones, which is all incredibly heart-wrenching, but I am wondering what the hell it has to do with me, especially as Old Mr Hughes appeared and showed me the way. Tomorrow I shall make it a priority to at least begin to read the book from the Book Barn as I call it, ha-ha.

I am absolutely shattered, the wind is battering the cottage and making me even more sleepy, so I will bid you a goodnight,

Until tomorrow,

As always Xxx.

CHAPTER EIGHTEEN

Once the children had been ferried off to school by Bronwyn, Lois caught up on the household chores, lit a large fire and sat with her book which she read studiously not realising just how long she had been reading, so engrossed was she that she could not quite believe her eyes when she looked at the clock and realised that it was now two in the afternoon. She placed the book on the shelf and ran to the coat hook, making a quick exit out of the cottage.

She parked in the small car park which was to the right of the small cottage hospital, climbed out of the car and checked her watch, it was now half two, so hurriedly she walked to the entrance and stepped inside. There was a reception desk manned by an older, smartly dressed lady, who looked up from her paperwork and smiled,

"Can I help you?" she asked,

"Would it be possible to speak to Agnes McBride, I was supposed to pop in this morning, but unfortunately something came up," Lois lied and smiled sweetly, praying that Agnes was still there,

"Ah yes, you must be Lois," the woman said and picked up the telephone receiver which was on the desk beside her, "Lois is here," she then said, replaced the handset and again smiled,

"It's the forth door on the left, just along the corridor," she said and pointed,

"Thank you very much," Lois said as she walked in the direction that had been shown to her. She stopped at the door and inhaled deeply, she had no idea why but Agnes McBride unnerved her somewhat, a little like Jackie, her old department manager, she then gently tapped on the door,

"Come," she heard, so she opened the door and stepped inside the small but tastefully furnished office.

She walked up to the school gates and stood beside Bronwyn, "Well, how did it go?" she asked excitedly,

"I am on a trial shift tomorrow," Lois replied and grinned,

"Well that is wonderful, I tell you what, why don't we all go to the pub for dinner as a little celebration?" Bronwyn suggested,

"I'm in," Ruth said as she stepped up behind them,

"Yeah, why not," Lois said and smiled, she and the children would only be returning to an empty cottage and she had promised them that this was the beginning of their new life together,

"I'll get Gar to do the driving, so he can come and pick you up and we can have a couple of glasses of wine, what do you think?" Bronwyn said excitedly,

"I had better not, first day back at work for weeks, I had better keep a clear head, besides Mark and Will are coming for the weekend, so I was going to invite you all for dinner on Saturday, we can have a drink then," Lois replied, erring on the side of caution, Ruth, and Bronwyn both nodded as the door opened and the excitable children ran out of the small school building in search of their parents,

"Shall we say seven at the pub?" Bronwyn asked as she began to usher her two girls towards the gate, Lois and Ruth nodded,

"What are you doing here? I didn't know that you had little ones," Lois asked as Jake grabbed the belt of her coat and began using it as a swinging rope,

"I don't, I came to see you," Ruth replied, Lois nodded suspiciously, "I know that we didn't really get off on the right foot, but I likes you and I just wanted you to know, that if you are ever fed up or need a friend, you knows where to find me," Ruth said awkwardly as Lois smiled and wrapped her arms around her, Jake still attached by the belt almost took Lois off of her feet as he dragged her backwards causing them all to laugh.

Thursday 11th February 96,
Dear Lois,

I have a trial shift at the cottage hospital tomorrow and I am a complete bag of nerves, honestly, you would think that I haven't worked for years but it's only been a matter of weeks since I left my post in A&E, I suppose it's the old adage, better the devil you know eh. We had dinner at the pub tonight by way of a cause for celebration, the food was lovely, and the children had the best time as they sat with Tiggy and Jess, while Bronwyn, Ruth and I put the world to rights! I love them both dearly, I have never in my life experienced such a wonderful sense of community. I have, since moving here always been a little weary of Ruth but since getting to know her properly, she is one of the most down-to-earth, caring people that I have ever known, we have so much to talk about, which is weird, in my former life, my only true friend was Mark, who still is I might add, but you know what I mean, all the girls at school and the countless women that I have worked with have all been bitchy backstabbers, so meeting genuine women truly is a breath of fresh air (I only hope that the staff at the hospital are the same).

And now I sit here on my lonely bed, the children are sound asleep and this is the hour of heartbreak for me, the time when my thoughts are filled with nothing but Alex, how I miss him, his strong arms keeping me safe, his rubbish jokes, causing us all to roll our eyes, but more

than anything just knowing that he was there in the bed beside me, gave life a whole new meaning for me, and now, now I must train myself to enjoy life without him, which for me will be the hardest thing that I have ever had to do. I shall go now before my falling tears drop on the pages and stick them together,
As always Xxx

The alarm shrilled out, causing Lois to jump from her slumber, she had only just dropped back off after waking in the middle of the night because of her horrific dream. She swung her legs out of the bed, switched off the alarm and slouched her way down the stairs. Her first go-to was the kettle and she opened the back door while she waited for it to boil, the air was filled with the sound of the dawn chorus, which was incredible, the first time that she had heard it since living at Drift End, but then for once the sun was shining and the wind was gentle, she gulped in the fresh morning air, turned, and jumped as the spectre of Old Mr Hughes stood in the kitchen doorway, "Oh No!" Lois cried as she cast her eyes upon him, he frowned and shook his head as he placed a finger over his lips in a bid to quieten her, "Who is it, who is next, it's not one of the children is it?" she asked despairingly, "There were three," he whispered as he vanished as quickly as he had appeared.

She dropped the children at the shop and parked in the car park of the hospital, dressed in her new uniform she strolled confidently to the door and stepped inside. She greeted Mrs Hall, the receptionist and then made her way to the nurse's room to de-bag and such, then ready for her first shift she walked to the consultation area, where she was met by the in-house Doctor. "I have read great things about you," Dr Sian Murphy said as she smiled, Lois grinned as she shook the young doctor's hand, to say that she had always had a rather strained relationship with most Doctors over the years would be an understatement,

"Thank you, I endeavour to work to the best of my ability," Lois replied,

"Great, that's what I like to hear, now we have a student nurse coming in at nine, she has been here for a year, but if I am to be completely honest, she still hasn't a clue what she is doing, so you are going to have your work cut out with that one," the Doctor said, Lois chuckled,

"I am no stranger to that," she replied.

The morning dragged like you wouldn't believe, with only two patients attending in four hours, Lois got to work by reorganising the sluice and the medicine cupboard, much to the disgust of Anna Morgan, student nurse and full-time layabout. Sian was not joking when she said that she was useless, all that she was interested in was drinking tea and reading a fashion magazine whilst perched behind the small nurse's station.

After spending an hour having lunch with Ruth at Kyle's office, Lois was determined to get some work out of lazy Anna that afternoon, she stepped inside and smiled as she looked at not one, not two, but three people waiting in the reception area, Anna returned late from her lunch and huffed when she saw the people waiting.

"Go and call the first patient please," Lois asked and looked directly at Anna, who huffed and dragged her feet as she slouched towards the reception, where she led the lady to the consultation area and sat her behind the screen, Lois, and

Doctor Sian (which she insisted on being called) waited for
Anna to report her problem,
"She can't feel her fingers," Anna said as she read from the
notes she had scribbled on a scrap piece of paper,
"Which hand?" Lois asked Anna shrugged her shoulders,
Doctor Sian shook her head in disbelief,
"Do you have her records to hand?" Lois then asked as Anna
shook her head,
"Why not?" Doctor Sian asked,
"I didn't know that I had to," Anna mumbled,
"Well of course you did, how long have you worked here?
Over a year, you should know by now that you lead the patient
to the consultation area and then hand the notes to us,"
Doctor Sian growled as she looked at the young woman
disdainfully, Anna began to cry as she ran towards the
reception to collect the notes that she had left on the small
coffee table along with the old magazines and newspapers,
"Highly strung as well!" Sian huffed as she snatched the notes
from Anna and marched towards the screened area.
After Doctor Sian had examined the woman both she and Lois
sat at the desk in the consultation room,
"Well her heart rate is normal, and all her vital signs are good,
do you have any suggestions?" the Doctor asked,
"Do we know what she does for a living or her hobbies, I have
seen similar cases where it is caused by repetition," Lois
replied, the Doctor smiled,
"Well way you go, she is all yours," she said and handed the
notes to Lois, who smiled and walked back around the screen,
where after asking a series of questions learned that Mrs
Matthews was a keen crafter and was constantly using scissors
which would explain why the base of her thumb and index
finger were numb.

"Can you prescribe me something for it, it's just that I am in the process of making the bunting for the spring fair," Mrs Matthews asked, Lois chuckled,
"Medically no, but my Mum was a crafter and she had scissors which had no handles, I will bring them into work tomorrow and you can give them a try, I'll leave them at the reception desk for you," Lois said and smiled,
"But how do they work, if they've no handles?" she asked,
"They are sprung," Lois replied as she continued to fill in the paperwork,
"Oh, well thank you very much nurse," Mrs Matthews said as she gathered her belongings and left.

That evening Lois and the children were sitting around the dinner table, Jake was pushing his food around his plate, which considering that it was spaghetti was rather odd, Lois thought, she looked at Amber, who shrugged her shoulders and then frowned,
"Are you not hungry Jakey?" Lois asked, Jake shook his head as he looked at his plate still full of spaghetti,
"Do you feel unwell?" Lois asked as she placed the back of her hand over his brow, again he shook his head,
"Why aren't you eating then, it's your favourite," Lois asked desperate to get to the bottom of it, sometimes with Jake the situation had to be forced,
"Because someone is going to die!" he shouted agitatedly,
Amber gasped and Lois sat up straight in her chair,
"What makes you say that?" Lois asked,
"That man was there again, standing right there!" Jake said wide-eyed as he pointed to the fireplace,
"What old Mr Hughes?" Amber asked as she placed her cutlery on her plate her appetite too was now diminished, Jake slowly

and definitely nodded his head, Lois looked at Amber and then Jake,

"That doesn't mean that someone is going to die, this was his home, maybe he is just visiting," Lois said trying to be the voice of reason,

"You said that he comes to warn people, he kept saying three," Jake said defiantly as he sat upright in his chair and folded his arms,

"We shouldn't read too much into it, I think he just wants to say hello, that's all," Lois replied,

"Well, why didn't he then, he said three not hello!" Jake scorned, as he pushed his chair back and promptly left the table.

Later that night Lois walked into Jake's room to find him fast asleep, she pulled the covers over him and turned out the light, she then walked to Amber's room, who was sitting up in bed drawing,

"Come on you, lights out, it's late," Lois said as she walked to the bed, Amber huffed and placed the sketch pad and pencil on the floor as Lois pulled up the covers,

"Do you think that one of us or all of us are going to die Mum?" Amber asked anxiously, Lois smiled,

"Of course not, I think that he just wants to stay around the place, wouldn't you," Lois asked, Amber smiled and snuggled down. Lois turned out the light and walked to her bedroom and as she slid beneath the duvet, thoughts of Alex filled her mind as she cried herself to sleep.

She was in a small bedroom sitting on a metal-framed single bed looking at his photograph as tears fell from her eyes in utter despair, spilling all over his image, the acid in the tears causing the image to fade, just as his life had. She climbed to her feet and walked to the cabinet which sat above a small vanity sink in the corner of the small room. Slowly she opened the door and took out a small bottle, closing the door she walked back to the bed, sat down and removed the cork from the top of the bottle as she then closed her eyes and she held it to her mouth, choking as the contents filled her throat the burning sensation was unbearable, within minutes after severe jerking, her body lay still and motionless as the last breath left her body, the bottle fell to the floor, rolling as it hit the linoleum surface revealing its contents, Arsenic.

She sat upright as she gasped for breath, the dream was so lucid, so real, so lifelike that for a minute she believed it to be true, she slowed her rapid breathing and wiped the perspiration from her brow as she then turned on the small bedside lamp and looked at the clock, it was twelve-thirty, she had only been asleep for an hour, she gulped from the glass of water on her bedside table, the taste of arsenic remained on her tongue as then a mist appeared from under the door, it was moving rapidly towards the bed and as it reached her a vision of Alex appeared as the mist dissipated,

"I'm sorry I left you, please stop this from happening, break the cycle," he cried as he vanished back into the mist before he and the mist disappeared completely.

She sat for a while absorbing everything that she had just experienced, then took her dream journal from the drawer, and read the dream that she had the night before, it was the same except that she hadn't drank from the bottle. What did it all mean? She just didn't understand, why were her dreams taking her back through layers of time? Did it cement the thought that she had been in love with Alex in a previous life? She sighed as she placed the dream journal back in the drawer and switched off the lamp and as she became encased in the warmth of the duvet she felt the side of the bed lower as though someone was sitting and as she closed her eyes and drifted into sleep she felt the loving touch of Alex's hand as her brow was tenderly stroked, she fought sleep, wanting to never lose the moment, to feel his gentle touch once more was all that she could ask for, "I will never leave you, I will be with you always," she heard him whisper before the bed returned to normal and she placed her face into the tear-soaked pillow and slipped into sleep.

CHAPTER NINETEEN

She woke to the shrill of the alarm but felt like she had not slept a wink, her heavy eyelids refusing to remain open, it wasn't until Amber bellowed from the open door that she truly woke,

"Mum, It's Friday, Mark and Will are coming today," She shrieked excitedly, Lois chuckled as she reluctantly climbed out of bed and slid her feet inside her slippers,

"I know, come on, I am in need of coffee," Lois said as she touched Amber's glowing cheek and made her way down the stairs towards the kitchen.

As the children sat at the table eating breakfast, she noticed that Jake appeared to be miles away, just staring into space,

"What's wrong Jake?" she asked apprehensively, silently praying that he wasn't ailing in any way, Jake remained silent, still encased in a trance-like state, Lois crouched beside him and gently nudged him, "Jake," she said again, this time he turned his head slowly to face her,

"I had a bad dream," Jake sulked, this was not something that Lois wished to hear, he hadn't had a night terror since Kevin had left,

"It's probably because you saw Mr Hughes last night," Amber said as she removed the bowl from her mouth, Lois gave her a look of disapproval, Jake shook his head,

"It wasn't him, it was Mum, she turned into a monster and then jumped into the river trying to drag me in with her," he said wearing a look of terror, Lois frowned, how on earth did she come back from that? What could she say to ease his troubled mind, for Jake, Lois had always been his safety net, but knowing him only too well and knowing how much association influenced his thinking, she was now mortified,

"Sometimes, when we worry about things, our mind plays it back in a dream but gets a little muddled, that's all," Lois said and stroked his face causing him to flinch away,

"Do you promise that you are not a monster?" Jake asked gravely causing Amber to snigger, Lois glared at her and then turned her gaze back to Jake,

"I promise you, Jake, that I am not a monster," she said as she began to pull at the skin on her face, "Look it's real, there is nothing beneath it," she added trying her hardest to reassure him, Jake smiled a small smile, pushed his chair away from the table and skipped out of the kitchen,

"He's such a weirdo," Amber said as she laughed and shook her head,

"Amber! Don't speak about your brother like that," Lois scorned as Amber then huffed loudly and left the kitchen.

As Lois stood at the sink washing the dishes flashbacks from her dream began to fill her thoughts, the vision of the faded photograph swam around her head and very soon she was sobbing into the dishcloth as the realisation that she would never see Alex again finally hit her head on. Amber returned to the kitchen and on seeing how distraught she was put her arms around her,

"Mum, come on don't cry, it was just a dream," Amber said by way of comforting her, Lois stopped sobbing, wiped her eyes, and looked at Amber,

"How do you know about the dream?" Lois asked in bewilderment,

"Eh? Jake told us about it in the kitchen, are you all right Mum?" Amber asked anxiously, Lois shook her head and marched towards the stairs, after looking at the clock and realising that she was going to be late for work.

The journey into the village was one of silence, Amber worrying about Lois's mental state, Jake worrying that his mum was a monster and Lois, well she was still distraught as her

mind was filled with visions of Alex, she pulled up outside the
shop and the children jumped out of the car, saying not a
word, and entering the shop, Lois pulled away and drove onto
the car park and as the vehicle ground to a halt she turned off
the engine and rested her head on the steering wheel. She was
trying so hard to fight the compulsion to give way to her
emotions, not to dissolve into a wreck of despair, but at that
moment in time, misery was most definitely winning the battle,
that was until there was a large knock on the driver's side
window, forcing her from the depths of despair, she turned to
see Dr Sian smiling at her. Quickly composing herself, she
wiped the rogue tears away, smiled widely and opened the car
door,
"For a minute there, I thought that you were asleep," Dr Sian
said as Lois climbed out of the car,
"No, I was just having a moment that's all," Lois said as she
locked the car and followed the Doctor into the entrance.
A while later she walked to the reception and grabbed the
notes for the next waiting patient and was slightly traumatised
when she read the name on the file, she stepped into the
waiting area, "Mrs Hughes," she called out and grimaced as
Ethel Hughes climbed to her feet and walked towards her,
"I had no idea that you worked here," she said as she walked
towards the consultation area,
"It's my second day," Lois replied and smiled as Mrs Hughes
sat behind the screen waiting patiently for Dr Sian,
"How lovely. How's the cottage, I hope my Emlyn hasn't been
bothering you, mind he need not now that it has happened,"
she said,
"What has happened?" Dr Sian asked as she stepped behind
the screen,
"Her fiancé and his parents were mowed down by a lorry, my
Emlyn appeared to warn her, that's what he does you know,
still I bet that you're relieved it wasn't your little ones," she said

and turned her gaze to a now completely distraught Lois who was struggling to hold back for fear of unleashing all manner of frustration out on Old Mrs Hughes, Dr Sian took one look at Lois, then at Mrs Hughes,

"Lois, go and have your break now," Dr Sian said gently, Lois shook her head as she fought back the tears, "Really, I insist," Dr Sian then said more sternly, Lois turned and sprinted to the nurse's room where she slammed the door closed and buried her head into her coat to muffle the sound of her cries. "Pull it together for goodness sake, don't allow it to consume you, it will only happen again," she heard a familiar voice say, she looked around the room, but she was the only person in there, "Who are you?" she called out as the door opened and Agnes McBride stepped inside,

"Dr Sian has just told me what happened, I suggest that you go home now and come back on Monday, give yourself a few days of R&R," Agnes said sweetly, Lois smiled and nodded, she knew that she could not cope with much more,

"Thank you for being so understanding," Lois said as she grabbed her coat and bag,

"Think nothing of it, besides it might force that lazy wee madam to do some work," She replied and winked referring of course to lazy Anna the student nurse.

She closed the door of the cottage and sighed with relief, for a few hours, she had only herself to contend with, she placed her coat on the hook and walked to the kitchen, filled the kettle, and opened the back door, as the telephone began to ring, sighing she plodded into the lounge and lifted the receiver, "Hello,"

"Mrs Parker?" a female voice asked,

"Yes," Lois replied reluctantly,

"This is Sister Kelly from the stroke ward, I am afraid that I have some upsetting news," Lois said nothing, "A little short of an hour ago, Kevin lost the battle and died," she continued, still Lois remained silent, "Mrs Parker are you there?" she asked,

"Er yes sorry, ok well thanks for letting me know," she replied vaguely,

"What about the funeral arrangements, you are noted as next of kin?"

"No not any more, I received the final divorce papers yesterday," Lois replied,

"Oh, that's awkward, whom should I contact?" she asked,

"His mother," Lois said as she replaced the receiver and walked back to the kitchen, her head began to spin and soon everything was shrouded in darkness.

She was sitting beside the stream at the ravine, watching the water as it travelled on its journey towards the vastness of the ocean, "That was me, I entered Jake's dream state, he needs to know that you are the monster Lois not me," Kevin said as his apparition towered over her,

"Go Away!" she screamed, "I thought that at least now we would be rid of your vile attacks," she cried, he grabbed her face squeezing it in his cold lifeless fingers,

"You will NEVER be free of me!" he roared in her face as she began to scream hysterically,

"Lois, Lois, it's me, Mark," she heard as light filled her vision and she opened her eyes to find herself on the kitchen floor with Mark and Will kneeling beside her, she sighed with relief as she reached out to Mark, needing so much for him to comfort her, which of course he did, folding his arms around her as she breathed heavily.

Dear Lois...

Friday 12th February 96,

Dear Lois,

Oh Lois, I need your help, I am trying so hard to fight the feelings of utter despair, but at present it is winning the battle, thank goodness for Mark. So much has happened in such a short space of time, my first day at work went well, well, I was offered the job, so I must have done something right, to be honest, I thoroughly enjoyed it, it is completely different from the A&E but I enjoyed having the time to converse with people, that was until this morning when Old Mrs Hughes came in banging on about Alex's demise, I went to pieces and was sent home, to find out that Kevin died this morning, but then after taking that phone call something weird happened, I fainted in the kitchen and was down in the ravine sitting beside the stream when Kevin appeared and told me that he had entered Jake's dream state to show him that I was the true monster, he grabbed my face and told me that I will never be free of him, what the fuck am I going to do? How do I explain to Jake that his nightmare was caused by his dying father?

I need guidance on this but have no idea where to find it, who do I ask, maybe I should seek solace in the book that I borrowed from The Book Barn. I must go now because Mark and Will are downstairs amusing the children and I need to at least try and gain some of Jake's trust back, so for now,

As always Xxx

Lois took herself down the stairs and sat on the sofa watching the flames of the roaring fire as Will and Mark played

Monopoly with the children, she became lost in the dancing flames that is until Jake threw himself down beside her and rested his head on her shoulder,

"I'm happy that he is dead, now me, you, and Amber are safe," he said and smiled,

"Me too," she replied and hugged him tightly, ecstatic that he was not flinching every time that she touched him, she desperately wanted to tell him about what she had experienced that afternoon, but knew deep in her heart that it would frighten the living daylights out of him, knowing that his dead father could infiltrate his dreams and portray his Mum as a monster, "But hey, at least now we know why Old Mr Hughes appeared again," Lois said and winked, Jake smiled widely and snuggled into her side.

The following morning Lois woke with a fresh outlook, a new lease of life as she had not experienced any dreams or visions. She drew back the curtains and smiled as bright sunlight filled the room, warming her face, she opened the window to allow the fresh air to seep inside and engulf any remnants of negative stagnant energy.

Downstairs the kitchen was a hive of activity as Mark and Will had set about preparing the cottage for the forthcoming dinner party, the children were tidying their bedrooms and as she walked into the kitchen Will passed her a steaming mug of coffee,

"Really guys, there is no need, I'll do it once I have had my coffee," Lois said and smiled an empty smile, which Mark noticed and walked to her, she had always been a fighter, one of life's survivors, but Mark could see a degree of hollowness within her eyes and it was giving him great cause for concern. He placed his arm around her shoulder and hugged her tightly,

"No sorry, after that coffee, you and I have a date at the supermarket," he said and winked,
"Yay, can't wait," Lois replied with more than a hint of sarcasm in her tone.

Saturday 13th February 96,

Dear Lois,

Hey, I am writing this and I can't even see straight, the evening was a roaring success, well it was until the shit hit the fan, but that's what copious amounts of alcohol does to people isn't it? I did say to Mark that we had brought too much, but Mark being Mark insisted that it was always better to have too much as opposed to not enough!

Anyway, I digress, the food was lovely and everyone seemed to enjoy it, after dinner, the children disappeared upstairs to play on Jake's console and we (the adults) (Maybe not!) sat around chatting, which was all right until we got on the subject of Kevin, I mean I had to tell them, I was left with no choice when Trudy asked about him. Bronwyn gasped when I revealed that he had died and Ruth mumbled good riddance, as I had already spoken to her about his toxic behaviour. Gareth and Bronwyn then launched a verbal attack on Ruth, which I thought was unfair, so I intervened on Ruth's behalf, as too did Will, but then Mark took offence to that and all hell broke loose. Bronwyn and Gareth promptly left with the girls, awkwardly Trudy and Bryn followed soon after and Mark stormed off upstairs in a sulk, leaving me, Ruth, and Will to clear up. Charming! After we finished washing up we sat around the table and I told them about

what I had experienced when I passed out. They both told
me that I needed to seek the advice of someone
knowledgeable in the realm of spirits, but I don't have a
clue where to begin the search.
But that's enough of me for now, my eyes do not wish to
remain open any longer so I will bid you a goodnight,
As always Xxx

She opened her eyes and sighed heavily when she heard Jake
calling out to all the occupants 'Happy Valentine's Day!' which
was something she did not wish to be reminded of at that
particular moment in time, especially as she had the mother of
all hangovers and her head was still reeling from the events of
the night before. She climbed out of bed and opened her
bedroom door to be met by Amber who was grinning like a
Cheshire cat as she held a single red rose out to Lois, "It's
from Alex," she said and skipped down the stairs, Lois now
taken aback held the thorny rose to her chest and even though
the sharp spikey spines began to tear at her skin, she could not
feel a thing, just the essence of Alex surrounding her, she
breathed him in not wishing to move for fear of losing his
essence until Jake appeared and began tugging at the belt of
her dressing gown, beckoning for her to walk down the stairs.
She walked into the kitchen, her head was light and swimmy,
she was not sure if it was due to the effects of the alcohol, or
the sensation of Alex, so quickly she made her way to a stool
and perched herself on it. Will, who was whistling as he
prepared croissants turned and smiled,
"Where's Mark?" Lois asked as he passed her a coffee,
"Gone to Kyle's," Will replied and raised his eyebrows, "Says
he needs some breathing space, away from us," he continued,
"Did he say us or you?" Lois asked as she frowned,

"Definitely us," Will replied as he placed the tray of croissants into the hot oven,

"What did I do?" Lois asked in bewilderment,

"To be honest Lo, he has been acting weird since the funeral, he hardly says a word these days," Will said as he sat opposite Lois,

"I know he can be moody, but I have never known him to act like this, in all the years that I have known him," Lois said as she shook her head in disbelief.

After a soothing shower, Lois stepped into her bedroom and looked out of the window, the weather was particularly kind for February, the sun was shining and only a whisper of a breeze filled the air. Lois dressed and then called the children,

"Come on, let's go for a wander," she said as they both appeared from the staircase,

"Do we have to?" Amber sulked,

"Yes, yes we do, grab your coats," Lois insisted as she opened the front door and then turned to look at Jake who was standing in defiance with his arms folded,

"What is it?" she asked as she rolled her eyes,

"Well, if I had a dog then I would go for a walk, I must have a purpose!" Jake stated adamantly,

"Yes you must, and the purpose is spending time in nature and filling your lungs with fresh air, now come on," Lois replied insistently as Jake huffed and walked to the coat hook.

CHAPTER TWENTY

After spending a couple of hours meandering through the woods, they sat beside the stream, "Can we go to the bookshop?" Jake asked and pointed to the barn at the top of the hill, Lois shook her head,

"No not today Jakey, we need to get back I have lots to do," Lois replied and looked at Will who was wearing an expression of bewilderment as he gazed at the old barn,

"That's never a bookshop," he said as he continued to look, Lois nodded,

"It certainly is, I have had three books since we moved in," she replied,

"No way! I don't believe you," Will replied and shook his head,

"It is, Jake and me have seen it," Amber replied adamantly, Will shook his head as they began to walk the path back up to the cottage, every now and then turning back to look up at the barn.

The afternoon was spent washing and ironing school and work uniforms as well as prepping dinner, Will was in the lounge with Jake helping him with his homework when there was a hefty knock on the front door, Will slowly walked to the door and answered it,

"Hey, come on in, is Mark not with you?" Lois heard Will say, she turned off the iron and walked into the lounge to see Kyle standing beside the fire,

"Why would he be with me? I came here to speak to him, our Mum is poorly," Kyle replied wearing an expression of confusion,

"He left here first thing this morning, to stay at yours," Will replied and looked anxiously at Lois,

"Why?" Kyle asked and looked at Will suspiciously,

"We had words last night, I think that Mark just wanted to clear his head," Lois jumped in and said,
"He must have found somewhere else to go because he certainly hasn't been at mine," Kyle said and scratched his chin whilst in deep thought.

Kyle left in pursuit of his brother, Lois and Will continued with the afternoon and once the children were in bed and they were in the lounge, Will looked at the clock,
"I wonder if Kyle managed to get hold of Mark," he sighed,
"I was just about to say the same thing, should I give Kyle a call?" Lois asked it had been playing on her mind since Kyle had visited earlier, it was totally out of character of Mark to just disappear, she was thinking,
"It's up to you, I'm not doing it, there is no way I am backing down on this one," Will said defiantly, Lois rolled her eyes and walked to the telephone and a couple of minutes later returned to her seat,
"He hasn't been able to track him down, he has spent the entire afternoon travelling around the village and surrounding area, but he is nowhere to be found," Lois said as she chewed her lip anxiously,
"Try our house number, he could have gone home," Will suggested and Lois did just that after a few minutes of constant ringing she replaced the receiver, sat down, and shook her head,
"Well, he could have gone home and being the stubborn sod that he is has chosen to ignore incoming calls," Will said and yawned, "I'm going to call it a night, I need to head off early in the morning," he said as he climbed up from the sofa, Lois nodded her head,
"I won't be up much later, goodnight," she said as Will walked to the spare room and closed the door.

She made herself a mug of tea, switched everything off and made her way up to bed, after checking the children she climbed into bed and took out her journal, which she was about to write in when she heard a low growling noise coming from the corner of her room, she placed the journal down beside her and slipped out from beneath the duvet, she had read stories about foxes coming into houses and had now convinced herself that there was one in her room, she slowly edged towards the corner of the room, the sound was coming from behind the small armchair, so quickly she tipped the chair forward and jumped back to reveal nothing, the noise had stopped completely, so now, well and truly baffled she walked back to the bed, drank her tea and turned off the light, too tired and on edge she decided that the journal could wait as she buried her head beneath the duvet and slipped into sleep.

She was in an unfamiliar house in the kitchen arguing with a woman, the same woman from the canteen where they worked, "You need to snap out of it, Mum needs us to work what with Dad being ill," she shouted over and over again. She ran to a room beside the kitchen and peeped through the open door where she watched a woman lovingly tend to an incredibly frail and feeble man who was lying lifeless on a bed, every so often he began to cough, she turned away as tears fell from her eyes and ran up the stairs to her room, the room with the bed and the sink in the corner, she sat on the bed and looked at the photo as she wept uncontrollably, then as before she walked to the cabinet and took out the same bottle. A shadow crossed the room and towered over her, "Go on do it, do us all a favour, we are sick of you moping around," he growled as he pushed the bottle to her lips.

She turned over and opened her eyes, breathing heavily from the rush of adrenaline and was faced with the apparition of

Kevin, his face pushed against hers, "Have you ever thought to yourself that it cannot be a coincidence that every person you become close to dies, it's no coincidence, you are cursed, it's your fault, whose next Lois, Amber, Jake?" he growled and then vanished. She pushed herself up and jumped out of bed, for fear of him still being there, she ran to the light, quickly switched it on and looked all around the room and then at the clock, 12.30, there it was again, what on earth was happening to her? She walked to the kitchen to get a glass of water to clear the vile taste in her mouth, she took out the large bottle of spring water from the fridge and poured a large glassful and as she turned to put the bottle back she saw him, standing in the kitchen doorway, the spectre of Old Mr Hughes and he was sobbing, "Oh no! Please, please, not again, what can I do to stop it?" she cried and as she did he vanished.

She decided by four thirty am that she was not going to sleep, so she had a shower and walked down to the kitchen to make a coffee, she noticed that the door to the spare room was open so slowly she walked and peered in, the bed was empty, all of Mark and Wills things were still strewn across the room yet there was no sign of either of them.

After looking out of the windows and door to see if there was any sign of either of them for the umpteenth time, Lois walked up the stairs to wake the children and an hour later they were standing in the lounge ready to leave but unsure as to what to do,

"They have a key Mum, come on we are going to be late," Amber implored, Lois looked at Amber and then Jake, walked to the coat hook,

"Come on then," she said and opened the door.

Monday 15th February 96,

Dear Lois,

What a fucking few days, my head is all over the place, I thought at one point today that I was going to be sent home yet again, my thoughts were miles away, worrying about Mark and Will, and hearing those haunting words from last night's dream, whose next Lois Amber, Jake???? Am I cursed, is it me, I saw Old Mr Hughes last night and yes you guessed it, he was sobbing, which can mean only one thing, but what can I do to stop it? Move out I hear you say, if only it were that simple, my parents died before we had even set eyes on this place, so I can definitely rule out the cottage, if it is me then how do I break the curse how do I stop all these unnecessary deaths? I am truly at my wit's end.

However, you will be pleased to know that when we returned home this evening Will and Mark were here, thankfully they had kissed and made up and are leaving first thing in the morning, all day I worried about them, a simple phone call would have been nice, but no, I woke Will when I saw Old Mr Hughes, he then couldn't sleep, so he went out in search of Mark, who he found tucked up in a bed of straw in a nearby barn, apparently the Book barn! I argued with Will that he must have been mistaken, but he was having none of it, they were both insistent that it was one of the same! Never mind eh, at least they are both safe and well, and I endeavour to prove them wrong tomorrow when I walk up to pay Cerys a visit.

I am so tired but so afraid to sleep, I even contemplated sleeping on the sofa, but that would worry the children so I guess I just have to be brave and pray that I don't get a visit from the big bad wolf, which reminds me, something has been playing heavily on my mind since he began to appear, there has been no sign of Alex, I mean surely he being a spirit also should be able to keep him away from me, yet not one of them has, not Mum, Dad, Alex, Treena or Norman, where are they all?

Anyhow, I am going to attempt to sleep now, wish me luck,

As always Xxx

She woke the following morning and sighed happily when she realised that she had slept soundly and wasn't plagued by the ex from hell, she skipped down to the kitchen where Mark and Will were sitting at the table, both wore an expression of great angst,

"Ok, what's happened?" she asked as she filled the kettle,

"Mark saw Old Mr Hughes last night and he has just had a call from the Nursing home, his Mum died last night at twelve-thirty, the exact time that Mark saw Mr Hughes," Will said sadly,

"I am so sorry Mark," Lois said as she walked to him and wrapped her arms around him, he smiled a small smile and wiped away his falling tears,

"I went to see her yesterday, and she seemed to have perked up, I cannot believe it Lo," he said and tapped Lois's hand, she sighed and made herself a coffee,

"Well the car is loaded so I suppose that we had better get a shift on if we want to miss the morning rush hour," Will said as he walked inside the cottage, Lois walked to Mark and wrapped her arms around him,

"I am always here if you need me or a shoulder, goodness knows you have always been there for me," she whispered,

"Lo, maybe you should think about selling this place," he said as he looked around the lounge and shuddered,

"Hmm, I'll think about it," she replied as they left, she had no intention of selling the cottage, she loved it and so did the children.

She dropped the children off at school, she and Bronwyn were still not on speaking terms and given that it was her day off and the weather was not too bad, she drove back and began the walk to the Book Barn. As she neared the brow of the steep hill she looked to the sky and watched as dark clouds loomed ever closer, she put up her hood and walked towards the barn, there was no open sign outside and as she reached the door she stepped back and gasped, there were no Dickensian style windows, just a rundown old barn, with two large wooden doors, which she forced open to find scurrying rats and a few bales of straw. She quickly closed the door and sat on a nearby boulder, what was happening, had she invented it all, she couldn't have, she had the book in her possession, and the children had seen the bookshop in all its former glory. What was she going to do now? Who could she seek advice from? Cerys was her guide and she said that she could visit whenever she wished, but where was she? Frantic and desperate she began to run back down the path, as despair once again took hold of her and threw in a good dose of hopelessness to boot she stopped running when breathlessness got the better of her she bent double to regain some breath and when she looked up she saw Alex standing beside the stream. She hurried her pace but as she reached him she suddenly realised that it was not Alex, it was Kevin,

"You can run but you can't hide Lois," he sneered,

"GO AWAY!" she screamed into his translucent face, he began to laugh, and blocked her path,

"Another one to add to the list, what's the total now, oh let me see, yes seven, wow at this rate you will soon become one of the most notorious serial killers in history," he said as he laughed,

"LEAVE ME," she roared as she did the apparition began to fade,

"Tell Amber that I'll see her later," he said as still he laughed and vanished,

"STAY AWAY FROM HER YOU BASTARD!" she screamed hysterically as she sobbed and then she turned to look at the water, she leaned over, it was not her reflection looking back, it was Alex,

"Come and join me, jump in, then it will all stop," he said as he beckoned to her, her eyes filled with tears as the compulsion to jump was overwhelming, "It will all stop if you end your life, Lois," she heard, she looked again as she was contemplating the suggestion, after all, she trusted Alex implicitly and if it broke the curse then maybe, just maybe she should, but then when she looked once more she saw Kevin's reflection glaring at her, not Alex's,

"BASTARD," she cried as she took to her heels and began to run up the path towards the cottage, and as soon as she stepped inside and slammed the door closed she slid down the door and sobbed.

Was she losing her mind? How would she ever know if Alex were around her now, now that the bastard had appeared as him she would never know, all these and multiple thoughts swam around her mind as she wept, the phone began to ring, and filled with dread she slowly walked to it and answered it,

"Hello," she sniffed,

"Lo, are you free?" Ruth said with an air of concern in her voice, Lois nodded until she realised that Ruth couldn't see her,

"Yes why, what's up?" she sniffed again and rubbed her sore swollen eyes,

"I needs to talk to you, can you drop into the office this afternoon?"

"Yeah, but Ruth," Lois said and then hesitated,

"What?"

"What was my significator?" Lois asked,

"The High Priestess why?"

"I was just making sure it was you," Lois replied and sighed with relief,

"Are you all right Lo?" Ruth asked,

"I'll see you in half an hour," Lois replied and replaced the receiver.

She climbed to her feet and walked to the kitchen and no sooner than she stepped inside she heard laughter, it surrounded her, she ran to the spare room and the laughter followed, she ran up the stairs and still she could not escape the menacing sound,

"You are not real, this is not happening," she cried as she ran out of the kitchen door and into the garden where large droplets of rain fell upon her, she stood, her face taking the force of the deluge of rain as a relief then swept over her, the rain was clearing her thoughts, grounding her as a fierce wind then swept around her almost knocking her from her feet. She stood for a while and allowed the rain to wash over her and then soaked to the skin, she ran back inside, grabbed the car keys, jumped in the car, and drove to the village, too scared to stay in the cottage for a fragment of a second.

She drove through the narrow lanes, soaked to the skin and shivering from the icy rain which had soaked her to the very core and just as she reached the turning for the village the spectre of Old Mr Hughes stepped out in front of her forcing her to slam on the brakes,

"There were three, you must listen," he implored, Lois shook her head and he vanished, she put her foot down hard on the accelerator and raced through the village, stopped half on half off the pavement, jumped out and ran to Kyle's office, twice slipping off of the narrow pavement.

She stepped inside and Ruth looked up from her paperwork and gasped, "Oh fuck, what has happened to you?" she said as she walked quickly to the door, turned the sign to closed and locked it.

CHAPTER TWENTY-ONE

Ruth lit the portable gas fire and sat Lois in its line of heat before she walked to the small back room, which served as a staffroom, in the corner was a small kitchenette, which she walked to and boiled the kettle,

"So, start from the beginning," Ruth said as she handed her a steaming mug of sweet tea, Lois cradled her ice-cold hands around the mug and told Ruth exactly what had happened,

"Hmm, I think that I ought to take you to see an old friend of mine, well she was my mother's best friend if truth be known, but she can communicate with spirits and I believe that she will know how you can protect yourself, I'll give her a call," Ruth said as she rummaged through her over-sized handbag and after a while took out her address book, as Ruth spoke on the phone Lois gazed out of the large office window onto the narrow pavement outside where the heavy rainfall was jumping up and down on the pavement.

"She said we could visit at half two," Ruth said and smiled as she replaced the receiver,

"I can't I have to collect the children from school at three," Lois replied as she shivered violently, the cold had somehow now crept into every bone in her body,

"What about Bron, I thought that she brought them home,

215

can't you ask her to keep hold of them?"

"No, she isn't speaking to me,"

"Why?"

"Because of what happened at the dinner party," Lois replied,

"But she's speaking to me, and it was me and her that had the row, no, I'm not having it, come on," she said as she turned off the heater pulled Lois up from her seat and led her out of the door, which she locked and marched towards Bronwyn's shop,

"Ruth there is no need, I will just have to see your friend another time," Lois said as she pulled back away from the door, Ruth being Ruth would not take no for an answer and forcefully pulled Lois into the shop, where Bronwyn looked at them both wearing an expression of shock,

"What brings you here?" she asked her face now slightly reddened with anger,

"I have come to find out why you are giving Lo the cold shoulder?" Ruth said as she stood tall with her hands on her hips,

"I don't appreciate being spoken to that way by a newcomer," Bronwyn replied and glared at Lois, who was dripping water all over the shop floor,

"Don't be so bloody ridiculous Bron, it was me and you that were arguing, Lois just wanted to back me up because she had told me all about her ex and what a complete bastard he was to her and the kids,"

"Oh, I see, so she can tell you, but not me, I was the first person to make her feel welcome in the village, she came to my house for dinner, and I took her children to school, yet she trusts you, the village gossip, more than me, I see how it is!" Bronwyn fumed,

"For crying out loud! It's not a fucking competition, I told Ruth because we were chatting Bronwyn, I never told you because the opportunity never arose," Lois scowled,

"What do you mean? We have had many a chat," Bronwyn gasped,

"Yes about the children or Gareth or the shop," Lois replied as she shook her head in disbelief, all she wanted was to get out of her soaked clothes, Bronwyn stood, mouth gaped open in shock,

"You're catching flies Bron," Ruth said and laughed, making both Bronwyn and Lois laugh,

"I'm sorry Lois, I know that I can overreact a bit, I think that I am just a little over-sensitive," Bronwyn said and curled her arms around Lois, "Urgh, you are soaked to the skin, what's happened love?" she asked as she stepped back, Lois and Ruth then, over coffee told Bronwyn everything.

They pulled up outside of Drift End and Ruth shuddered as Lois switched off the ignition and climbed out of the car, "Come on, I'm freezing," she shouted at Ruth who was reluctant to get out, she sighed heavily, unclipped the seatbelt and climbed out,

"I'll be a few minutes, make yourself at home," Lois said as she ran up the stairs to change,

"I'd rather not," Ruth mumbled as she stood perfectly still in the lounge beside the window, every small sound giving her cause for alarm. In the bedroom, Lois searched her wardrobe for the warmest clothes that she could find and hurriedly changed, and once the feeling of warmth began to return to her frozen body, she made her way down the stairs to find Ruth in the same position that she was when she left her, they both then hurried back out to the car.

As Lois drove she turned and looked at Ruth, "Why did you want to see me?" she asked, having previously forgotten all about the earlier phone call,

"Oh that, it can wait," Ruth replied as she gazed out of the car window,

"It must have been important, come on, what was it, the suspense is killing me," Lois replied and tapped Ruth's leg, Ruth huffed and turned to face Lois,

"I had a call from Will this morning," she said as she again turned her gaze to the window, Lois nodded,

"Turn left here," Ruth said, "He said that he can't stop thinking about me and asked if I would meet up with him for a drink," she continued, Lois immediately slammed her foot on the brake,

"What? Oh my God, poor Mark," Lois said exasperatingly,

"I know, that's why I called you see, didn't want to tell you over the phone," Ruth said and smiled awkwardly,

"Shit! What did you say?"

"We are here, just pull up over there on the left," Ruth said and pointed to a row of three council houses,

"What, she lives there?" Lois asked in bewilderment,

"Lois don't be so naive, not all witches live in a cottage in the middle of the woods you know," Ruth scorned and tutted.

They walked up the path towards the front door and as Ruth rang the doorbell Lois looked at her,

"Well?" Lois asked,

"What?"

"You haven't told me what you said to Will," Lois said as the door opened and a middle-aged woman smiled at them, she had bleach blonde hair and looked incredibly similar to Trudy from the pub, Lois was thinking as she welcomed them both inside.

Wednesday 16th February 96,

Dear Lois,

I think that I may be losing my mind! I have seen visions of The big bad wolf, of Alex, and Mr Hughes and I went up the hill to the Book Barn today to find that it was exactly as Mark and Will had described it, there was no shop, no Cerys, I simply do not understand it, both me and the children saw it as clear as day! How can it just disappear?

Dear Lois...

I ran back towards the stream where I was met by the wolf himself, telling me that I was cursed, then Alex appeared and told me that if I joined him and ended my life, all of the deaths would stop, but it wasn't Alex, it was the wolf! The Wolf then said that he would be visiting Amber, and I completely lost it, I could hear his sinister laughter throughout the cottage and subsequently, I ran out into the worst rain storm just to escape it.

I went to see Ruth as she phoned and asked me to pop in, she took me to see Eileen, her mother's best friend, sister of Trudy from the pub, and resident witch, from the outside her house looked like the others on the terrace, but inside, it was completely different, and I was blown away! She had a wood burner in her L-shaped lounge, there were pretty throws hanging from the walls, and plants a plenty, anyway, she held my hand and went into a deep trance, she began to pull strange faces, grimacing and yelping out as though in pain and then she released my hand and came out from the trance. She told me that she had seen Alex, Mum, Dad, Treena, and Norman, but something was blocking them, something powerful, namely the big bad wolf, she explained that when someone nasty crosses over, they take the bad energy with them, he has used his as a blockade, stopping all other spirits from getting close or making contact with me. She prepared a large pouch of herbs which I must place in every corner of every room, she then made three pouches, one each for the children and one for me to place under our pillows, I have no idea what she put inside but any help will be truly appreciated.

Ruth then told me that Will had phoned her, he told her that he was wildly attracted to her and asked her out for a drink! Poor Mark. She told me on the way home that although she liked Mark, she too felt a strong attraction to Will and was considering his invitation, she asked me if it would spoil our friendship, to which I had no reply, I love Mark with all of my heart, but in all honesty, if it wasn't Ruth it would be someone else that Will was attracted to, so obviously he isn't in love with Mark as he first claimed to be, I cannot judge other people and although I know that Mark will be heartbroken, I love Ruth as a friend and would be devastated if I were to lose her friendship, she is the only person around here that I feel I can confide in.

Anyway, I shall bore you no longer with my dilemmas and bid you a good night, I am slightly nervous about tonight, especially for Amber, let's just hope that the pouches work eh,

As always Xxx

The children were already asleep when she crept into their rooms and slipped the pouches beneath their pillows, she placed the pouch under hers and snuggled down, the exhaustion had now completely engulfed her, and no sooner had her head hit the pillow than she was sound asleep.

She was in a field walking with a band of men some dressed in white robes, others dressed for battle, Alex included, they walked side by side for many miles, crossing borders and boundaries, one of the robed men approached her and linked her arm, she instinctively knew that at that specific time, he was her father, now and then she would casually look around and then at Alex, who would be watching her, smiling his gorgeous smile when she caught his eye, how beautiful he was, how kind and considerate, she was filled with hope when her father walked with Alex and they conversed and laughed as they marched forward, she had a feeling that he would allow her to marry him. They crossed another boundary line and this time the air was filled with trepidation, what would lie ahead of them? They were all secretly asking themselves. They came to a valley nestled below a mountain range and hid amongst the gorse bushes, she was hiding with Alex, who after a while grabbed her by the hand and led her to the Loch where they sat at the water's edge and gazed into one another's eyes, "I asked your father's permission and he said that if we are successful on our plight that he would be happy for us to marry," he said as he held her face gently within his hands,

"That's wonderful," she purred, only to have the perfect moment marred by the sound of horses' hooves, quickly they scurried back toward the gorse, climbing amongst the sharp thorns for sanctuary. Men dressed in jackets of the brightest red rode into the valley and looked studiously around for signs of human habitation, suddenly an arm reached into the gorse and grabbed Alex, dragging him through the thorns which tore deeply at his flesh before they stood him beside a boulder and launched a vicious attack on him, his lifeless body falling to the ground, before her cries could leave her mouth a hand came over and blocked any sound, it was her father and very quickly he led her away from the enemy, hiding halfway up a mountain.

The sound of high-pitched screaming brought her swiftly from her dream state as she opened her eyes to see both Jake and Amber on her bed screaming hysterically, she sat up and reached out for them, but they jumped back, fear emanating from them, "What is it? What's happened?" Lois asked frantically,

"Stay away, why did you do that?" Amber screamed as Jake sat at the corner of the bed trembling,

"What? I was asleep, what do you mean?" Lois asked in bewilderment,

"You tried to strangle me," Amber cried,

"I did not, I couldn't, I was asl…" Lois said as she looked at Jake who was nodding his head as he sobbed.

After finally calming them down, they walked to the kitchen for milk and cookies, Lois looked at the clock 12.38 am, at the table Jake and Amber sat on one side and Lois on the other,

"Amber, tell me slowly what happened,"

"I was dreaming about Alex, he was still alive, then I woke up and heard Jake screaming, I ran to his room, where he was sitting in bed screaming because he had seen Old Mr Hughes," Amber said as her voice trembled,

"Go on," Lois said gently,

"I ran to his bed and grabbed his hand and we both ran to your room, you were fast asleep so we climbed into your bed and hid under the covers, then as I went back to sleep I felt like I couldn't breathe, I opened my eyes and you were strangling me, Jake woke up and saw it too," Amber said as again she burst into tears because of the trauma,

"That wasn't me, you must believe me, I am going to tell you both something, but you must promise not to be afraid," she said trying her hardest to convince them that it wasn't her, they nodded, "I keep seeing the big bad wolf, he is haunting me, he told me that he was going to appear to you tonight Amber, so Ruth took me to see a magic lady, she gave me pouches of herbs to put under our pillows which I did when you were asleep, but because you left them and got into my bed you were no longer protected, don't you see it wasn't me, it was the big bad wolf pretending to be me," Lois implored,

"But how did Old Mr Hughes get in my room then?" Jake asked as he frowned,

"Because the herbs are there to protect you from the big bad wolf and him only, not Old Mr Hughes," Lois replied,

"So why didn't your herbs protect us?" Amber asked as she wiped the tears away, Lois shrugged,

"I'm not sure, shall we go and take a look? Do you feel brave enough?" she asked, they both reluctantly nodded, she took their hands and led them up the stairs and they slowly walked towards Lois's bedroom, in the doorway, they could see a shadow, Jake hid behind Lois as she approached she realised that it was her mum, who pointed to the floor beside Lois's bed, Lois nodded as she led the children to the bag of herbs which lay on the floor beside the bed, "See, they must have slipped out when I slept," she said as she reached down and picked up the hessian pouch, placing it securely inside her pillowcase, "You do believe me don't you?" she asked as her eyes filled with tears of hopelessness, they nodded unconvincingly and Lois sighed, "What can I do to make you believe me?" she asked despairingly, Jake yawned,

"Can I go back to bed now?" he asked, Lois wiped the falling tears away and nodded,

"Are you sure you don't want to stay in here with me?" she asked,

"No thanks," Jake replied as he yawned again, Amber just shook her head. Lois led them both back to bed, securing their pouches within the pillowcases and tucked them both in, she then returned to her room and climbed into bed, as an emotional tsunami released itself and she wailed into her pillow, tears of unrelenting despair and hopelessness, how could this be happening? Was it her? Was she the perpetrator in all of this? All these thoughts were travelling through her mind at speed, spiralling out of control as the grip of hysteria set in and she sat on her bedroom floor listening to the menacing laughter that filled the air she began to scream.

She felt the sting of a hand hitting her sharply across the face, forcing her back from hysteria, she opened her eyes and looked into the familiar eyes of Mark, "Lois, for fucks sake, what is happening to you?" he asked as tears filled his eyes,

"Wha.. how?" she asked in a dazed-like state,

"I came here as I had nowhere else to go, I have been driving for hours, I drove to Kyle's, but all the lights were out, and then I realised that I still had your key, I have left Will," Mark cried,

"Oh, Mark, I am so sorry," Lois cried, she wiped her tears away and then saw something out of the corner of her eye, Jake and Amber were standing in the doorway, trembling, and weeping, she looked at them and beckoned them to her, but they both shook their heads too afraid to step into the room, too afraid to look at their Mum, their rock, as the visions of recent events replayed constantly throughout their minds.

CHAPTER TWENTY-TWO

She opened her eyes to bright sunlight beaming through the bedroom window and after only three hours of sleep it was not a welcoming sight for her already sore and swollen eyes, she could feel something at the foot of the bed, she pushed herself up and looked, Jake and Amber were curled up fast asleep at the foot of her bed, tears formed as the memories of the night before flashed into her mind, she leaned forward and gently stroked their small faces, her babies, her life, what was happening to them? She gently climbed out of bed, so as not to wake them, after what they had just experienced she wanted them to rest, school could wait, she thought as she crept down the stairs to the kitchen.

Mark was already up and dressed sitting at the table nursing a now cold cup of tea, Lois attempted to smile and switched the kettle on, "Do you want a fresh one?" she asked, Mark looked down at the cold tea, pulled a face and nodded,

"You haven't asked me why I have left Will," Mark said as Lois passed him a mug of tea, Lois nodded, "So, I take it that you already know," he continued, again Lois nodded, "So you know who she is then?" he asked, and reluctantly Lois nodded, "Well, who is the bitch?" he asked angrily,

"You mean, you don't know?" Mark shook his head, his face reddened as he filled with rage, "It's Ruth," Lois replied and flinched,

"What the local gossip, big hips, tits and a mouth to match,"

Mark roared,

"Shh, you'll wake the children,"

"They should be up now, what about school?" Mark shouted,

"They're not going today, not after last night," Lois whispered in a vain attempt for Mark to get the hint, she then heard footsteps as both children walked into the kitchen,

"But I want to go to school, Miss is telling us about the school trip today," Jake sulked and walked to the cupboard in search of Rice Krispies, Amber nodded in agreement, she loved school and did not want to miss a day,

"Really? Don't you want a day to rest and get over what happened last night?" Lois sighed, both children shook their heads,

"What and stay here with who knows what," Amber mumbled as she took a bowl from the cupboard, Lois rolled her eyes and looked at Mark.

They dropped the children off at school and as Lois climbed back into the car, she was unsure what to do, should they return to the house, where she could sit and watch Mark fester in his anger, while she wallowed in her despair? Or should they do something more productive? She was thinking as she took the local newspaper out from her bag and turned to the classified Ads pages,

"What are you looking for? A new love?" Mark smirked as he shook his head,

"Ouch!" Lois replied as she frowned, "As a matter of fact I am looking for a dog," she then retorted,

"Why?"

"Because I think that now that the children and I are living in a remote area on our own we should have a dog for extra protection,"

"So, you're not trying to buy Jake's affection then," Mark said as he stared out of the window, "There she is the fucking tart!" he then roared as he opened the car door and raced along the pavement towards Ruth, who was walking to work,

"Prick," Lois mumbled as she climbed out of the car and ran towards the ongoing slanging match on the narrow pavement,

"It's not my fault that he is more attracted to me is it? Maybe if you weren't so fucking miserable, you may have kept him interested," Ruth said as she stood tall and fearless,

"Are you going to let her speak to me like that?" Mark asked as he turned and looked at Lois,

"It's not my place to stop her, you provoked her," Lois replied, and Ruth smirked,

"That's it, I have had it with the lot of you!" Mark roared as he stormed away.

She drove to the small estate which took her half an hour and pulled up outside of the address that the lady on the telephone had given her, she walked up the path and knocked on the door, listening to the sound of many dogs barking, the door opened, and a miserable looking woman answered,

"I called earlier about the puppy," Lois said awkwardly to the woman who looked as though she had just crawled out of bed, without saying a word she swung the door open and gestured with her head for Lois to enter, which she did to be almost taken out by a large German shepherd who jumped up at her with full force,

"GET DOWN!" the woman screamed as the dogs tail then nestled between its legs as it ran out of the hallway and into the kitchen, "They're in there," she grunted and pointed to a door, slowly, Lois opened the door and grinned there were seven puppies completely wrecking the place, "Bitch or dog?" the woman asked abruptly,

"Er, a girl," Lois replied, the woman shook her head,

"Have you had this breed before?" she asked, Lois shook her head, "Then I would have a dog, they has a much better temperament," she advised, and Lois being Lois nodded her head in agreement.

As she drove back towards the cottage she looked at the puppy who sat in the dog carrier that the woman had kindly lent her for an extra twenty pounds. Its big brown eyes timidly looked back at her, and she then wondered what on earth she had just done, was it for security, or was Mark right, had she done it to win Jake's trust back, she thought as she drove up the uneven lane toward the cottage, something ran out in front of the car and she slammed on the brakes, quickly jumping out of the car after she had felt a thud, she ran around the car, nothing, not a soul to be seen, but then she heard weeping and she turned to look at the cottage, where Old Mr Hughes was standing at the porch crying, the puppy began to whimper, so she quickly climbed in, drove and parked outside, to find thankfully that the spectre had vanished. She grabbed the carrier and stepped inside, letting the dog free once she had closed the door and as he sniffed around, she was thinking about the children's reaction when they met him. The sound of a ringing telephone broke her thoughts and she walked to the phone and answered,

"Mrs Parker?"

"Well it's actually Ms Stone now," Lois replied,

"It's Mrs Partridge, Jake's teacher,"

"Oh hello, is everything all right?" Lois asked anxiously,

"No, I'm afraid we have had to call an ambulance, at playtime, Jake ran out of the school gates, he said that he saw you across the road holding a puppy, calling to him, he ran into the path of oncoming traffic and a car hit him,"

"Oh my God, is he okay, what hospital have they taken him to?" Lois cried,

"Bangor,"

With that, Lois dropped the receiver grabbed the puppy placed him back in the carrier and made a detour to Kyles's office en route, where she ran in threw the carrier at Ruth and ran out.

She parked the car and ran as fast as her legs would carry her towards the A&E department, where she ran to the reception desk and demanded to know where her son was, an older nurse stepped out and led Lois to the relative's room, where she explained what was happening, he was in the fracture clinic having his arm put in a cast, his arm taking the full force of the accident, luckily they were no other injuries apart from minor grazes, however, the Doctor wanted him to stay in for observation for twenty-four hours, just to be sure.

"Can I see him, I want to be with him?" Lois asked anxiously as she chewed at her fingernails, the nurse smiled and led her toward the fracture clinic where, as she arrived, met Jake who was being wheeled to the children's ward by a nurse accompanied by his TA, Lois ran in front of the wheelchair and kneeled on the floor in front,

"Oh Jake, how many times have I told you not to run across the road," Lois sighed as she looked at his tear-stained face, she took hold of his hand which he forcefully drew back,

"Get away from me!" he screamed alarming all around him to stop and stare,

"Don't be silly Jakey, it's me, Mummy," Lois cried,

"Get AWAY from ME!" he screamed again, the nurse who was with Lois led her away to a side room as she sobbed. They sat in the room, waiting for the paediatrician to come and have a chat, Lois was in a state of dazed confusion, at that moment in time she had never felt so lonely, Jake was her boy, her little star, he, and Amber gave her a reason to live, to fight, to strive for a better existence and now she was losing them, what was the point in living, she thought as the door opened and a young Doctor stepped inside, accompanied by a security guard, Lois wiped her eyes and frowned,

"Mrs Parker, I'm Doctor James, I have just had a long conversation with Jake, and I have been left with no other option than to refer him to the emergency team at Social Services, I believe that Jake and his sister Amber are at great risk in your care," the words faded away as she sprinted through the door, through the hospital and as far away as she could, finding herself at the sea. She walked toward the rising tide, as the wind blew violently in her face, she had nothing left to give, the only thing worth living for had now been taken away, and she had no more fight, she stepped into the icy water, wading through the large waves until they took her into the watery abyss.

She had no intention of fighting for survival, she allowed the water to take her as a vision filled her mind her body became swollen, full of salty water, a vision of the dream, the dream where Alex was slain in battle, she ran to the Loch and jumped into the dark water, no fight left, then she saw Jake and Amber, Jake was in a unit, locked in a room, sitting on a bed, rocking to and fro, Amber was in a room full of children of similar ages, they were taunting her, she was distraught, "Mum, WHY?" she screamed as she cried. As her heavily water-laden body began to sink to the depths she heard a voice a familiar voice, "Break the chain, do not allow it to become three or it will never change," she heard Cerys say, at that moment she could feel electrical charge soar through her body, the pain was excruciating as then she began to choke as her lungs could take no more.

Meanwhile…..

Kyle walked into the office and glared at the puppy which was sitting beside Ruth's desk as she fed him strips of dog treats, "Why the bloody hell is there a dog in my office?" he shouted and shot Ruth a look which could have possibly turned her to stone,

"Lois ran in, threw him at me and ran out, what was I supposed to do," Ruth said matter of factly,

"Get bloody rid!" Kyle roared,

"Fine, I shall take it home," Ruth scorned as she stood, put on her coat, and placed the puppy in the carrier,

"If you walk out now, that's it, you are finished," Kyle fumed,

"You were looking for an excuse to get me out because of Mark so I will make it easy for you Kyle, you can shove your job up your arse," Ruth shouted as she picked up the carrier and walked out of the office, marching towards her small flat. Mumbling to herself about how much Kyle pissed her off anyway she walked straight into the path of Bronwyn, who was walking back from school with the girls,

"Oh my God Ruth, it's terrible isn't it?" Bronwyn said stifling back tears,

"I know, he was a prick to work for anyways," Ruth fumed,

"What are you talking about?" Bronwyn asked in bewilderment,

"Kyle, I have had it with him, honestly Bron, the bloke is an arsehole," Ruth growled,

"No, no, no, haven't you heard about Jake?"

"What, what about him?"

"He was run down by a car, and now social services have taken Amber into care, Jake is still in hospital," Bronwyn cried the tears now running freely,

"What? What about Lois? Where is she?"

"Nobody knows, she ran out of the hospital in a terrible state, apparently Jake told the Doctor that Lois tried to strangle Amber in her sleep and then turned up outside opposite the school gates with a puppy..." Bronwyn stopped mid-sentence and looked at what Ruth was holding in her hand, "What's that?" she asked,

"It's a puppy,"

"I can see that, where did you get it from?"

"Lois ran into the office, threw it at me then ran out,"

"Oh my God! It must be true! She tried to kill them both," Bronwyn cried,

"Don't be ridiculous! Lois isn't capable of that," Ruth growled,

"The proof is right there in your hand Ruth," Bronwyn said and pointed at the puppy.

She opened her eyes thinking that she had passed to the other side, a man and woman were on either side of her peering over her, "It's okay, the ambulance is on its way," The woman said as she stroked the soaked hair from Lois's face, Lois nodded slightly, that was all her energy used as she slipped into unconsciousness.

Ruth sat in the armchair of her sparsely furnished flat, she had never felt the need to over-fuss things, so long as she had the essentials that was all that mattered, she thought about her childhood, growing up with just her Mum, who liked a drink, a little too much, which was why Ruth was happy with the simpler things in life, that was all she had ever had, she spent her childhood, pretty much taking care of herself, forcing her to grow up before her years and now in her thirties she believed that she had met the man of her dreams, but even that was masked by darkness, he belonged to someone else, and a man at that! He was Lois's best friend, but Ruth had grown to love Lois, like the sister she had never had, both of them being only children had an empty space that a sibling could have filled, and they found one another.

What should she do? should she fulfil her dream of finding true love or fill the gaping hole in her life and retain Lois's friendship? What if Lois had tried to kill the children, then she would be forsaking true love for a murderer? She had never felt so torn in her life, the phone rang, causing her to jump, she tutted and slowly walked to answer it,

"Hello,"

"It's me, Will,"

"Oh, how are you?" she asked hesitantly, still unsure as to what to do,

"I'm calling about Lois,"

"What about her, have they found her?" she asked as her heart began to thump out of her chest, she simply could not accept that Lois was guilty of what she was being accused of,

"Yes, Mark just called me from the hospital in Chester, which is why I am calling, to ask you to stay away," he said awkwardly,

"Stay away from where?"

"The hospital, she is in a bad way, they are not sure if she will make it, I am leaving to join Mark in a bit,"

"You can piss off if you think that I am not going to be there for her," Ruth said before she replaced the receiver and placed the puppy back in the carrier, her mind now well and truly made up as she walked out of the flat towards the shop.

"Absolutely not! No, I am not harbouring a convict!" Bronwyn stated adamantly when Ruth asked her to look after the puppy,

"He's not a convict Bron, he is an innocent Puppy, please I needs to go to the hospital," Ruth pleaded,

"Why do want to go and see her, she tried to kill her children, they should lock her up and throw away the key," she scorned, "Well that's if she makes it, with any luck she won't," she added,

"It's a good job that you're not judge and jury, whatever happened to innocent until proven guilty?" Ruth exclaimed,

"That dog there, that's proof enough for me," Bronwyn scorned and looked at the dog carrier as the puppy cried,

"Let's not be hasty Bronwyn, of course we'll look after him Ruth, the girls will love it, go on, you go and send Lois our love," Gareth said as he took the dog carrier from Ruth, who smiled relievedly and scowled at Bronwyn,

"You can send his love all you want but do not include me in that, vile bloody woman, I always knew there was something not quite right about her," she said, Ruth shook her head in disbelief as she walked to the door,

"That's a lie right there, you were all over her when she arrived," Gareth said and chuckled as he headed upstairs to their apartment.

CHAPTER TWENTY-THREE

Ruth's legs buckled when she walked through the double doors of the hospital, she stopped to steady herself for a few minutes, then reluctantly walked to the large reception desk and just above a whisper gave Lois's name, the young receptionist typed the name into the computer and looked at Ruth, "She's in ICU, but they are rather strict when it comes to visitors," she said in an overly sympathetic albeit equivocal manner,
"I don't give a toss if truth be known," Ruth sneered as she noticed the huge directions board hanging in front of her,
"No really, they won't let you in," the receptionist called out as Ruth took to her heels in search of the blue zone, she ran up three flights of stairs and finally with no breath left she huffed and puffed her way to a locked door, she pressed the buzzer and a rather stern voice called out from the speaker,
"Yes,"
"I'm here to see my friend Lois Stone," Ruth said awkwardly,
"Sorry, we have no one here by that name," the voice bellowed as other visitors passed by, taking far too much notice of the booming voice,
"Sorry, I meant Lois Parker," Ruth said as her face reddened with pure embarrassment,
"I'm afraid that she already has her allocated visitors with her at the moment," the voice replied snootily,
"Well could you ask one of them to leave I have just driven from Wales you know," Ruth said as her patience was now well and truly opaquely thin,
"I'll go and ask," the voice huffed, Ruth turned to see a young couple staring at her,
"What?" she sneered, as they quickly moved away from the corridor and towards the stairwell.

After what seemed like an eternity, the door opened and Will stepped out and walked towards her,

"Finally, what fucking took you," she sighed as she walked to the door, Will grabbed her arm,

"Can we go and grab a coffee and I can fill you in," he said as he began to pull Ruth in the direction of the stairs,

"Do I have a choice," she huffed and she reluctantly followed him.

Mark was sitting beside the bed as the doctor checked the machines and recorded his findings on Lois's many charts, once finished he sighed and looked at Mark,

"Any change?" Mark asked, his voice overflowing with hopelessness,

"There is a slight improvement in brain activity, but at present, I haven't got anything else to offer,

"So what are her chances of survival?" Mark asked, dreading the reply, the Doctor sighed,

"Luckily she was discovered quite soon after the accident, meaning that any reduction in oxygen saturation was minimal, unfortunately, it all now depends on how much of a fighter she is," he replied as his pager beeped, "I have to go, but you will be updated on any changes," he said as he switched the pager off and left the room. Mark turned and watched as machines breathed for Lois, allowing her lungs to heal, she lay there lifeless, pallid, her usually rosy lips tinged with blue, he grabbed her cold hand and held it to his face, it was at that very moment that the realisation hit of how important she was to him, how she brightened his life, how strong and steadfast she always was, she was a prime example of the meaning of the word survivor, and the inspiration of everything good about him and if she didn't fight, she ceased to be, how would he cope without her,

"Lois, please sweetheart, please fight, if not for me, for Amber and Jake, they need you, Lo, I need you," he wept, his falling tears soaking her cold hand as it rested on his face.

They finished their coffee and pushed the chairs back under the table when someone grabbed Ruth from behind, she quickly turned to see an unfamiliar woman smiling at her, "Are you Ruth?" she asked as she held out her hand, Ruth scowled,
"Who wants to know?" she asked suspiciously,
"I am Heather White, Amber and Jake's social worker, could I have a word?" she asked as she awkwardly moved her unshaken hand back to her side,
"Well that depends, if you are going to slate Lois or ask me to condemn her then no," Ruth said as she glared at the now nervous woman,
"No, it's nothing like that, please, if you could spare me a moment I can explain what is happening on our side," she asked anxiously, Ruth raised an eyebrow and looked at Will, who was nodding, gesturing for Ruth to follow her as she walked to one of the rooms marked as PRIVATE.
"Please take a seat," she said as they entered the small room, Ruth did as she asked and sat with her arms folded in a show of defensiveness,
"Now if I could just explain, when we have a report that a child or children are at risk, following legal guidelines, we must take each and every one seriously, I have spoken to Amber and Jake's school, where they have stated that they have no concerns about the welfare of the children and did, in fact, sing the highest of praises about Lois as a parent," Heather White said as she read from her notebook, Ruth raised an eyebrow,
"Which brings me to you, I am led to believe that you have become firm friends with Lois since she moved to your village, is that correct?" she asked as she looked over the rim of her

glasses, Ruth nodded, "Could you give me your opinion on the family?" she asked awkwardly,

"Lois is the best Mum that any child could wish for, her entire existence revolves around her children, what you lot don't know, is that Lois is being haunted by her dead husband, he uses Lois's appearance to haunt the children making them believe that it is Lois, the bastard, he was a bastard in life and is a bastard in death," Ruth seethed as Heather White scribbled frantically in her notebook,

"Now that's interesting that you should say that, as you know Amber is in a residential unit and Jake is in hospital, last night they both reported that their mum had been to them and attempted to kill them, which is impossible, you'll agree," Heather White stated, Ruth nodded,

"Do they know how seriously ill their Mum is?" Ruth asked, Heather White shook her head, "You haven't told them? What if she doesn't make it? Are you going to tell them then?" Ruth roared as she climbed to her feet, "They needs to know that their Mum is hanging in the balance, they needs to know that she is not hurting them, their bastard father is the culprit of that!" Ruth fumed as she walked to the door all the while Heather White nervously nodded her head.

She could not, no matter how hard she tried, open her eyes. She could hear voices and sounds but she felt detached, almost as though she were listening from another dimension. Within the darkness came a dull light, she could feel nothing, but in that light, she could see scenarios being played, memories of what led her to be where she was at that moment in time. Painfully she watched again as Alex's life was taken, and her parents' lives were taken, and then how her children had grown so quickly from loving her to fearing her, she could see Kevin standing on the opposite side of the road to the school, holding a puppy, beckoning to Jake and she watched in horror as Jake fled the playground and ran into the path of an oncoming car, she wanted to scream but could make no sound, she could see Kevin, in her bedroom, his hands tight around Amber's neck, forcing the breath from her, again she could make no sound, and this was constantly replaying, over and over again, torturing her mind as her ailing body had no more fight to give. She desperately wanted it to stop, she wanted the machines to stop breathing for her, she could not bear to witness it all repeatedly, but how could she stop it, maybe if she moved toward the light, that is what they did in movies to end existence on this mortal coil, they would enter the light. She tried to move but was paralysed, again she wanted to scream out, but nothing.

Ruth entered the room and Mark climbed to his feet, showing no sign of malice, he smiled sadly and walked to the door, "Maybe you can talk some sense into her, bring back her fighting spirit, please Ruth," he asked as tears filled his eyes and he closed the door behind him, leaving Ruth alone with Lois,
"Lo, they know that it's not you that tried to hurt the children, the social worker told me, come on, you needs to fight this, come back your kids need you," Ruth said as she fought her emotions and choked back the tears.
After a while there was a gentle knock on the door and a nurse peered around and beckoned to Ruth, who reluctantly stood, kissed Lois's head, and walked to the door, she gasped when she saw Jake and Amber standing with Heather White,
"They desperately want to see her," Heather said sadly, Ruth winked and then kissed both children on the cheek,
"You need to tell your Mum to wake up, you hear," Ruth said and winked at them as they then entered the room, upon

seeing his Mum, Jake stopped in his tracks and turned to look
at Ruth,

"Can Ruth come in, I'm scared," Jake asked anxiously as he
gazed at Lois, Heather looked at Ruth, who nodded and smiled
as she stepped backwards and allowed Ruth to take Jake's
hand, she could feel the tremors of his body as fear coursed
through his veins, she tightened her grip and bent down to face
him,

"She is still you're Mum Jake," Ruth said gently and smiled,
Jake attempted to smile and walked to stand beside his big
sister, his only alliance at that moment in time, tears rolled
down Amber's cheeks as she looked at her barely recognisable
Mum lying lifeless in the bed, attached to no end of machinery,

"Mum, Mummy, we know that it wasn't you, please come back
we don't know what to do," Amber sobbed and laid her head
beside Lois,

"Please Mummy, he keeps coming back, we are scared, you are
the only one who knows how to stop him," Jake said as his
voice trembled, suddenly the machinery alarms began to ring
out, bleeping, Jake covered his ears as the deafening noises
seemed to become louder, reems of staff ran into the room
ushering the children and Ruth outside as they all crowded
around Lois.

She was finally released from whatever was holding her back,
the light was calling to her, beckoning her forth to freedom,
calling her to be unbound from the torturous visions, and
gladly she stood up and began to run towards the brightest of
lights, familiar silhouettes of those gone before were now
visible, she had never felt so free from the restraints of life, she
was as light as a feather as she continued to run towards Alex
who was waiting for her, but as she neared the light, a
cacophonous bone-chilling shriek filled the air and the spectre
of Old Mr Hughes stood before her, blocking her entrance,

"No! You must fight it, if you enter now, it will replay over and over, do not let it become three, learn from the past," he cried as his apparition faded to nothing and the light once again beckoned her to enter, Alex smiled and then turned and disappeared within the light as too did the many souls who were awaiting her arrival, slowly she turned and looked at the tunnel which stood in front of her, she could see two small figures, who were distraught, it was Amber and Jake, she began to run towards them when Kevin appeared behind them and placed his colossal arms around them binding them to him, Lois screamed out as her legs sped into overdrive, and when she reached him, she opened her mouth and the same bone-chilling shriek screamed out forcing Kevin to crumble to dust.

Ruth, Amber, Jake, Mark, and Will sat in the relative's room, the silence was most deafening as they waited for news, Jake rocked back and forth as Amber chewed her fingernails until there was no nail left, the door opened and Ruth leapt from her seat, her heart racing as she looked at two desperate children, dreading what the doctor was going to say, he smiled awkwardly and closed the door,
"Well?" Ruth asked impatiently,
"Please, take a seat," he directed to Ruth, who looked at Will and took a seat, "It was touch and go for a moment we thought that we had lost her, but, she has proven herself to be a fighter and I am thrilled to tell you that she is awake and asking for you all," The Doctor announced as Jake leapt from his seat and glory punched the air, all the while Amber slid to the floor as she wept tears of joy and relief, "So, if you would like to follow me," he continued as he opened the door and walked back towards Lois's room, as they reached the door the Doctor turned and smiled, "Try not to get her too excited," he said as Jake opened the door and ran to the bed where his

Mum was sitting up smiling, Amber followed, Mark stood to
the side to allow Ruth to enter, she shook her head,
"Let them have their time with her, they have been through
enough," she said and leaned against the wall, Will smiled at
her usually unseen thoughtfulness, and Mark looked at first
Will, then Ruth, the realisation that they were meant to be was
apparent, he had never looked at Mark in that way, so resigned
to being once again single, Mark smiled at them and edged up
the corridor, Will walked to Ruth and leaned in as Mark looked
in the opposite direction and smiled at the Doctor who was
walking towards him,
"Mark," he said quietly, Mark smiled and nodded, "I know that
this might come across as somewhat forthright, but I was
wondering, are you in a relationship?" he asked coyly, Mark
sighed, looked at Ruth and Will, who were enjoying one
another's company and shook his head,
"No, no I'm not, why do you ask?" he replied,
"I was wondering if you would maybe like to go out for dinner
one night?" he asked hesitantly, Mark grinned,
"I'd love to," he replied as they began to swap numbers.

Jake was sitting on one side of Lois, while Amber perched on
the other side, Lois looked at them and was overcome with
emotion, with gratitude, with unconditional love, as Jake
chatted away about his school trip and Amber held her hand in
a vice-like grip.
"We are going on a real train that goes around the edge of a
giant lake, I told Mrs Partridge that you would come too, but
you have to have swimming lessons first," Jake announced,
Lois looked at him in bewilderment,
"Why? I can swim," Lois asked in bemusement, Jake sighed
and tutted, which caused Amber to chuckle,

"Because you nearly drowned, so you can't swim can you?" he said and shook his head as Lois and Amber laughed, which then caused Lois's lungs to burn as she began to cough.

Heather White approached Ruth and Will, "Sorry to interrupt, but I need to ask about provisions for the children, as far as we are concerned the children can return to Lois's care, but what should we do whilst she is hospitalised?" she asked,
"You should ask Mark, he is Lois's closest friend," Ruth replied and looked in Mark's direction, smiling as he swooned over the handsome Doctor, Mark overheard and looked at Ruth and smiled gratefully as Heather White walked towards him,
"I am staying at Lois's house for the time being, so the children will be perfectly safe with me," Mark stated as the Doctor tapped his shoulder and then walked in to check on Lois,
"Wonderful, thank you, here's my card in case you run into any problems," Heather said and smiled as she passed Mark her card.

"So are me and Amber staying here with you?" Jake asked as the doctor took Lois's blood pressure,
"Er, I'm not sure what's happening yet Jakey," Lois replied and looked at the Doctor as Mark then entered the room,
"No, you are coming home with me," Mark said and grinned, Jake scowled and shook his head,
"But I don't want to, not without Mummy, what if the big bad wolf comes back?" Jake sulked,
"Sweetheart, he's never coming back, I promise, I stopped him once and for all," Lois said as she held up her hand victoriously, Jake laughed,

"Did you have a gigantic battle? Did you get dragons to slay him?" Jake asked excitedly, Lois chuckled as did the Doctor and Mark,

"No I showed him how much I love you both and that scared him until he crumbled away like sand," Lois said,

"Cool, okay Mark, but I am only going home if you promise to cook spaghetti," Jake said,

"I promise, but if you want spaghetti for dinner, we need to go now, I need to get some shopping in," Mark said and glanced at Lois, watching as sadness swept across her face,

"How long will I be here for?" she asked the Doctor,

"I need to run a few tests tomorrow just to ensure there is no lasting damage, and if they are all good, you can probably be discharged," he said and grinned,

"Thank you," Lois said and sighed with relief as Mark readied the children for the journey home, she needed to speak to him about the puppy but they had gone before she had a chance to say anything. The door opened and Ruth and Will stepped into the room,

"Would you look at that, an hour ago she looked as though she was going to pop her clogs and now she is sitting up sipping tea!" Ruth exclaimed as she walked to Lois and kissed her cheek,

"Where is the puppy?" she asked and looked at Ruth,

"He's at Bron's, I will collect him on the way home," Ruth said and glanced at Will who was wantonly staring in her direction,

"Are you sure, what about work?" Lois asked,

"I quit," Ruth replied as she smiled and shrugged her shoulders, Lois frowned,

"It wasn't because of me was it?" She asked anxiously, Ruth grinned and shook her head,

"Nah, it was a dead-end job and Kyle is a bit of a prick to work for if truth be known," Ruth said, she could feel Will's eyes burning a hole into her and she was desperate to get her hands on him, but now this time was for Lois, pleasure had to take a back seat for a while, "Will, why don't you go and grab me and Lo a cappuccino," Ruth said and winked, taking the hint, Will nodded and left the room,

"I see that you two have got the ball rolling then," Lois said and chuckled as Ruth blushed,

"I don't know what you mean," she replied bashfully.

CHAPTER TWENTY-FOUR

Monday 21st February 96,

Dear Lois,

Sorry, it's been a while but so much has happened in such a short space of time. I attempted suicide, the thought of losing my children was too much to bear, so I walked into the freezing cold sea and asked it to carry me away (of course now I feel a complete fool and regret it, feeling so ashamed of myself). Luckily I had a vision of Jake and Amber and something happened, my body filled with electricity and I was washed up on the beach, a couple found me and called for help, which is why I am now able to write to you. Apparently, in the hospital, it was touch and go for a while, but I pulled through and for that, I am utterly thankful.

While I was unconscious I saw Old Mr Hughes, it was at the moment when I was happy to walk into the light, but he blocked my way and screamed, it was the most horrific sound I have ever heard, then, he said not to allow it to become three. I now understand the message he was trying to put across, then there were three, there were three, it always happened at 12.30, 1,2,3,0, in my two previous lives I had been planning to marry Alex, but sadly his life was cut short on both occasions, and I, not being able to face life without him, took my own life. If I had been successful this time it would have been three, and we would never be released from that particular cycle, but now, this time, I truly believe that if I live out the rest of my days, focusing purely on the children living a happy and fulfilled life, then in the next life, Alex and I will not be separated and will live a lifetime with one another just as we both desperately yearn for.

Now enough of my emotional ramblings, we have called the puppy Mr Hughes as we believe that he is our protector, Jake wanted to call him cat, but he was outvoted by Amber, Mark, and myself, thank goodness, he is an adorable creature, very loving and loyal, the look on the children's faces when Ruth brought him in was priceless, I think that Jake is still recovering from the shock.

On an even lighter note, Mark is staying with us for a while, he is swooning over the handsome Doctor David, they have had two dates already, and now Will seems nothing but a distant memory, well to Mark anyway, Ruth on the other hand is completely smitten by Will and they visit every day, which at first I thought could be awkward, but is lovely. Bronwyn and Gareth popped in this morning with a beautiful bouquet and a large pot of homemade stew, which I was thrilled about, meaning that I can take Mr Hughes out for a walk and not have to worry about rushing back to cook.

I have been signed off of work for the remainder of the week, so I endeavour to rest, walk, and enjoy my new lease of life, well except for Friday when Jake has volunteered me to help out on the school trip to Bala Lake, yippee!

I shall sign off for now as the hills are a calling,

As ever Xxx

She held the journal close to her heart and sighed, she had read through her words and couldn't quite believe how much had happened, she placed the journal in her bedside drawer and walked down the stairs, to find Mark in the lounge ironing whilst watching daytime TV, which gave her cause to chuckle, it reminded her of the times she would come in from school and her Mum would be doing the same thing. Quietly she walked to the coat hook and took down her winter jacket, Mark looked in her direction and scowled, "And just where exactly, do you think you are going?" he asked, hands on hips, "I am taking Mr Hughes for a walk," she replied as she placed her scarf around her neck,

"David said that you needed to rest," Mark scowled and shook his head disapprovingly,

"Since when has gentle exercise been bad for you, I am a nurse, I know my body and I am fully aware that I feel well enough to get some fresh air," Lois replied adamantly. Mark unplugged the iron, tutted, and walked to the coat hook,

"I am not letting you go alone, your lungs have only just started to recover from great trauma," he mumbled as he put on his coat and shivered as Lois opened the door.

Mark insisted on holding the lead as Mr Hughes was so excited that he pulled incessantly, so they walked down to the ravine and sat beside the stream, all the while, Mr Hughes was desperate to jump into the icy water. Lois looked up the hill in the direction of the 'Book shop' and sighed,

"What's wrong?" Mark asked anxiously,

"I just don't understand Mark, how can it be a bookshop for weeks and then suddenly turn into a disused barn? It just doesn't make sense," Lois uttered vaguely as still she stared at the abandoned old building,

"Maybe Kevin planted the thought in your head?"

"The children saw it too, it wasn't just me," Lois replied as she shook her head,

"But he convinced them that he was you, did he not," Mark said with a raised eyebrow,

"Yes, but when we first came across the bookshop Kevin was still very much alive," Lois said and chuckled as Mr Hughes ran around her tying her up in the lead,

"Ah, true," Mark replied as Lois unravelled herself and began to walk up the hill, "Lois, don't be daft, you will push yourself too hard and land yourself back in the hospital," he sighed, she stopped walking and turned to face him, whatever would she do if she didn't have him in her life, she was incredibly lucky to have a friend like Mark, he was always there for her, he gave her sound advice, he listened while she moaned, and oh how they laughed. She smiled and walked back to him, linking his arm as together they walked back to the cottage.

That afternoon Lois sat on the sofa reading a book while Mark continued to catch up with the ironing, he looked over in Lois's direction,

"Is that from the spectral bookshop?" he asked and chuckled, Lois placed the book down and sighed,

"Funny! No, Ruth brought it into the hospital for me, but it's a bit too raunchy for me," she said and laughed, "Actually, where is the book that I borrowed?" Lois said as she sat deep in thought, she threw her legs off of the sofa and walked to the staircase, and after an hour of searching, she could not locate the book anywhere in the house, she even checked the children's rooms in case they had taken it, but it was nowhere to be found.

She walked back into the lounge scratching her head, still bemused by the missing book,

"Are you sure that you ever had the book?" Mark asked as he put away the ironing board, Lois tutted,

"I am not stupid Mark, I definitely had the book here," Lois said as she took everything out of the magazine rack, frantically searching,
"What was it called?" Mark asked as he placed two mugs of coffee on the table,
"It didn't have a title," Lois replied as she moved to the sideboard and began to empty the contents, slowly turning to look in Mark's direction as he howled with laughter,
"So let me get this straight, we are looking for a book with no title from a non-existent bookshop," he said as he laughed,
"Believe what you want, but I know that it was real," Lois huffed as she stormed out of the lounge into the kitchen, placing the large saucepan of stew onto the hob, banging the cupboard doors as she did in a show of despondency. She was in the process of angrily peeling potatoes when Mark put his head around the door,
"I am going to collect the children, is there anything that we need from the shop?" he asked nervously, Lois remained silent shaking her head in answer to his question, he shrugged his shoulders and after a few seconds, Lois heard the front door close. She placed the potatoes on to boil, let Mr Hughes out of the kitchen door and then began to search again, it had to be there somewhere, she distinctly remembered its faded green woven cover, she placed the book in her bedside cabinet, she recalled doing it, yet it was not there, it wasn't anywhere.
Jake ran inside first to be greeted by Mr Hughes who had patiently waited all day for his best friend to return, knocking him to the floor as he eagerly licked his face, all the time Jake was calling for help as he laughed hysterically from the antics of the overly affectionate dog, Lois pulled Jake to his feet and sent him up to change, Amber followed Jake and Lois returned to the kitchen, Mark cautiously approached and smiled as he filled the kettle, Lois, knowing that she was behaving like a child, smiled back and walked to the sink to drain the potatoes,

"Jake's teacher asked me to return this to you, Jake took it in for show and tell," Mark said and grimaced, Lois took the book, with its aged, green woven cover and gasped, she looked at Mark and grinned,

"See! I told you that I had it," Lois exclaimed as Mark took the book from her and opened it, he began to read,

"Dear Lois, our venture is almost at an end, please use this book to write the first Chapter in what is the beginning of your new journey and return it to me at my home, Cerys." he read out loud, Lois slowly turned and frowned,

"It does not say that" she said as she walked to him and took the book from him, she opened the first page and true to his word, handwritten was a note from Cerys, "But, I, I don't understand, her home is not there, where am I supposed to take it?" Lois thought out loud,

"Lo, I don't mean to come across as rude, but after what you have been through, isn't it possible that you could have written it yourself?" Mark mumbled apprehensively,

"No Mark! It isn't possible, I met this woman, she owned the bookshop and made me the most amazing tasting tea, thanks ever so much for your confidence in my mental state," Lois fumed as she flicked through pages and pages of blankness, she slammed the book on the worktop, "Anyway, tea is ready," she said as she walked to the staircase to call the children.

Jake was preoccupied with trying to place as many chicken dippers into his mouth as he could (after point blank refusing to even try Bronwyn's stew), Mark watched him and shook his head,

"So Jake, what did your teacher think of the book that you took in for show and tell?" He asked and smirked at Lois, who rolled her eyes waiting for yet another round of ridicule,

"She loved it! There was a story about a dragon and how it helped the people in a village," Jake replied, his eyes as wide as saucers, Lois grinned,

"But there are no words inside the book, she most probably made the story up," Mark scoffed, Lois frowned,

"Really?" she sighed and shook her head as she watched Jake's expression change very quickly to one of rage,

"No, she did not! She showed us the pictures and everything!" Jake exclaimed angrily as he pushed his chair away from the table and stormed out of the room,

"Nice one Mark," Lois sneered as she too left the table in pursuit of Jake, she found him in the kitchen sitting in the dog's bed with Mr Hughes, telling him how much of a liar Mark was,

"Shall we take Mr Hughes for a small walk? You can hold the lead," Lois suggested and smiled, knowing that the distraction would help with Jake's now foul mood, Jake grinned widely and jumped to his feet, "We can't go too far because my lungs are still a bit tired," Lois added, Jake took no notice and ran to the cupboard to fetch the dog's lead, "Amber, Jake and I are taking Mr Hughes for a short walk, you coming?" Lois asked as she peered around the lounge door, Amber shook her head, so Lois and Jake left with Mr Hughes, excitedly pulling Jake down towards the ravine. The wind had gained momentum and poor Jake was struggling to walk through the biting gusts whilst holding onto the dog's lead, so quickly they turned and headed back towards the cottage. Small flakes of snow began to fall from the darkened sky as they reached the front porch, Lois looked at the drive and noticed that Mark's car had gone, she looked at Jake and frowned as they entered the warm, cosy cottage, relieved to be shielded from the wintry wind. Lois hung up the coats as Jake released Mr Hughes from his lead and ran into the lounge, Lois followed and looked at Amber who was huddled up on the sofa wearing an expression of terror,

"What's wrong? And where is Mark?" Lois asked as she walked to the sofa,

"Dr David called on the phone and Mark began to shout and then left," Amber said sorrowfully,
"What? He left you here on your own, what the hell is he playing at?" Lois fumed as she stroked Amber's face, "Did something happen while we were out?" she continued apprehensively, Amber shook her head,
"No I was too scared to move in case it did," she replied as she leaned into Lois, who wrapped her arms around her.
That night, with both children, tucked up in bed with hot water bottles and extra blankets, Mr Hughes in his usual position at the end of Jake's bed, Lois walked to her room and placed her mug of cocoa on her bedside cabinet, she pulled back the duvet and moved the hot water bottle to the other side of the bed and climbed inside the warm sheets. She opened the book and read the words once again before she flicked through the pages, still, they remained empty. She shook her head in disbelief as she recalled the conversation Mark had had with Jake at dinner time, what on earth had gotten into him, she thought, he was acting completely out of his usual caring character, she sighed, picked up her pen and began to write,

Chapter One of A New Life,

To wake up in a hospital after trying to take your own life is an inexplicable experience, one which I hope I will never have to go through again.....
Once upon a time, there was a lady called Lois, a lady who had been given a second chance. She was guided by an incredibly special woman on how to save her soul from eternal grief. Despite the emptiness and devastation which

257

grief brings, the story begins with Lois deciding not to waste the chance she has been given, to live the best life with her children, to go on many adventures, show them the world, and teach them to love the earth, the life-giver. Lois is fortunate to have some fabulous friends in her life, and she hopes that her new adventures will involve them too, making memories that they can all reflect upon and recall in their twilight years.

The first thing on the agenda is to research plants and their healing properties and try to incorporate that into her daily work life, odd as it may seem; Conventional medicine versus holistic medicine has always been at the centre of many arguments, however, Lois feels that she could practice in a way which would go unnoticed and all for the greater good!

She closed the book as she yawned and placed the pen and book on the cabinet beside her as she sipped the warm cocoa. She placed her empty mug down, switched off the light and snuggled into the bed, her eyes closing as she did.

She felt the empty side of the bed move, as though someone had sat on it, she turned and gasped, Alex was perched on the side of the bed grinning at her, his hand reached over as he swept the hair from her face, "I am so proud of you Lo, you have finally freed us from this awful cycle," he said still smiling, she held his cold hand in hers and held it to her face, where the tears were falling freely, "know this, where I watch from, there is no linear time, centuries pass like a day. I love watching you and the children, it fills me with hope for the next time, I want you to know that you are now free to do whatever you wish, and if that should involve someone else, then so be it," he continued as Lois shook her head in dispute,

"There will never be anyone else, I can promise you, Alex, I am happy to live out my days for the children, making a difference in the lives of others, trust me I am contented with sharing my life with friends," she wept, he smiled, "Sometimes friends are not who we think, some are only in it for their own means, remember that Lo, and wherever you are and whatever you are doing I am standing right beside you," he said as he slowly faded away. She sat up, switched on the light, and wiped the tears away, what a beautiful dream, it felt so real like he was back, she thought as her attention then turned to the book, which had moved and was now upside down, the pen was nowhere to be seen. She grabbed the book and opened it, the note from Cerys was still there, the start of the chapter was still there but there was something written on the next page, she could see through the age-worn paper, slowly she turned the page and instantly recognised the handwriting,

Dear Lois,
Always remember what I said, I will stand beside you wherever you are, all the time you want me to, your new journey will not be a lonesome one, because I will be with you every step of the way. I love you more than I ever have,
All my love
Alex xxx

CHAPTER TWENTY-FIVE

She opened her eyes, her bedroom was filled with light, she looked at the clock, it was six thirty, how was it so light? She asked herself as she climbed out of bed and shuddered as she walked to the window, upon opening the curtains she understood, the ground was covered in a thick layer of snow which was illuminated by the light of the moon. She wrapped herself in her thick dressing gown and walked downstairs, where she clicked on the kettle, and set about lighting a large toasty fire. She could hear the clumsy footsteps of Mr Hughes as he bolted down the narrow staircase and laughed as he greeted her with sloppy kisses. After her coffee was made she opened the back door, Mr Hughes ran, desperate to relieve himself, and all the while Lois stood at the door shivering from the biting wind. After what seemed like an eternity and no sign of the dog, Lois stepped out onto the path of icy snow and growled when she noticed that the side gate was open and the dog had bolted, she stepped back inside and pulled on her boots as she then walked out in search of the evasive Mr Hughes.

As luck would have it, he hadn't ventured far and was at the front of the house sniffing around the porch, she walked to him and clicked the lead into place as a precaution, it was then that she noticed tyre marks in the snow, two sets, one set in, and one set out, perplexed, she took the dog around the back and wiped his paws on an old towel as she entered the kitchen. She took her coffee into the lounge and warmed herself by the fire as notions of who the tyre marks were made by filled her thoughts, it had to be Mark, no one had knocked on the door she was sure of that, being the light sleeper that she was, she walked back into the kitchen and to Mark's bedroom, she gently tapped on the door, and after a few seconds she opened the door and walked through. All of Mark's belongings had gone, she was completely flabbergasted, not a word had he said about leaving, he hadn't left a note of explanation, nothing. She turned, shaking her head, and stepped into the kitchen as the phone began to ring, she hurriedly walked to the phone and answered, "Lois, it's Bron,"

"Hi Bron, everything okay?" Lois replied and frowned,

"I'm just calling to let you know that school is closed today because of the heavy snowfall last night,"

"Ah, I see, what about the trip on Friday? Do you think that will still go ahead as planned?" Lois asked,

"I don't see why not, there is no more snow forecast, in fact, I watched the weather forecast this morning and they said that the weather was set to turn mild tomorrow, so hopefully it will melt this blasted snow,"

"Right, well thanks for letting me know Bron,"

"No worries, oh before I go, Gareth said do you need anything he has to deliver some bits to the Makelin's house on the hill,"

"No thanks all the same but I am pretty well stocked up here," Lois replied as they said their goodbyes and Lois set about preparing pancakes for breakfast.

By the afternoon, the sun had made an appearance and just as Bronwyn had said the snow finally began to melt, "Can we take Mr Hughes for a walk?" Jake asked once he had finished playing his game, and was clearly bored,

"Really?" Lois replied as she rolled her eyes and looked at Amber who was snuggled on the sofa watching a movie,

"Before we had a dog you always made us go for a walk and now we have one you never want to go," Jake huffed and stamped his foot on the ground, Lois shook her head and sighed,

"I'll make a deal with you, you promise to eat a roast dinner today and I'll agree to take Mr Hughes out for a walk," Lois said thinking that it would be a game changer, Jake grinned and nodded,

"Okay," he said as he ran to the kitchen to grab the lead,

"Aww, do we have to," Amber huffed as Lois grabbed her hands and pulled her to her feet.

They sludged their way through the melting snow and ice and walked through the wood beside the ravine, everywhere was so peaceful, so serene, even the water in the stream ran gently and silently. Jake had released Mr Hughes from his lead and he was having the time of his life as he investigated yet more new surroundings, Amber was walking in front of Lois and she stopped when she came to a small cluster of saplings, "Look Mum, flowers," she said and pointed, Lois caught her up and looked down at a clutch of snowdrops who stood graciously in the sunlight, enjoying the warmth of the gentle rays of sunshine, "Can I pick them?" Amber asked, Lois shook her head,

"Leave them where they are, they brighten up the wood don't you think," Lois replied.

As they reached the top of the path and could see the cottage, Jake pointed and shouted, there was a figure inside the porch, slowly they approached and once within spitting distance Lois stopped and turned to the children, "You wait here, I'll call you once we know who it is," she said as she apprehensively stepped towards the porch, she quickly opened the door and gasped, Ruth was standing, frozen to the core, shivering, her tear-stained cheeks glowing red from the ice-filled air,

"Ruth! What on earth has happened?" Lois said as she beckoned for the children to come,

"Can we get inside Lo, I think I have got frostbite," Ruth quivered.

Inside, Lois sat Ruth beside the fire as she made them both a hot mug of cocoa which she took into the lounge, Ruth cradled the mug within her numb fingers and sniffed, "So, you are wondering why I am here and why I look like this yeah," Ruth began, Lois nodded, "Last night, Will and I decided to grab a Chinese from the town on our way home, we sat by the fire and had a glass or two of wine with our dinner, we were having a lovely evening, Will even offered me a job and we were planning that I should move to Liverpool, then there was a loud banging on the door, Will goes to see who it is when Mark storms into my flat, standing in front of me, bold as brass with his hands on his hips, giving it the biggun, turns out that Dishy David wasn't the man that Mark thought he was and has been sowing his wild oats all over the place, Mark went round his house after David called to tell him it was over and caught him in bed with a nurse, anyway, he's crying and wailing like a banshee, then he starts calling me every slut under the sun, storms out as he threatens to kill himself, so naturally Will follows him and I cleaned up and sat and waited for Will to come back as he hasn't got a key, I dozed off on the sofa and jumped up when the door was knocking, it was half past three in the morning. Will walked in followed by a smug-looking Mark and announced that they had decided to give it another go, they were catching a flight this morning to Singapore, where Will had been offered a new contract, fucking bastards! Anyways, I was in a bit of a state and while Will was packing I just walked out, I had no idea where I was going, it was snowing really bad and I just walked until I found myself here, I didn't know where else to go," Ruth said as fresh tears began to fall, Lois leaned in and placed her arms around her, holding her close.

"So they have just fucked off to Singapore? What a pair of arseholes!" Lois fumed as she watched her close friend fall to pieces.

After an afternoon of being the proverbial shoulder, Lois cooked the roast while Ruth sat in the lounge playing Sonic with Jake, Amber stayed in the kitchen with Lois and helped her prepare the food and then they sat at the table and enjoyed the wonderful roast lamb that Lois had cooked. Once they had finished eating Ruth sat back in her chair and rubbed her full tummy,
"I has to hand it to you, Lo, that was the best roast I has ever had in my life, nice one!" she said contentedly, Lois chuckled as Jake nodded in agreement, Lois looked at him in utter astonishment,
"You liked it?" She asked in bewilderment,
"I didn't like it Mum, I loved it," Jake roared as he then lifted his plate to his mouth and began to drink the remaining gravy.

Wednesday 23rd February 96,
Dear Lois,
What an unexpected turn of events! Isn't life full of twists and turns eh? So I currently have an incredibly distraught Ruth, snoring her head off in the spare room, I am worried about her as she is usually so headstrong and courageous, yet now she seems so fragile and broken. I am still not over the fact that one, Mark left Amber alone in the cottage because he had a row with his new boyfriend, and two, that he came here in the middle of the night to take his things without so much as a bye or leave and

three, do the one thing he swore he never would, take someone who was in a relationship with somebody else. Just goes to show, that you think you have known someone for many years and they are not the person that you thought they were. I couldn't allow Ruth to go back to her flat alone in that state so I suggested that she stay here for a while, I said that I needed the company, so she agreed.
I thought that Mark was a true friend, but it turns out that I was just a time filler for him until the right guy came along, which saddens me somewhat, even when I met Alex, still, I included Mark in everything, and yet he was happy to just blow me and the children off and piss off to Singapore, well sod him. Alex warned me about him last night.
I have started Chapter One in Cerys's book, author I am not, but I will write it from my heart, nevertheless.
Tomorrow Ruth and I are going to her flat to collect some of her things, then we are popping in to see Bronwyn, it seems ages since we have had a girly chinwag,
I shall sign off now as I want to sleep and hopefully, dream of my man as I did last night,
So I shall bid you a goodnight,
As always Xxx

Lois gasped silently when they entered Ruth's sparse flat, she looked around as Ruth walked into her bedroom to pack some clothes,
"How long have you lived here?" Lois asked, expecting Ruth to say no longer than a few months,
"Since I was sixteen, rents cheap and it suited me at the time," Ruth shouted, Lois shook her head in dismay,

"Pack all of your clothes, you are moving in with me!" Lois
replied Ruth peered around the door,
"Did you just say what I thought you said, you want me, the
village gossip and lifelong spinster to move into your beautiful
cottage?" Ruth asked in bewilderment, no one had ever shown
her kindness like that, ever! She thought as she looked at Lois,
someone she had not known long, yet felt like she had known
her for years,
"Yes, we can grow old as two miserable spinsters together,"
Lois replied and laughed Ruth took a run at her and threw her
arms around her,
"Really Lo, you mean it?" she asked again, Lois nodded,
"Yes really,"
"But what about the kids, shouldn't you ask them first?"
"They love you Ruth, who did they turn to when I was in the
hospital, you, you are the Auntie that they have never had,"
Lois said and ushered her back to her room to continue
packing they needed to be at Bronwyn's within the hour.

After an hour or so, bringing Bronwyn up to speed, they had
decided that they would have dinner together at the pub that
evening, so they collected the children from school, shared the
news about the newest edition of the family, went home,
changed, and met back at the pub. Trudy was most kind in
allowing Mr Hughes to join them and Jake was thrilled that he
got to show off his best friend to Tiggy and Jess.
"So girls what happens next I wonder?" Bronwyn said as
Trudy brought a fresh bottle of wine to the table,
"We start a new adventure, as the travelling spinsters," Ruth
said and held up her glass, Lois laughed and then placed her
hand over the top of her glass before Bronwyn could top it up,
"Come on Lo, this is a celebration," Bronwyn said as she tried
her hardest to prize Lois's hand away,

"I have to drive home Bron," Lois replied as she adamantly shook her head,

"Rubbish, Gar can drop you off before he takes me and the girls home, and I can pick you up in the morning," Bronwyn insisted, and of course, Lois caved and sipped at her very full glass of wine.

"What are you going to do about work Ruth?" Bronwyn asked as she finished her third glass and hiccupped, Ruth shrugged her shoulders,

"Haven't got a clue if truth be known,"

"Sorry to interrupt," they heard a man's voice say, they turned and saw Kyle standing at the bar close to their table, "Ruth, I am so sorry for the way I have treated you, I cannot cope in the office without you, please come back," Kyle pleaded,

"What's it worth," Ruth replied and winked at the girls,

"I'll give you a ten per cent pay rise,"

"Twenty?" Ruth said and grinned,

"Fifteen and that's my final offer,"

"Done!" Ruth shouted and walked to Kyle with an outstretched hand, they shook and the deal was sealed.

Chapter One of A New Life,

To wake up in a hospital after trying to take your own life is an inexplicable experience, one which I vow I will never go through again.....

Once upon a time, there was a lady called Lois, a lady who had been given a second chance. She was guided by an incredibly special woman on how to save her soul from eternal grief. Despite the emptiness and devastation which grief brings, the story begins with Lois deciding not to waste the chance she has been given, to live the best life with her children, to go on many adventures, show them the world, and teach them to love the earth, the life-giver. Lois is fortunate to have some fabulous friends in her life, and she hopes that her new adventures will involve them too, making memories that they can all reflect upon and recall in their twilight years.

The first thing on the agenda is to research plants and their healing properties and try to incorporate that into her daily work life, odd as it may seem; Conventional medicine versus holistic medicine has always been at the centre of many arguments, however, Lois feels that she could practice in a way which would go unnoticed and all for the greater good!

As all good stories do, this one has already taken a twist, Lois had hoped to share her new adventure with the person she believed to be her closest friend, but as ever life throws up many surprises. It turns out that Lois's friend has gone off to adventure elsewhere with somebody else, but she knows now that it is a blessing in disguise, and at times like this, you discover who the genuine people are. So Lois, Ruth and the children are ready to begin their new adventure and tomorrow they are going to the travel agents after Lois returns from the school trip to book a two-week holiday in France, they plan to travel through villages and explore all that they can, and who knows where they will have travelled to when she reaches Chapter two!

CHAPTER TWENTY-SIX

"Ruth, Bronwyn will be here in five minutes, we can't be late today, the coach leaves the school at half-eight," Lois called out as she closed the lunchboxes, after receiving no reply from Ruth, Lois walked to her room and knocked on the door and with no answer she pushed the door open, Ruth's bed was made, her things had been unpacked and put away, yet she was nowhere to be seen, Lois shrugged and walked back to the kitchen and heard the front door close and Ruth walked through and grinned,

"Where on earth have you been?" Lois asked as she grabbed the bookbags from the hook,

"Well a fresh start, new me, I got up at six, got ready and went for an early morning stroll, it was breathtaking, literally," she said and laughed,

"I have been meaning to ask, where is your car?" Lois asked as she grabbed her bag and walked to the bottom of the stairs,

"Oh, it's in the garage, should be ready this afternoon," Ruth replied as she called out to the children, and this time they raced down the stairs as soon as they were called,

"How do you do that, I have called them three times and they completely ignored me, you call them once and they come running," Lois said and shook her head,

"Well you've either got it or you haven't Lo," Ruth replied as she slipped past her and winked.

She ushered them all towards the door as the resonance of Bronwyn's horn was threatening to wake the dead, Amber tripped over something as she stepped out of the door, she bent down and frowned at Lois who was directly behind her, then handed her the book, Cerys's book.

As they travelled through the countryside on the coach Jake had his face glued to the window as he and his friend in the seat behind were having a pheasant counting competition, Lois sighed and checked her watch, then opened her bag to grab a tissue, she looked at the book and read the words of the Chapter, all the time wondering how she was supposed to return it to Cerys as the bookshop no longer existed, the coach ground to a halt, signalling that they had arrived, so she slipped the book back inside her bag as they all began to disembark. After a trip around the beautiful lake on the train (which Jake was ecstatic about) they ventured off on their own with their small groups, Lois only had Jake and his friend in her group, and she felt sure that Mrs Partridge had taken pity on her owing to her stint in hospital, so the three of them walked on the shoreline, Jake and William were searching for unusual stones and Lois looked all around her, taking everything in. She felt a sense of familiarity around the lake, the surrounding hills, and the looming mountains in the background, all seemed to know her as she did them. They walked for a while until they walked into the path of another small group, who were stopping to have their lunch, and although the sun was covered by a thick blanket of cloud, it felt mild enough to sit on a blanket and join them, which they did.
"Hi, Lois isn't it?" the leader of the group said as she smiled, Lois smiled and nodded,
"I'm Cheryl, Hope's Mum," she said as they shook hands, they chatted for a while, and after they had finished eating the

children decided on a game of hide and seek, Lois leaned back
and sighed,

"Beautiful isn't it?" Cheryl sighed and leaned back, Lois
nodded,

"It certainly is," she agreed, she felt someone watching her
from the corner of her eye, she turned and looked and rapidly
climbed to her feet, "Cheryl do you mind, I have just spotted
an old friend, would you keep an eye on the boys while I go
and have a chat?" Lois asked,

"Of course, we still have a few hours before we have to return
to the coach," she replied, Lois took to her heels and ran as
fast as her legs would carry her until she reached the familiar
face,

"I cannot believe that you are here, what are the chances of
that!" Lois exclaimed breathlessly,

"I asked you to return the book to my home, this is my home,"
Cerys said and smiled,

"I don't understand. What about the bookshop?" Lois asked in
bewilderment, Cerys chuckled,

"It was a temporary thing, do you have the book?" she asked,
Lois nodded, then remembered that she had left her bag with
Cheryl,

"I'll have to run back and grab it, it's in my bag," Lois said as
she positioned herself ready to sprint back,

"There is plenty of time, come let's walk," Cerys said as she
took Lois's arm and they walked along the shoreline, "You
have endured much pain and suffering Lois, and owing to your
courage you have changed an eternity of sorrow, to great
happiness, and I cannot tell you how I admire your strength
and your commitment to your children," Cerys said as they
stopped and looked into the darkened water of the lake, Lois
looked into the water as tears formed in her eyes, Cerys took
something from her satchel and handed it to Lois,

"I made this for you," she said as she handed her a flask,

"Tea?" Lois asked and smiled, Cerys nodded, while Lois wasted no time in unscrewing the lid and pouring herself a cup, making noises of complete satisfaction as she drank.
"Your children are a credit to you Lois and every day you should feel thankful that you are blessed to have them in your life," Cerys said, she watched as Jake looked at them from where they were picnicking,
"But, how did you know I would be here today?" Lois asked as she closed the lid of the flask,
"I know many things, as you will too, you must have faith in yourself and your ability," Cerys replied, Lois nodded,
"How can I learn, if you are not there to guide me?" Lois asked,
"I am always there, you just have to close your eyes and call upon me," Cerys replied and smiled, "Now, run back and grab the book," she continued, Lois nodded and sprinted back, grabbed her bag, promising Cheryl that she would only be a few minutes and returned to Cerys, she handed her the book and Cerys read Chapter One and once finished she smiled,
"I see great things ahead for you and your family, many adventures to be had, friendships to be forged, Amber will achieve great things as too will Jake," Cerys said as she looked in Jake's direction,
"Jake?" Lois said and frowned,
"Do not be led under the misapprehension that all is lost for Jake, children like Jake are like the most beautiful flowers, they bloom when they are ready," Cerys said gently, Lois nodded as tears fell freely down her cheeks, "Now, go back and enjoy your surroundings, remember the meditation techniques in the second book and when you wish to see me, follow what you have learned," Cerys said as she walked towards a small copse of trees,
"Wait! Cerys here's your..." she was going to say flask but at that moment, she realised that her hand was void of anything

except a small posy of snowdrops, she looked into the wood but Cerys had vanished.

As they walked back to the car park Ceryl told Lois the local legend of a Goddess who lived beside the shore of the lake, according to legend her name was Ceridwen, she was married to Lord Teghid and they had two children, a girl, and a boy. Her daughter was blessed with beauty and kindness, however, her son was disfigured and dark. Ceridwen called out to the earth to help her and she was shown the way to the island of Druids, where she learned how to create a potion to aid her son, the potion was called the Awen.
She had a cauldron cast especially and had two servants to watch over the brew for a year and a day, one was a young man called Gwion and the other a blind man called Mordor. A year went by and the day before the potion was ready, Ceridwen took her son to the cottage to eagerly await his potion of healing. Ceridwen, her son, and Mordor fell asleep, Gwion noticed that the fire was dying down so he added more wood, too much wood, the cauldron bubbled over and three drops hit Gwion's hand, which he licked, taking the power of the potion from Ceridwen's son. A great chase ensued, Gwion shapeshifted to a hare, Ceridwen a greyhound, Gwion then changed to a salmon, Ceridwen to an otter, then he changed to a grain of wheat, and she changed to a hen and consumed him. Nine months later she gave birth to a son, who she sent in a leather bag to the sea, he was discovered by a fisherman who took him in and named him Taliesin, he became the greatest bard this world had ever known.

The journey home was filled with thoughts of recent events as though it was all replaying once again, although this time, Lois felt no pain and the more she thought about the story of Ceridwen, she thought about Cerys, it couldn't be, could it?

Dear Lois…

Friday 25th February 96,

Dear Lois,

Wow! Today we went to Bala Lake, aka Teghid Shore, it was so beautiful, so serene and strangely so familiar. We travelled on the train around one side of the Lake and walked back to the car park, picnicking on the way. Jake absolutely loved every minute of it, but something extraordinary happened, I spotted Cerys along the shoreline, we chatted and I returned the book, she told me how to contact her if ever I need guidance and she had prepared me a flask of her amazing tea.

On the walk back, Cheryl, Hope's mum told me the legend of a Goddess called Ceridwen who had two children, I won't go into details because I want to research the story deeper, but it led me to think Ceridwen, Cerys? It can't be, can it? I had a long and meaningful chat with myself on the return journey as I realised that life is far too precious to waste, I need to live every minute of it and encourage the children to do the same, that is why the first week of March, Ruth and I have booked a two week holiday in France with the children. We are sailing to France and then hiring a camper, the children are so excited and so am I.

Every night, when I lay down and close my eyes, I feel him beside me, he stays all night, and for that, I am filled with gratitude, it gives me the drive to get up every morning and embrace the day as though it is the last. I

Dear Lois...

cannot wait for the next Chapter of my life to kick in and
I hope that you will join me every step of the way,
So for now, I will sign off,
Until the next time,
As ever xxx

THE END..... (Or is it?)

ABOUT THE AUTHOR

Louise lives on the edge of Dartmoor National Park with her fellow writer husband and their children. Drawing on life experiences, motherhood, nursing, autism etc. and her deep connection to nature, she finds inspiration for her stories, the family are keen walkers and explorers which sets the scene for many stories. You can find out more about Louise and her books on their publishing house website
www.undertheoaks.co.uk